COMING HOME

Before the quake it had been called Castle Minterl; but few outside Minterl remembered that. Small events drown in large ones. Atlantis itself, an entire continent, had drowned in the tectonic event that sank this small peninsula.

The lovely golden-haired woman ceased peering over the side of the boat. She lifted her eyes to watch the south tower come toward them. She murmured into Karskon's ear, "And that's all that's left."

But she *sounded* shaken. "It's all gone! Tapestries and banquet hall and bedrooms and the big ballroom...the gardens...all down to the fishes, and not even merpeople to enjoy them..." She shuddered, though her face still wore the mask of eager interest. "Maybe the riding-birds survived. Nihilil kept them on the roof."

Also by Larry Niven
Published by Ballantine Books:

ALL THE MYRIAD WAYS

CONVERGENT SERIES

FLIGHT OF THE HORSE

THE FLYING SORCERERS

A GIFT FROM EARTH

A HOLE IN SPACE

THE INTEGRAL TREES

THE LONG ARM OF GIL HAMILTON

NEUTRON STAR

RINGWORLD

THE RINGWORLD ENGINEERS

TALES OF KNOWN SPACE: THE UNIVERSE OF
LARRY NIVEN

WORLD OF PTAVVS

A WORLD OUT OF TIME

Limits

LARRY NIVEN

A Del Rey Book

BALLANTINE BOOKS • NEW YORK

A Del Rey Book
Published by Ballantine Books

Copyright © 1985 by Larry Niven

Library of Congress Catalog Card Number: 84-91741

ISBN 0-345-32142-1

Manufactured in the United States of America

First Edition: February 1985

Cover Art by Barclay Shaw

CONTENTS

MORE TALES FROM THE DRACO TAVERN...

INTRODUCTION

Half my output used to be short stories.

It's common knowledge in this field that the money is in novels; but it's also true that stories come in their own length. Stretching an idea beyond its length is even worse than over-compressing it. Ordinarily I would have continued to write short stories.

What happened was, I hit a bump in my career.

A novice writer should try anything, not just to pay the rent, but because he needs practice, versatility, skills. Later he must learn to turn down bad offers: the first bump.

The second bump comes when he learns to turn down *good* offers.

I'm a slow learner.

I learned to say *no*; but that was only a couple of years ago. Show me a contract and I flinch; but if I committed myself years ago, it gets signed; and then the book must be written.

Footfall, being written with Jerry Pournelle, is a year and a half overdue and finished. But everything else is backed up behind it.

I didn't know whether *The Integral Trees* and *The Smoke Ring* would be one book or two; it was conceived as Siamese twins. It's two, and *The Smoke Ring* is awaiting *Footfall*.

So are a children's book to be written with Jerry Pournelle and Wendy All; and *The Legacy of Heorot*, with Jerry (again) and Steven Barnes. A collection of the Warlock stories needed rewriting to remove redundancies. I've been rewriting speeches into articles for the Philcon.

Where would I find time to write short stories?

But I did.

In 1983, Fred Saberhagen wrote me with a strange proposal. How would I like to write a Berserker story?

The idea: Fred will ask half a dozen friends to write tales of human-Berserker encounters. Fred will shuffle them into the order he likes, and write a beginning and an ending to turn it all into a novel.

Sure I wanted to write a Berserker story! I didn't have to do any research; it was all in my head. I've been reading them long enough. I wrote "A Teardrop Falls" and sent copies to Fred and to *Omni*, which bought it for an indecently large sum considering that I hadn't even built my own background.

I've since seen other Berserker pastiches in the magazines, and I await the novel with some eagerness.

There was to be a new magazine on the stands, a meld of fact and fiction aimed at the general reading public. Its name: *Cosmos*. Its editor: Diana King.

Diana commissioned a story for that magazine from me and Jerry Pournelle. Topic: probably asteroid mining. Tone: space advocacy, and light. "What we'd really like to be writing," I said, "is 'To Bring Home the Steel,' by Don Kingsbury. Only it's already done."

Call it a character flaw: I have to be inspired. Jerry and I gathered one evening to plot the story. I didn't get going until we realized who it was that scared Jackie Halfie into leaving Earth.

What happened? *Cosmos* became *Omni*. Diana King resigned and was replaced by Ben Bova. Ben rejected "Spirals" because it was too long. The story ultimately appeared in Jim Baen's *Destinies*.

Collaborations are hard work. The only valid excuse for collaborating is this: there is a story you would like to write, and you don't have the skills you'd need to write it alone.

Exceptions? Sure! Jerry and I wrote "Spirals" together because it was more fun that way. And there is a classic exception, a way of collaborating that holds no risks at all.

Here's how it works. You've got a story in your trunk. Somewhere in there is a terrific story idea; but it never jelled. You broke your heart over it when you didn't yet have the skills, and now you can't throw it away and you can't bear to look at the damn thing either.

Then you meet a writer who seems to have the skills you would have needed. Hand him the manuscript! "Can you do anything with this?"

Look: you've *already* done your share of the work, and it's earned you nothing. He's done no work at all. If he says "No," you've lost nothing. He's lost nothing. If he says "Yes," it's his risk. Maybe you can get reinspired.

It was that way with "The Locusts." I'd only recently met Steven Barnes. The direction he was taking, he would soon become the best of the New Wave writers. Well, I couldn't have that . . .

I handed him "The Locusts," and he made it work. Ultimately I watched that story lose him his first Hugo Award. We've since written two novels together.

At the Phoenix World Science fiction convention in 1979, I told James Baen that I had run out of anything to say about the Warlock's Era.

Jim made me a proposal. "We'll invite some good people to write stories set in the Warlock's world. You be editor. I'll do all the work, you take all the credit."

I don't think either of us believed it would work out that way, and it didn't. (I *didn't* expect Jim to leave Ace Books!) I also had my doubts as to whether one writer would want to work in another's universe. But we tried it. I hoped, wistfully, that reading stories set in my own universe might reinspire me.

It did. Dian Girard is an old friend, and writing "Talisman" with her was a delightful experience. I wrote "The Lion in His Attic" on my own, by moving my favorite restaurant and res-tauranteur 14,000 years into the past. (That's *Mon Grenier*, in Reseda, owned and run by Andre Lion.) Both stories have appeared in *More Magic*, three years overdue.

* * *

"The Roentgen Standard" was party conversation among some of the craziest members of the Los Angeles Science Fantasy Society. Most of what I did that night was listen. When *Omni* bought the article, I earmarked half the money as a LASFS contribution.

The LASFS turned the money over to the Viking Fund, lest mankind sever communications with Mars.

Beginning around 1970, Harlan Ellison enlisted a team to build a solar system and to write stories within it. The project was to become a book, *Harlan's World: Medea*. When the book appears, Harlan will assuredly tell the tale of Medea's creation in detail; and so I need not.

But my patience is legendary—read: half imaginary—and I don't write stories to be read only by an editor. "Flare Time" must be ten years old by now. I managed to get Harlan's reluctant permission to publish "Flare Time" in a British anthology, *Andromeda*, and, some years later, in *Amazing Stories*. I *took* the right to publish it here.

I like bars. Gavagan's Bar, Jorkens and the Billiards Club, the White Hart, Callahan's Saloon: I like the ambience, the decor, the funny chemicals. I wanted one for my own.

I wanted a vehicle for dealing with philosophical questions.

I wanted to write vignettes. How else would I find time to write anything but novels?

I found it all in the Draco Tavern. The chirpsithra in particular claim to own the galaxy (though they only use tidally locked worlds of red dwarf stars) and to have been civilized for billions of years. It may be so. If confronted with any easily described, sufficiently universal philosophical question, the chirps may certainly claim to have solved it. Best yet, the Draco Tavern reminds me of those wonderful multispecies gatherings on the old Galaxy covers.*

On the subject of limits:

We are the creators. A writer accepts what limits he chooses, and no others. Often enough, it's the limits that *make* the story.

* Other tales in the Draco Tavern series may be found in my *Convergent Series*, published by Del Rey Books in 1979.

And we know it. In historical fiction the author may torture probability and even move dates around if it moves his main character into the most interesting event-points; but he would prefer not to, because events form the limits he has chosen. In fantasy he makes the rules, and is bound only by internal consistency. In science fiction he accepts limits set by the universe; and these are the most stringent of all; but only if he so chooses.

One penalty for so choosing is this: the readers may catch him in mistakes. I've been caught repeatedly. It's part of the game, and I'm willing to risk it.

I've also been known to give up a law or two for the sake of a story. I've broken the lightspeed barrier to move my characters about. I gave up conservation of rotation for a series of tales on teleportation.

You'll find fantasy here too; but observe how the stories are shaped by the limits I've set. Most of my stories have puzzles in them, and puzzles *require* rules. I seem to be happiest with science fiction, "the literature of the possible," where an army of scientists is busily defining my rules for me.

What have we here?

Long stories, short stories, *very* short stories, new and old. Collaborations. Science fiction and fantasy and economic theory.

Have fun.

THE
LION
IN HIS
ATTIC

Before the quake it had been called Castle Minterl; but few outside Minterl remembered that. Small events drown in large ones. Atlantis itself, an entire continent, had drowned in the tectonic event that sank this small peninsula.

For seventy years the seat of government had been at Beesh, and that place was called Castle Minterl. Outsiders called this drowned place Nihilil's Castle, for its last lord, if they remembered at all. Three and a fraction stories of what had been the south tower still stood above the waves. They bore a third name now: Rordray's Attic.

The sea was choppy today. Durily squinted against bright sunlight glinting off waves. Nothing of Nihilil's Castle showed beneath the froth.

The lovely golden-haired woman ceased peering over the side of the boat. She lifted her eyes to watch the south tower come toward them. She murmured into Karskon's ear, "And that's all that's left."

Thone was out of earshot, busy lowering the sails; but he might glance back. The boy was not likely to have seen a lovelier woman in his life; and as far as Thone was concerned, his passengers were seeing this place for the first time. Karskon turned to look at Durily, and was relieved. She looked interested, eager, even charmed.

But she *sounded* shaken. "It's all gone! Tapestries and banquet hall and bedrooms and the big ballroom . . . the gar-

1

dens . . . all down there with the fishes, and not even merpeople to enjoy them . . . that little knob of rock must have been Crown Hill . . . Oh, Karskon, I wish you could have seen it." She shuddered, though her face still wore the mask of eager interest. "Maybe the riding-birds survived. Nihilil kept them on the roof."

"You couldn't have been more than . . . ten? How can you remember so much?"

A shrug. "After the Torovan invasion, after we had to get out . . . Mother talked incessantly about palace life. I think she got lost in the past. I don't blame her much, considering what the present was like. What she told me and what I saw myself, it's all a little mixed up after so long. I saw the travelling eye, though."

"How did that happen?"

"Mother was there when a messenger passed it to the king. She snatched it out of his hand, playfully, you know, and admired it and showed it to me. Maybe she thought he'd give it to her. He got very angry, and he was trying not to show it, and that was even more frightening. We left the palace the next day. Twelve days before the quake."

Karskon asked, "What about the other—?" But warning pressure from her hand cut him off.

Thone had finished rolling up the sail. As the boat thumped against the stone wall he sprang upward, onto what had been a balcony, and moored the bow line fast. A girl in her teens came from within the tower to fasten the stern line for him. She was big as Thone was big: not yet fat, but hefty, rounded of feature. Thone's sister, Karskon thought, a year or two older.

Durily, seeing no easier way out of the boat, reached hands up to them. They heaved as she jumped. Karskon passed their luggage up, leaving the cargo for others to move, and joined them.

Thone made introduction. "Sir Karskon, Lady Durily, this is Estrayle, my sister. Estrayle, they'll be our guests for a month. I'll have to tell Father. We bring red meat in trade."

The girl said, "Oh, very good! Father will love that. How was the trip?"

"Well enough. Sometimes the spells for wind just don't do anything. Then there's no telling where you wind up." To

Karskon and Durily he said, "We live on this floor. These outside stairs take you right up past us. You'll be staying on the floor above. The top floor is the restaurant."

Durily asked, "And the roof?"

"It's flat. Very convenient. We raise rabbits and poultry there." Thone didn't see the look that passed across Durily's face. "Shall I show you to your rooms? And then I'll have to speak to Father."

Nihilil's Castle dated from the last days of real magic. The South Tower was a wide cylindrical structure twelve stories tall, with several rooms on each floor. In this age nobody would have tried to build anything so ambitious.

When Rordray petitioned for the right to occupy these ruins, he had already done so. Perhaps the idea amused Minterl's new rulers. A restaurant in Nihilil's Castle! Reached only by boats! At any rate, nobody else wanted the probably haunted tower.

The restaurant was the top floor. The floor below would serve as an inn; but as custom decreed that the main meal was served at noon, it was rare for guests to stay over. Rordray and his wife and eight children lived on the third floor down.

Though "Rordray's Attic" was gaining some reputation on the mainland, the majority of Rordray's guests were fishermen. They often paid their score in fish or in smuggled wines. So it was that Thone found Rordray and Merle hauling in lines through the big kitchen window.

Even Rordray looked small next to Merle. Merle was two and a half yards tall, and rounded everywhere, with no corners and no indentations: his chin curved in one graceful sweep down to his wishbone, his torso expanded around him like a tethered balloon. There was just enough solidity, enough muscle in the fat, that none of it sagged at all.

And that was considerable muscle. The flat-topped fish they were wrestling through the window was as big as a normal man; but Merle and Rordray handled it easily. They settled the corpse on its side on the center table, and Merle asked, "Don't you wish you had an oven that size?"

"I do," said Rordray. "What is it?"

"Dwarf island-fish. See the frilly spines all over the top of the thing? Meant to be trees. Moor at an island, go ashore. When you're all settled the island dives under you, then snaps the crew up one by one while you're trying to swim. But they're magical, these fish, and with the magic dying away—"

"I'm wondering how to cook the beast."

That really wasn't Merle's department, but he was willing to advise. "Low heat in an oven, for a long time, maybe an eighth of an arc," meaning an eighth of the sun's path from horizon to horizon.

Rordray nodded. "Low heat, covered. I'll filet it first. I can fiddle up a sauce, but I'll have to see how fatty the meat is . . . All right, Merle. Six meals in trade. Anyone else could have a dozen, but you—"

Merle nodded placidly. He never argued price. "I'll start now." He went through into the restaurant section, scraping the door on both sides, and Rordray turned to greet his son.

"We have guests," said Thone, "and we have red meat, and we have a bigger boat. I thought it proper to bargain for you."

"Guests, good. Red meat, good. What have you committed me to?"

"Let me tell you the way of it." Thone was not used to making business judgments in his father's name. He looked down at his hands and said, "Most of the gold you gave me, I had spent. I had spices and dried meat and vegetables and pickle and the rest. Then a boat pulled in with sides of ox for sale. I was wondering what I could sell, to buy some of that beef, when these two found me at the dock."

"Was it you they were looking for?"

"I think so. The lady Durily is of the old Minterl nobility, judging by her accent. Karskon speaks Minterl but he might be of the new nobility, the invaders from Torov. Odd to find them together—"

"You didn't trust them. Why did you deal with them?"

Thone smiled. "Their offer. The fame of Rordray's Attic has spread throughout Minterl, so they say. They want a place to honeymoon; they had married that same day. For two weeks' stay they offered . . . well, enough to buy four sides of ox and enough left over to trade *Strandhugger* in on a larger boat, large enough for the beef and two extra passengers."

"Where are they now? And where's the beef?"

"I told . . . eep. It's still aboard."

Rordray roared. *"Arilta!"*

"I meant to tell Estrayle to do something about that, but it—"

"Never mind, you've done well."

Arilta came hurrying from the restaurant area. Rordray's wife resembled her husband to some extent: big-boned, heavy, placid of disposition, carrying her weight well. "What is it?"

"Set the boys to unloading the new boat. Four sides of beef. Get those into the meatbox fast; they can take their time with the other goods."

She left, calling loudly for the boys. Rordray said, "The guests?"

"I gave them the two leeward rooms, as a suite."

"Good. Why don't you tell them dinner is being served? And then you can have your own meal."

The dining hall was a roar of voices, but when Rordray's guests appeared the noise dropped markedly. Both were wearing court dress of a style which had not yet reached the provinces. The man was imposing in black and silver, with a figured silver patch over his right eye. The lady was eerily beautiful, dressed in flowing sea-green, and a thumblength taller than her escort. They were conversation stoppers, and they knew it.

And here a man came hurrying to greet them, clapping his hands in delight. "Lady Durily, Lord Karskon? I am Rordray. Are your quarters comfortable? Most of the middle floor is empty, we can offer a variety of choices—"

"Quite comfortable, thank you," Karskon said. Rordray had taken him by surprise. Rumor said that Rordray was a werelion. He was large, and his short reddish-blond hair might be the color of a lion's mane; but Rordray was balding on top, and smooth-shaven, and well-fed, with a round and happy face. He looked far from ferocious—

"Rordray! Bring 'em here!"

Rordray looked around, disconcerted. "I have an empty table in the corner, but if you would prefer Merle's company . . . ?"

The man who had called was tremendous. The huge platter

before him bore an entire swordfish fillet. Durily stared in what might have been awe or admiration. "Merle, by all means! And can you be persuaded to join us?"

"I would be delighted." Rordray escorted them to the huge man's table and seated them. "The swordfish is good—"

"The swordfish is *wonderful*!" Merle boomed. He'd made amazing progress with the half-swordfish while they were approaching. "It's baked with apricots and slivered nuts and . . . something else, I can't tell. Rordray?"

"The nuts are soaked in a liqueur called *brosa*, from Rynildissen, and dried in the oven."

"I'll try it," Karskon said, and Durily nodded. Rordray disappeared into the kitchen.

The noise level was rising toward its previous pitch. Durily raised her voice just high enough. "Most of you seem to be fishers. It must have been hard for you after the merpeople went away."

"It was, Lady. They had to learn to catch their own fish instead of trading. All the techniques had to be invented from scratch. They tell me they tried magic at first. To breath water, you know. Some of them drowned. Then came fishing-spears, and special boats, and nets—"

"You said *they*?"

"I'm a whale," said Merle. "I came later."

"Oh. There aren't many were-folk around these days. Anywhere."

"We aren't all gone," Merle said, while Karskon smiled at how easily they had broached the subject. "The merpeople went away, all right, but it wasn't just because they're magical creatures. Their life *styles* include a lot of magic. Whales don't practice much magic."

"Even so," Karskon wondered, "what are you doing on land? Aren't you afraid you might, ah, change? Magic isn't dependable any more—"

"But Rordray is. Rordray would get me out in time. Anyway, I spend most of my time aboard *Shrimp*. See, if the change comes over me there, it's no problem. A whale's weight would swamp my little boat and leave me floating."

"I still don't see—"

"Sharks."

"Ah."

"Damn brainless toothy wandering weapons! The more you kill the more the blood draws more till—" Merle shifted restlessly. "Anyway, there are no sharks ashore. And there are books, and people to talk to. Out on the sea there's only the whale songs. Now, I like the singing; who wouldn't? But it's only family gossip, and weather patterns, and shoreline changes, and where are the fish."

"That sounds useful."

"Sure it is. Fisherfolk learn the whale songs to find out where the fish are. But for any kind of intelligent conversation you have to come ashore. Ah, here's Rordray."

Rordray set three plates in place, bearing generous slabs of swordfish and vegetables cooked in elaborate fashions. "What's under discussion?"

"Were-creatures," Karskon said. "They're having a terrible time of it almost everywhere."

Rordray sat down. "Even in Rynildissen? The wolf people sector?"

"Well," Durily said uncomfortably, "they're changing. You know, there are people who can change into animals, but that's because there are were-folk among their ancestors. Most were-folk are animals who learned how to take human form. The human shape has magic in it, you know." Rordray nodded, and she continued. "In places where the magic's gone, it's terrible. The animals lose their minds. Even human folk with some animal ancestry, they can't make the change, but their minds aren't quite human either. Wolf ancestry makes for good soldiers, but it's hard for them to stop. A touch of hyena or raccoon makes for thieves. A man with a touch of lion makes a good general, but—"

Merle shifted restlessly, as if the subject were painful to him. His platter was quite clean now. "Oh, to hell with the problems of were-folk. Tell me how you lost your eye."

Karskon jumped, but he answered. "Happened in the baths when I was thirteen. We were having a fight with wet towels and one of my half-brothers flicked my eye out with the corner of a towel. Dull story."

"You should make up a better one. Want some help?"

Karskon shook his head, smiling despite himself. "Where are you from?"

"Inland. It's been years since I tasted fresh fish. You were right, it's wonderful." He paused, but the silence forced him to continue. "I'm half Torovan, half Minterl. Duke Chamil of Konth made me his librarian, and I teach his legitimate children. Lady Durily descends from the old Minterl nobility. She's one of Duchess Chamil's ladies-in-waiting. That's how we met."

"I never understood shoreside politics," Merle said. "There was a war, wasn't there, long ago?"

Karskon answered for fear that Durily would. "Torov invaded after the quake. It was an obvious power vacuum. The tales tell that the Torovan armies never got this far south. What was left of the dukes surrendered first. You'll find a good many of the old Minterls hereabouts. The Torovans have to go in packs when they come here."

Merle was looking disgusted. "Whales don't play at war."

"It's not a game," Karskon said.

Rordray added, "Or at least the stakes are too high for ordinary people."

There was murky darkness, black with a hint of green. Blocky shapes. Motion flicked past, drifted back more slowly. Too dark to see, but Karskon sensed something looking back at him. A fish? A ghost?

Karskon opened his good eye.

Durily was at the window, looking out to sea. Leftward, waves washed the spike of island that had been Crown Hill. "There was grass almost to the top," Durily said, "but the peak was always a bare knob. We picnicked there once, the whole family—"

"What else do you remember? Anything we can use?"

"Two flights of stairs," Durily said. "You've seen the one that winds up the outside of the tower, like a snake. Snake-headed, it used to be, but the quake must have knocked off the head."

"Animated?"

"No, just a big carving...um...it could have been animated once. The magic was going out of everything. The merpeople were all gone; the mainlanders were trying to learn to catch their own fish, and we had trouble getting food. Nihilil was thinking of moving the whole court to Beesh. Am I rambling too much, darling?"

"No telling what we can use. Keep it up."

"The inside stairs lead down from the kitchen, through the laundry room on this floor, and through Thone's room on the lower floor."

"Thone." Karskon's hand strayed to his belt buckle, which was silver, and massive; which was in fact the hilt of a concealed dagger. "He's not as big as Rordray, but I'd hate to have him angry with me. They're all too big. We'd best not be caught . . . unless we, or *you*, can find a legitimate reason for being in Thone's room?"

Durily scowled. "He's just not interested. He sees me, he knows I'm a woman, but he doesn't seem to care . . . or else he's very stupid about suggestions. That's possible."

"If he's part of a were-lion family—"

"He wouldn't mate with human beings?" Durily laughed, and it sounded like silver coins falling. No, he thought, she wouldn't have had trouble seducing a young man . . . or *anything* male. *I* gave her no trouble. Even now, knowing the truth . . .

"Our host isn't a were-lion," she said. "Lions eat red meat. We've brought red meat to his table, but he was eating fish. Lions don't lust for a varied diet, and they aren't particular about what they eat. Our host has exquisite taste. If I'd known how fine a cook he is, I'd have come for that alone."

"He shows some other signs. The whole family's big, but he's a lot bigger. Why does he shave his face and clip his hair short? Is it to hide a mane?"

"Does it matter if they're lions? We don't want to be caught," Durily said. "Any one of them is big enough to be a threat. Stop fondling that canape sticker, dear. This trip we use stealth and magic."

Oddly reluctant, Karskon said, "Speaking of magic . . . ?"

"Yes. It's time."

"You're quite right. They're hiding something," Rordray said absently. He was carving the meat from a quarter of ox and cutting it into chunks, briskly, apparently risking his fingers at every stroke. "What of it? Don't we all have something to hide? They are my guests. They appreciate my food."

"Well," said his wife, "don't we all have something worth gossipping about? And for a honeymooning couple—"

At which point Estrayle burst into a peal of laughter.

Arilta asked, "Now what brought that on?" But Estrayle only shook her head and bent over the pale yellow roots she was cutting. Arilta turned back to her husband. "They don't seem loving enough, somehow. And she so beautiful, too."

"It makes a pattern," Rordray said. "The woman is beautiful, as you noticed. She is the Duchess's lady-in-waiting. The man serves the Duke. Could Lady Durily be the Duke's mistress? Might the Duke have married her to one of his men? It would provide for her if she's pregnant. It might keep the Duchess happy. It happens."

Arilta said, "Ah." She began dumping double handfuls of meat into a pot. Estrayle added the chopped root.

"On the other hand," Rordray said, "she is of the old Minterl aristocracy. Karskon may be too, half anyway. Perhaps they're not welcome near Beesh because of some failed plot. The people around here are of the old Minterl blood. They'd protect them, if it came to that."

"Well," his wife said with some irritation, "which is it?"

Rordray teased her with a third choice. "They spend money freely. Where does it come from? They could be involved in a theft we will presently hear about."

Estrayle looked up from cutting onions, tears dripping past a mischievous smile. "Listen for word of a large cat's-eye emerald."

"Estrayle, you will explain that!" said her mother.

Estrayle hesitated; but her father's hands had stopped moving, and he was looking up. "It was after supper," she said. "I was turning down the beds. Karskon found me. We talked a bit, and then he, well, made advances. Poor little man, he weighs less than I do. I slapped him hard enough to knock that lovely patch right off his face. Then I informed him that if he's interested in marriage he should be talking to my father, and in any case there are problems he should be aware of . . ." Her eyes were dancing. "I must say he took it well. He asked about my dowry! I hinted at undersea treasures. When I said we'd have to live here, he said at least he'd never have to worry about the cooking, but his religion permitted him only one wife, and I said what a pity—"

"The jewel," Rordray reminded her.

"Oh, it's beautiful! Deep green, with a blazing vertical line, just like a cat's eye. He wears it in the socket of his right eye."

Arilta considered. "If he thinks that's a safe place to hide it, he should get a less flamboyant patch. Someone might steal that silver thing."

"Whatever their secret, it's unlikely to disturb us," Rordray said. "And this is their old seat of royalty. Even the ghost . . . which reminds me. Jarper?"

The empty air he spoke to remained empty. He said, "I haven't seen Jarper since lunch. Has anyone?"

Nobody answered. Rordray continued, "I noticed him hovering behind Karskon at lunch. Karskon must be carrying something magical. Maybe the jewel? Oh, never mind, Jarper can take care of himself. I was saying Jarper probably won't bother our guests. He's of old Minterl blood himself. If he had blood."

They stuffed wool around the door and around the windows. They propped a chair under the doorknob. Karskon and Durily had no intention of being disturbed at this point. An innkeeper who found his guests marking patterns on the floor with powdered bone, and heating almost-fresh blood over a small flame, could rightly be expected to show annoyance.

Durily spoke in a language once common to the Sorcerer's Guild, now common to nobody. The words seemed to hurt her throat, and no wonder, Karskon thought. He had doffed his silver eye patch. He tended the flame and the pot of blood, and stayed near Durily, as instructed.

He closed his good eye and saw green-tinged darkness. Something darker drifted past, slowly, something huge and rounded, that suddenly vanished with a flick of finny tail. Now a drifting current of luminescence . . . congealing, somehow, to a vaguely human shape . . .

The night he robbed the jewel merchant's shop, this sight had almost killed him.

The Movement had wealth to buy the emerald, but Durily

swore that the Torovan lords must not learn that the jewel existed. She hadn't told him why. It wasn't for the Movement that he had obeyed her. The Movement would destroy the Torovan invaders, would punish his father and his half-brothers for their arrogance, for the way they had treated him...for the loss of his eye. But he had obeyed *her*. He was her slave in those days, the slave of his lust for the Lady Durily, his father's mistress.

He had guessed that it was *glamour* that held him: magic. It hadn't seemed to matter. He had invaded the jeweler's shop expecting to die, and it hadn't mattered.

The merchant had heard some sound and come to investigate. Karskon had already scooped up everything he could find of value, to distract attention from the single missing stone. Waiting for discovery in the dark cellar, he had pushed the jewel into his empty eye socket.

Greenish darkness, drifting motion, a sudden flicker that might be a fish's tail. Karskon was seeing with his missing eye.

The jeweler had found him while he was distracted, but Karskon had killed him after all. Afterward, knowing that much, he had forced Durily to tell the rest. She had lost a good deal of her power over him. He had outgrown his terror of that greenish-dark place. He had seen it every night while he waited for sleep, these past two years.

Karskon opened his good eye to find that they had company. The color of fading fog, it took the wavering form of a wiry old man garbed for war, with his helmet tucked under his arm.

"I want to speak to King Nihilil," Durily said. "Fetch him."

"Your pardon, Lady." The voice was less than a whisper, clearer than a memory. "I c-can't leave here."

"Who were you?"

The fog-wisp straightened to attention. "Sergeant Jarper Sleen, serving Minterl and the King. I was on duty in the watchtower when the land th-th-thrashed like an island-fish submerging. The wall broke my arm and some ribs. After things got quiet again there were only these three floors left, and no food anywhere. I s-starved to death."

Durily examined him with a critical eye. "You seem nicely solid after seventy-six years."

The ghost smiled. "That's Rordray's doing. He lets me take the smells of his cooking as offerings. But I can't leave where I d-died."

"Was the King home that day?"

"Lady, I have to say that he was. The quake came fast. I don't doubt he drowned in his throne room."

"Drowned," Durily said thoughtfully. "All right." She poured a small flask of seawater into the blood, which was now bubbling. Something must have been added to keep it from clotting. She spoke high and fast in the Sorcerer's Guild tongue.

The ghost of Jarper Sleen sank to its knees. Karskon saw the draperies wavering as if heated air was moving there; and when he realised what that meant, he knelt too.

An unimaginative man would have seen nothing. This ghost was more imagination than substance; in fact the foggy crown had more definition, more reality, than the head beneath. Its voice was very much like a memory surfacing from the past . . . not even Karskon's past, but Durily's.

"You have dared to waken Minterl's king."

Seventy-six years after the loss of Atlantis, and the almost incidental drowning of the seat of government of Minterl, the ghost of Minterl's king seemed harmless enough. But Durily's voice quavered. "You knew me. Durily. Lady Tinylla of Beesh was my mother."

"Durily. You've grown," said the ghost. "Well, what do you want of me?"

"The barbarians of Torov have invaded Minterl."

"Have you ever been tired unto death, when the pain in an old wound keeps you awake nonetheless? Well, tell me of these invaders. If you can lure them here, I and my army will pull them under the water."

Karskon thought that Minterl's ancient king couldn't have drowned a bumblebee. Again he kept silent, while Durily said, "They invaded the year after the great quake. They have ruled Minterl for seventy-four years. The palace is drowned but for these top floors." Durily's voice became a whip. "They are used as an inn! Rabbits and chickens are kept where the fighting-birds roosted!"

The ghost-king's voice grew stronger. "Why was I not told?"

This time Karskon spoke. "We can't lure them here, to a drowned island. We must fight them where they rule, in Beesh."

"And who are you?"

"I am Karskon Lor, Your Majesty. My mother was of Beesh. My father, a Torovan calling himself a lord, Chamil of Konth. Lord Chamil raised me to be his librarian. His legitimate sons he—" Karskon fell silent.

"You're a Torovan's bastard?"

"Yes."

"But you would strike against the Torovan invaders. How?"

Durily seemed minded to let him speak. Karskon lifted the silver eye patch to show the great green gem. "There were two of these, weren't there?"

"Yes."

"Durily tells me they were used for spying."

The King said, "What you keep in your eye socket was the traveling stone. Usually I had it mounted in a ring. If I thought a lord needed watching, I made him a present of it. If he was innocent I made him another present and took it back."

Karskon heaved a shuddering sigh. He had *almost* believed; always he had *almost* believed.

Durily asked, "Where was the other stone?"

"Did your mother tell you of my secret suite? For times when I wanted company away from the Queen? It was a very badly kept secret. Many ladies could describe that room. Your mother was one."

"Yes."

The ghost smiled. "But it stood empty most of the time, except for the man on watch in the bathing chamber. There is a statue of the one-eyed god in the bathing chamber, and its eye is a cat's-eye emerald."

Durily nodded. "Can you guide us there?"

"I can. Can you breath under water?"

Durily smiled. "Yes."

"The gem holds *mana*. If it leaves Minterl castle, the ghosts will fade."

Durily lost her smile. "King Nihilil—"

"I will show you. Duty runs two ways between a king and his subjects. Now?"

"A day or two. We'll have to reach the stairwell, past the innkeeper's family."

The ghosts went where ghosts go. Karskon and Durily pulled the wool loose from the windows and opened them wide. A brisk sea wind whipped away the smell of scorched blood. "I wish we could have done this on the roof," she said viciously. "Among Rordray's damned chickens. Used their blood."

It happened the second day after their arrival. Karskon was expecting it.

The dining room was jammed before noon. Rordray's huge pot of stew dwindled almost to nothing. He set his older children to frying thick steaks with black pepper and cream and essence of wine, his younger children to serving. Providentially Merle showed up, and Rordray set him to moving tables and chairs to the roof. The younger children set the extra tables.

Karskon and Durily found themselves squeezing through a host of seamen to reach the roof. Rordray laughed as he apologized. "But after all, it's your own doing! I have red meat! Usually there is nothing but fish and shellfish. What do you prefer? My stew has evaporated, *poof*, but I can offer—"

Durily asked, "Is there still fish?" Rordray nodded happily and vanished.

Cages of rabbits and pigeons and large, bewildered-looking *moas* had been clustered in the center of the roof, to give the diners a sea view. A salvo of torpedoes shot from the sea: bottlenosed mammals with a laughing expression. They acted like they were trying to get someone's attention. Merle, carrying a table and chairs, said, "Merpeople. They must be lost. Where the magic's been used up they lose their half-human shape, and their sense too. If they're still around when I put out I'll lead them out to sea."

Rordray served them himself, but didn't join them. Today he was too busy. Under a brilliant blue sky they ate island-fish baked with slivered nuts and some kind of liqueur, and vegetables treated with respect. They ate quickly. Butterflies fluttered in Karskon's belly, but he was jubilant.

Rordray had red meat. Of *course* the Attic was jammed, of *course* Rordray and his family were busy as a fallen beehive. The third floor would be entirely deserted.

* * *

Water, black and stagnant, covered the sixth step down. Durily stopped before she reached it. "Come closer," she said. "Stay close to me."

Karskon's protective urge responded to her fear and her beauty. But, he reminded himself, it wasn't *his* nearness she needed; it was the gem. . . . He moved down to join Durily and her ally.

She arrayed her equipment on the steps. No blood this time: King Nihilil was already with them, barely, like an intrusive memory at her side.

She began to chant in the Sorcerer's Guild tongue.

The water sank, step by step. What had been done seventy-odd years ago could be undone, partially, temporarily.

Durily's voice grew deep and rusty. Karskon watched as her hair faded from golden to white, as the curves of her body drooped. Wrinkles formed on her face, her neck, her arms.

Glamour is a lesser magic, but it takes *mana*. The magic that was Durily's youth was being used to move seawater now. Karskon had thought he was ready for this. Now he found himself staring, flinching back, until Durily, without interrupting herself, snarled (teeth brown or missing) and gestured him down.

He descended the wet stone stairs. Durily followed, moving stiffly. King Nihilil floated ahead of them like foxfire on the water.

The sea had left the upper floors, but water still sluiced from the landings. Karskon's torch illuminated dripping walls, and once a stranded fish. Within his chest his heart was fighting for its freedom.

On the fifth floor down there were side corridors. Karskon, peering into their darkness, shied violently from a glimpse of motion. An eel thrashed as it drowned in air.

Eighth floor down.

Behind him, Durily moved as if her joints hurt. Her appearance repelled him. The deep lines in her face weren't smile wrinkles; they were selfishness, sulks, rage. And her voice ran on, and her hands danced in creaky curves.

She can't hurry. She'd fall. Can't leave her behind. Her spells, my jewel: keep them together, or we drown. But the ghost was drawing ahead of them. *Would he leave us? Here?* Worse, King Nihilil was becoming hard to see. Blurring. The whole corridor seemed filled with the restless fog that was the King's ghost . . .

No. The King's ghost had *multiplied*. A horde of irritated or curious ghosts had joined the procession. Karskon shivered from the cold, and wondered how much the cold was due to ghosts rubbing up against him.

Tenth floor down . . . and the procession had become a crowd. Karskon, trailing, could no longer pick out the King. But the ghosts streamed out of the stairwell, flowed away down a corridor, and Karskon followed. A murmuring was in the air, barely audible, a hundred ghosts whispering gibberish in his ear.

The sea had not retreated from the walls and ceiling here. Water surrounded them, ankle deep as they walked, rounding up the corridor walls and curving over their heads to form a huge, complex bubble. Carpet disintegrated under Karskon's boots.

To his right the wall ended. Karskon looked over a stone railing, down into the water, into a drowned ballroom. There were bones at the bottom. Swamp-fires formed on the water's surface. More ghosts.

The ghosts had paused. Now they were like a swirling, continuous, glowing fog. Here and there the motion suggested features . . . and Karskon suddenly realised that he was watching a riot, ghost against ghost. They'd realised why he was here. Drowning the intruders would save the jewel, save their fading lives. *Not* drowning them would repel Minterl's enemies.

Karskon nerved himself and waded into them. Hands tried to clutch him . . . a broadsword-shape struck his throat and broke into mist . . .

He was through them, standing before a heavy, ornately carved door. The King's ghost was waiting. Silently he showed Karskon how to manipulate a complex lock. Presently he mimed turning a brass knob and threw his weight back. Karskon imitated him. The door swung open.

A bedchamber, and a canopied bed like a throne. If this place was a ruse, Nihilil must have acted his part with verve.

The sea was here, pushing in against the bubble. Karskon could see a bewildered school of minnows in a corner of the chamber. The leader took a wrong turn, and the whole school whipped around to follow him, through the water interface and suddenly into the air. They flopped as they fell, splashed into more water and scattered.

A bead of sweat ran down Durily's cheek.

The King's ghost waited patiently at another door.

Terror was swelling in Karskon's throat. Fighting fear with self-directed rage, he strode soggily to the door and threw it open, before the King's warning gesture could register.

He was looking at a loaded crossbow aimed throat-high. The string had rotted and snapped. Karskon remembered to breathe, forced himself to breathe...

It was a tiled bathroom, sure enough. There was a considerable array of erotic statuary, some quite good. The Roze-Kattee statue would have been better for less detail, Karskon thought. A skeleton in the pool wore a rotting bath-attendant's kilt; that would be Nihilil's spy. The one-eyed god in a corner... yes. The eye not covered by a patch gleamed even in this dim, watery light. Gleamed green, with a bright vertical pupil.

Karskon closed his good eye and found himself looking at himself.

Grinning, eye closed, he moved toward the statue. Fumbling in his pouch for the chisel. Odd, to see himself coming toward himself like this. And Durily behind him, the triumph beginning to show through the exhaustion. And behind her—

He drew his sword as he spun. Durily froze in shock as he seemed to leap at her. The bubble of water trembled, the sea began to flow down the walls, before she recovered herself. But by then Karskon was past her and trying to skewer the intruder, who danced back, laughing, through the bedroom and through its ornate door, while Karskon—

Karskon checked himself. The emerald in his eye socket was supplying the magical energy to run the spell that held back the water. It had to stay near Durily. She'd drilled him on this, over and over, until he could recite it in his sleep.

Rordray stood in the doorway, comfortably out of reach. He threw his arms wide, careless of the big, broad-bladed kitchen knife in one hand, and said, "But what a place to spend a honeymoon!"

"Tastes differ," Karskon said. "Innkeeper, this is none of your business."

"There is a thing of power down here. I've known that for a long time. You're here for it, aren't you?"

"The spying stone," Karskon said. "You don't even know what it is?"

"Whatever it is, I'm afraid you can't have it," Rordray said. "Perhaps you haven't considered the implications—"

"Oh, but I have. We'll sell the traveling stone to the barbarian king in Beesh. From that moment on the Movement will know everything he does."

"Can you think of any reason why I should care?"

Karskon made a sound of disgust. "So you support the Torovans!"

"I support nobody. Am I a lord, or a soldier? No, I feed people. If someone should supplant the Torovans, I will feed the new conquerors. I don't care who is at the top."

"We care."

"Who? You, because you haven't the rank of your half-brothers? The elderly Lady Durily, who wants vengeance on her enemies' grandchildren? Or the ghosts? It was a ghost who told me you were down here."

Beyond Rordray, Karskon watched faintly luminous fog swirling in the corridor. The war of ghosts continued. And Durily was tiring. He couldn't stay here, he had to pry out the jewel. He asked, "Is it the jewel you want? You couldn't have reached it without Durily's magic. If you distract her now you'll never reach the air, with or without the jewel. We'll all drown." Karskon kept his sword's point at eye level. If Rordray was a were-lion—

But he didn't eat red meat.

"The jewel has to stay," Rordray said. "Why do you think these walls are still standing?"

Karskon didn't answer.

"The quake that sank Atlantis, the quake that put this entire peninsula under water. Wouldn't it have shaken down stone walls? But this palace dates from the Sorcerer's Guild period. Magic spells were failing, but not always. The masons built this palace of good, solid stone. Then they had the structure blessed by a competent magician."

"Oh."

"Yes. The walls would have been shaken down without the blessing and some source of *mana* to power it. You see the problem. Remove the talisman, the castle crumbles."

He might be right, Karskon thought. But not until both emeralds were gone, and Karskon too.

Rordray was still out of reach. He didn't handle that kitchen knife like a swordsman, and in any case it was too short to be effective. At a dead run Karskon thought he could catch the beefy chef . . . but what of Durily, and the spell that held back the water?

Fool! She had the other jewel, the spying-stone!

He charged.

Rordray whirled and ran down the hall. The ghost-fog swirled apart as he burst through. He was faster than he looked, but Karskon was faster still. His sword was nearly pricking Rordray's buttocks when Rordray suddenly leapt over the bannister.

Karskon leaned over the dark water. The ghosts crowded around him were his only light source now.

Rordray surfaced, thirty feet above the ballroom floor and well out into the water, laughing. "Well, my guest, can you swim? Many mainlanders can't."

Karskon removed his boots. He might wait, let Rordray tire himself treading water; but Durily must be tiring even faster, and growing panicky as she wondered where he had gone. He couldn't leave Rordray at their backs.

He didn't dive; he lowered himself carefully into the water, then swam toward Rordray. Rordray backstroked, grinning. Karskon followed. He was a fine swimmer.

Rordray was swimming backward into a corner of the ballroom. Trapping himself. The water surface rose behind him, curving up the wall. Could Rordray swim uphill?

Rordray didn't try. He dove. Karskon dove after him, kicking, peering down. There were patches of luminosity, confusing . . . and a dark shape far below . . . darting away at a speed Karskon couldn't hope to match. Appalled, Karskon lunged to the surface, blinked, and saw Rordray clamber over the railing.

He threw Karskon's boots at his head and dashed back toward the King's "secret" bedroom.

The old woman was still waiting, with the King's ghost for her companion. Rordray tapped her shoulder. He said, "Boo."

She froze, then tottered creakily around to face him. "Where is Karskon?"

"In the ballroom."

Water was flowing down the walls, knee-high and rising. Rordray was smiling as at a secret joke, as he'd smiled while watching her savor her first bite of his incredible swordfish. It meant something different now.

Durily said, "Very well, you killed him. Now, if you want to live, get me that jewel and I will resume the spells. If our plans succeed I can offer Karskon's place in the new nobility to you or your son. Otherwise we both drown."

"Karskon could tell you why I refuse. I need the magic in the jewel to maintain my inn. With the traveling jewel Karskon brought me, this structure will remain stable for many years." Rordray didn't seem to notice that the King's ghost was clawing at his eyes.

The water was chest high. "Both jewels, or we don't leave," the old woman said, and immediately resumed her spell, hands waving wildly, voice raspy with effort. She felt Rordray's hands on her body and squeaked in outrage, then in terror, as she realised he was tickling her. Then she doubled in helpless laughter.

The water walls were collapsing, flowing down. The odd, magical bubble was collapsing around him. Clawing at the stone bannister, Karskon heard his air supply roaring back up the stairwell, out through the broken windows, away. A wave threw him over the bannister, and he tried to find his footing, but already it was too deep. Then the air was only a few silver patches on the ceiling, and the seawash was turning him over and over.

A big dark shape brushed past him, fantastically agile in the roiling currents, gone before his sword-arm could react. Rordray had escaped him. He swam toward one of the smashed ballroom windows, knowing he wouldn't make it, trying anyway. The faint glow ahead might be King Nihilil, guiding him. Then it all seemed to fade, and he was breathing water, strangling.

Rordray pulled himself over the top step, his flippers already altering to hands. He was gasping, blowing. It was a long trip, even for a sea lion.

The returning sea had surged up the steps and sloshed along the halls and into the rooms where Rordray and his family dwelt. Rordray shook his head. For a few days they must needs occupy the next level up: the inn, which was now empty.

The change to human form was not so great a change, for Rordray. He became aware of one last wisp of fog standing beside him.

"Well," it said, "how's the King?"

"Furious," Rordray said. "But after all, what can he do? I thank you for the warning."

"I'm glad you could stop them. My curse on their crazy rebellion. We'll all f-fade away in time, I guess, with the magic dwindling and dwindling. But not just yet, if you please!"

"War is bad for everyone," said Rordray.

SPIRALS

by Larry Niven and Jerry Pournelle

There are always people who want to revise history. No hero is so great that someone won't take a shot at him. Not even Jack Halfey.

Yes, I knew Jack Halfey. You may not remember my name. But in the main airlock of Industrial Station One there's an inscribed block of industrial diamond, and my name is sixth down: Cornelius L. Riggs, Metallurgist. And you might have seen my face at the funeral.

You *must* remember the funeral. All across the solar system work stopped while Jack Halfey took his final trek into the sun. He wanted it that way, and no spacer was going to refuse Jack Halfey's last request, no matter how expensive it might be. Even the downers got in the act. They didn't help pay the cost, but they spent hundreds of millions on sending reporters and cameras to the Moon.

That funeral damned near killed me. The kids who took me to the Moon weren't supposed to let the ship take more than half a gravity. My bones are over a hundred years old, and they're fragile. For that young squirt of a pilot the landing may have been smooth, but she hit a full gee for a second there, and I thought my time had come.

I had to go, of course. The records say I was Jack's best friend, the man who'd saved his life, and being one of the last survivors of the Great Trek makes me somebody special. Nothing would do but that I push the button to send Jack on his "final spiral into the sun," to quote a downer reporter.

I still see TriVee programs about ships "spiraling" into the sun. You'd think seventy years and more after the Great Trek the schools would teach kids something about space.

When I staggered outside in lunar gravity—lighter than the 20% gravity we keep in the Skylark, just enough to feel the difference—the reporters were all over me. Why, they demanded, did Jack want to go into the sun? Cremation and scattering of ashes is good enough for most spacers. It was good enough for Jack's wife. Some send their ashes back to Earth; some are scattered into the solar wind, to be flung throughout the universe; some prefer to go back into the soil of a colony sphere. But why the sun?

I've wondered myself. I never was good at reading Jack's mind. The question that nearly drove me crazy, and did drive me to murder, was: why did Jack Halfey make the Great Trek in the first place?

I finally did learn the answer to that one. Be patient.

Probably there will never be another funeral like Jack's. The Big Push is only a third finished, and it's still two hundred miles of the biggest linear accelerator ever built, an electronic-powered railway crawling across the Earthside face of the Moon. One day we'll use it to launch starships. We'll fire when the Moon is full, to add the Earth's and Moon's orbital velocities to the speed of the starship, and to give the downers a thrill. But we launched Jack when the Moon was new, with precisely enough velocity to cancel the Earth's orbital speed of eighteen miles per second. It would have cost less to send him into interstellar space.

Jack didn't drop in any spiral. The Earth went on and the coffin stayed behind, then it started to fall into the Sun. It fell ninety-three million miles just like a falling safe, except for that peculiar wiggle when he really got into the sun's magnetic field. Moonbase is going to do it again with a probe. They want to know more about that wiggle.

The pilot was a lot more careful getting me home, and now I'm back aboard the Skylark, in a room near the axis where the heart patients stay; and on my desk is this pile of garbage from a history professor at Harvard who has absolutely proved that we would have had space industries and space colonies without Jack Halfey. There are no indispensible men.

In the words of a famous American president: Bullshit! We've made all the downers so rich that they can't remember what it was like back then.

And it was grim. If we hadn't got space industries established before 2020 we'd never have been able to afford them at all. Things were that thin. By 2020 A.D. there wouldn't have been any resources to invest. They'd have all gone into keeping eleven billion downers alive (barely!) and anybody who proposed "throwing money into outer space" would have been lynched.

God knows it was that way when Jack Halfey started.

I first met Jack Halfey at UCLA. He was a grad student in architecture, having got his engineering physics degree from Cal Tech. He'd also been involved in a number of construction jobs—among them Hale Observatory's big orbital telescope while he was still an undergrad at Cal Tech—and he was already famous. Everyone knows he was brilliant, and they're right, but he had another secret weapon: he worked his arse off. He had to. Insomnia. Jack couldn't sleep more than a couple of hours a night, and to get even that much sleep he had to get laid first.

I know about this because when I met Jack he was living with my sister. Ruthie told me that they'd go to bed, and Jack would sleep a couple of hours, and up he'd be, back at work, because once he woke up there was no point in lying in bed.

On nights when they couldn't make out he never went to bed at all, and he was pure hell to live with the next day.

She also told me he was one mercenary son of a bitch. That doesn't square with the public image of Jack Halfey, savior of mankind, but it happens to be true, and he never made much of a secret of it. He wanted to get rich fast. His ambition was to lie around Rio de Janeiro's beaches and sample the local wines and women; and he had his life all mapped out so that he'd be able to retire before he was forty.

I knew him for a couple of months, then he left UCLA to be a department head in the construction of the big Tucson arcology. There was a tearful scene with Ruthie: she didn't fit into Jack's image for the future, and he wasn't very gentle about how he told her he was leaving. He stormed out of her apartment carrying his suitcase while Ruthie and I shouted curses at him, and that was that.

I never expected to see him again.

When I graduated there was this problem: I was a metallurgist, and there were a lot of us. Metallurgists had been in big demand when I started UCLA, so naturally everybody studied metallurgy and materials science; by the time I graduated it was damned tough getting a job.

The depression didn't help much either. I graduated right in the middle of it. Runaway inflation, research chopped to the bone, environmentalists and Only One Earthers and Friends of Man and the Earth and other such yo-yo's on the rise; in those days there was a new energy crisis every couple of years, and when I got my sheepskin we were in the middle of, I think, number 6. Industry was laying off, not hiring.

There was one job I knew of. A notice on the UCLA careers board. "Metallurgist wanted. High pay, long hours, high risk. Guaranteed wealthy in ten years if you live through it."

That doesn't sound very attractive just now, but in those days it looked better. Better than welfare, anyway, especially since the welfare offices were having trouble meeting their staff payrolls, so there wasn't a lot left over to hand out to their clients.

So, I sent in an application and found myself one of about a hundred who'd got past the paperwork screening. The interview was on campus with a standard personnel officer type who seemed more interested in my sports record than my abilities as a metallurgist. He also liked my employment history: I'd done summer jobs in heavy steel construction. He wouldn't tell me what the job was for.

"Not secret work," he said. "But we'd as soon not let it out to anyone we're not seriously interested in." He smiled and stood up, indicating the interview was over. "We'll let you know."

A couple of days later I got a call at the fraternity house. They wanted me at the Wilshire headquarters of United Space Industries.

I checked around the house but didn't get any new information. USI had contracts for a good bit of space work, including the lunar mines. Maybe that's it, I thought. I could hope, anyway.

When I got to USI the receptionist led me into a comfortable room and asked me to sit down in a big Eames chair. The chair faced an enormous TV screen (flat: TriVee wasn't common in those days. Maybe it was before TriVee at all; it's been a long time, and I don't remember). She typed something on an input console, and we waited a few minutes, and the screen came to life.

It showed an old man floating in mid-air.

The background looked like a spacecraft, which wasn't surprising. I recognized Admiral Robert McLeve. He had to be eighty or more, but he didn't look it.

"Good morning," he said.

The receptionist left. "Good morning," I told the screen. There was a faint red light on a lens by the screen, and I assumed he could see me as well as I could see him. "I'd kind of hoped for the Moon. I didn't expect the O'Neill colony," I added.

It took a while before he reacted, confirming my guess: a second and a half each way for the message, and the way he was floating meant zero gravity. I couldn't think of anything but the Construction Shack (that's what they called it then) that fit the description.

"This is where we are," McLeve said. "The duty tour is five years. High pay, and you save it all. Not much to spend money on out here. Unless you drink. Good liquor costs like transplant rights on your kidneys. So does bad liquor, because you still have to lift it."

"Savings don't mean much," I said.

"True." McLeve grimaced at the thought. Inflation was running better than 20%. The politicians said they would have it whipped Real Soon Now, but nobody believed them. "We've got arrangements to have three quarters of your money banked in Swiss francs. If you go back early, you lose that part of your pay. We need somebody in your field, part time on the Moon, part time up here in the Shack. From your record I think you'd do. Still want the job?"

* * *

I wanted it all right. I was never a nut on the space industries bit—I was never a nut on anything—but it sounded like good work. Exciting, a chance to see something of the solar system (well, of near-Earth space and the Moon; nobody had gone further than that) as well as to save a lot of money. And with that job on my record I'd be in demand when I came home.

As to why me, it was obvious when I thought about it. There were lots of good metallurgists, but not many had been finalists in the Olympic gymnastics team trials. I hadn't won a place on the team, but I'd sure proved I knew how to handle myself. Add to that the heavy construction work experience and I was a natural. I sweated out the job appointment, but it came through, and pretty soon I was at Canaveral, strapping myself into a Shuttle seat, and having second and third thoughts about the whole thing.

There were five of us. We lifted out from the Cape in the Shuttle, then transferred in Earth orbit to a tug that wasn't a lot bigger than the old Apollo capsules had been. The trip was three days, and crowded. The others were going to Moon base. They refueled my tug in lunar orbit and sent me off alone to the Construction Shack. The ship was guided from the Shack, and it was scary as hell because there wasn't anything to do but wonder if they knew what they were doing. It took as long to get from the Moon to the Shack as it had to get to the Moon from Earth, which isn't surprising because it's the same distance: the Shack was in one of the stable libration points that make an equilateral triangle with the Earth and the Moon. Anything put there will stay there forever.

The only viewport was a small thing in the forward end of the tug. Naturally we came in ass-backwards so I didn't see much.

Today we call it the Skylark, and what you see as you approach is a sphere half a kilometer across. It rotates every two minutes, and there's all kinds of junk moored to the axis of rotation. Mirrors, the laser and power targets, the long thin spine of the mass driver, the ring of agricultural pods, the big telescope; a confusion of equipment.

It wasn't that way when I first saw it. The sphere was nearly all there was, except for a spiderweb framework to hold the solar power panels. The frame was bigger than the sphere, but it didn't look very substantial. At first sight the Shack was a pebbled sphere, a golf ball stuck in a spider's web.

McLeve met me at the airlock. He was long of limb, and startlingly thin, and his face and neck were a maze of wrinkles. But his back was straight, and when he smiled the wrinkles all aligned themselves. Laugh-lines.

Before I left Earth I read up on his history: Annapolis, engineer with the space program (didn't make astronaut because of his eyes); retired with a bad heart; wrote a lot of science fiction. I'd read most of his novels in high school, and I suppose half the people in the space program were pulled in by his stories.

When his wife died he had another heart attack. The Old Boys network came to the rescue. His classmates wangled an assignment in space for him. He hadn't been to Earth for seven years, and low gravity was all that kept him alive. He didn't even dare go to the Moon. A reporter with a flair for mythological phraseology called him "The Old Man of Space." It was certain that he'd never go home again, but if he missed Earth he didn't show it.

"Welcome aboard." He sounded glad to see me. "What do they call you?" he asked.

A good question. Cornelius might sound a dignified name to a Roman, but it makes for ribald comments in the USA. "Corky," I told him. I shrugged, which was a mistake: we were at the center of the sphere, and there wasn't any gravity at all. I drifted free from the grabhandle I'd been clinging to and drifted around the airlock.

After a moment of panic it turned out to be fun. There hadn't been room for any violent maneuvers in the tug, but the airlock was built to get tugs and rocket motors inside for repairs; it was big, nine meters across, and I could twirl around in the zero gravity. I flapped my arms and found I could swim.

McLeve was watching with a critical air. He must have liked what he saw because he grinned slightly. "Come on," he said. He turned in the air and drifted without apparent motion— it looked like levitation. "I'll show you around." He led the way out of the airlock into the sphere itself.

We were at the center of rotation. All around, above and

below, were fields of dirt, some plowed, some planted with grass and grains.

There were wings attached to hooks at the entrance. McLeve took down a set and began strapping them on. Black bat wings. They made him look like a fallen angel, Milton's style. He handed me another pair. "Like to fly?" he asked.

I returned the grin. "Why not?" I hadn't the remotest idea of what I was doing, but if I could swim in the air with my hands, I ought to be able to handle wings in no gravity. He helped me strap in, and when I had them he gave some quick instructions.

"Main thing is to stay high," he said. "The further down the higher the gravity, and the tougher it is to control these things." He launched himself into space, gliding across the center of the sphere. After a moment I followed him.

I was a tiny chick in a vast eggshell. The landscape was wrapped around me: fields and houses, and layout yards of construction gear, and machinery, and vats of algae, and three huge windows opening on blackness. Every direction was down, millions of light years down when a window caught my attention. For a moment that was terrifying. But McLeve held himself in place with tiny motions of his wings, and his eyes were on me. I swallowed my fear and looked.

There were few roads. Mostly the colonists flew with their wings, flew like birds, and if they didn't need roads, they didn't need squared-off patterns for the buildings either. The "houses" looked like they'd been dropped at random among the green fields. They were fragile partitions of sheet metal (wood was far more costly than sheet steel here), and they could not have borne their own weight on Earth, let alone stand up to a stiff breeze. They didn't have to. They existed for privacy alone.

I wondered about the weather. Along the axis of the sphere I could see scores of white puffballs. Clouds? I gathered my courage and flapped my way over to the white patch. It was a flock of hens. Their feet were drawn up, their heads were tucked under their wings, and they roosted on nothing.

"They like it in zero gravity," McLeve said. "Only thing is, when you're below them you have to watch out."

He pointed. A blob of chicken splat had left the flock and moved away from us. It fell in a spiral pattern. Of course the splat was actually going in a straight line—we were the ones who were rotating, and that made the falling stuff look as if it were spiraling to the ground below.

"Automatic fertilizer machine," I said.

McLeve nodded.

"I wonder you don't keep them caged," I said.

"Some people like their sky dotted with fleecy white hens."

"Oh. Where is everybody?" I asked.

"Most are outside working," McLeve said. "You'll meet them at dinner."

We stayed at the axis, drifting with the air currents, literally floating on air. I knew already why people who came here wanted to stay. I'd never experienced anything like it, soaring like a bird. It wasn't even like a sail plane: you wore the wings and you flew with them, you didn't sit in a cockpit and move controls around.

There were lights along part of the axis. The mirrors would take over their job when they were installed; for the moment the lights ran off solar power cells plastered over the outside of the sphere. At the far end of the sphere was an enormous cloud of dust. We didn't get close to it. I pointed and looked a question.

"Rock grinder," McLeve said. "Making soil. We spread it over the northern end." He laughed at my frown. "North is the end toward the sun. We get our rocks from the Moon. It's our radiation shielding. Works just as well if we break it up and spread it around, and that way we can grow crops in it. Later on we'll get the agricultural compartments built, but there's always five times as much work as we have people to do it with."

They'd done pretty well already. There was grass, and millet and wheat for the chickens, and salad greens and other vegetable crops. Streams ran through the fields down to a ring-shaped pond at the equator. There was also a lot of bare soil that had just been put in place and hadn't been planted. The Shack wasn't anywhere near finished.

"How thick is that soil?" I asked.

"Not thick enough. I was coming to that. If you hear the flare warnings, get to my house. North pole."

I thought that one over. The only way to ward yourself

from a solar flare is to put a lot of mass between you and the sun. On Earth that mass is a hundred miles of air. On the Moon they burrow ten meters into the regolith. The Shack had only the rock we could get from the Moon, and Moonbase had problems of its own. When they had the manpower and spare energy they'd throw more rock our way, and we'd plaster it across the outer shell of the Shack, or grind it up and put it inside; but for now there wasn't enough, and come flare time McLeve was host to an involuntary lawn party.

But what the hell, I thought. It's beautiful. Streams rushing in spirals from pole to equator. Green fields and houses, skies dotted with fleecy white hens; and I was flying as man flies in dreams.

I decided it was going to be fun, but there was one possible hitch.

"There are only ten women aboard," I said.

McLeve nodded gravely.

"And nine of them are married."

He nodded again. "Up to now we've mostly needed muscle. Heavy construction experience and muscle. The next big crew shipment's in six months, and the company's trying like hell to recruit women to balance things off. Think you can hold out that long?"

"Guess I have to."

"Sure. I'm old navy. We didn't have women aboard ships and we lived through it."

I was thinking that I'd like to meet the one unmarried woman aboard. Also that she must be awfully popular. McLeve must have read my thoughts, because he waved me toward a big structure perched on a ledge partway down from the north pole. "You're doing all right on the flying. Take it easy and let's go over there."

We soared down, and I began to feel a definite "up" and "down"; before that any direction I wanted it to be was "up." We landed in front of the building.

"Combination mess hall and administration offices," McLeve said. "Ten percent level."

It took a moment before I realized what he meant. Ten percent level—ten percent of Earth's gravity.

"It's as heavy as I care to go," McLeve said. "And any

lighter makes it hard to eat. The labs are scattered around the ring at the same level."

He helped me off with my wings and we went inside. There were several people, all men, scurrying about purposefully. They didn't stop to meet me.

They weren't wearing much, and I soon found that was the custom in the Shack; why wear clothes inside? There wasn't any weather. It was always warm and dry and comfortable. You mostly needed clothes for pockets.

At the end of the corridor was a room that hummed; inside there was a bank of computer screens, all active. In front of them sat a homely girl.

"Miss Hoffman," McLeve said. "Our new metallurgist, Corky Riggs."

"Hi." She looked at me for a moment, then back at the computer console. She was mumbling something to herself as her fingers flew over the keys.

"Dot Hoffman is our resident genius," McLeve said. "Anything from stores and inventories to orbit control, if a computer can figure it out she can make the brains work the problem."

She looked up with a smile. "We give necessity the praise of virtue," she said.

McLeve looked thoughtful. "Cicero?"

"Quintilian." She turned back to her console again.

"See you at dinner," McLeve said. He led me out.

"Miss Hoffman," I said.

He nodded.

"I suppose she wears baggy britches and blue wool stockings and that shirt because it's cool in the computer room," I said.

"No, she always dresses that way."

"Oh."

"Only six months, Riggs," the Admiral said. "Well, maybe a year. You'll survive."

I was thinking I'd damned well have to.

I fell in love during dinner.

The chief engineer was named Ty Plauger, a long, lean chap with startling blue eyes. The chief ecologist was his wife, Jill. They had been married about a year before they came up, and they'd been aboard the Shack for three, ever since it started up. Neither was a lot older than me, maybe thirty then.

At my present age the concept of love at first sight seems both trite and incredible, but it was true enough. I suppose I could have named you reasons then, but I don't feel them now. Take this instead:

There were ten women aboard out of ninety total. Nine were married, and the tenth was Dot Hoffman. My first impression of her was more than correct. Dot never would be married. Not only was she homely, but she thought she was homelier still. She was terrified of physical contact with men, and the blue wool stockings and blouse buttoned to the neck were the least of her defenses.

If I had to be in love—and at that age, maybe I did—I could choose among nine married women. Jill was certainly the prettiest of the lot. Pug nose, brown hair chopped off short, green eyes, and a compact muscular shape, very much the shape of a woman. She liked to talk, and I liked to listen.

She and Ty had stars in their eyes. Their talk was full of what space would do for mankind.

Jill was an ex-Fromate; she'd been an officer in the Friends of Man and the Earth. But while the Fromates down below were running around sabotaging industries and arcologies and nuclear plants and anything else they didn't like, Jill went to space. Her heart bled no less than any for the baby fur seals and the three-spined stickleback and all the fish killed by mine tailings, but she'd thought of something to do about it all.

"We'll put all the dirty industries into space," she told me. "Throw the pollution into the solar wind and let it go out to the cometary halo. The Fromates think they can talk everyone into letting Kansas go back to buffalo grass—"

"You can't *make* people want to be poor," Ty put in.

"Right! If we want to clean up the Earth and save the wild things, we'll have to give people a way to get rich without harming the environment. This is it! Someday we'll send down enough power from space that we can tear down the dams and put the snail darter back where he came from."

And more. Jill tended to do most of the talking. I wondered about Ty. He always seemed to have the words that would set her off again.

And one day, when we were clustered around McLeve's house with, for a few restful hours, nothing to do, and Jill was well out of earshot flying around and among the chickens in her wonderfully graceful wingstyle, Ty said to me, "I don't *care* if we turn the Earth into a park. I like space. I like flying, and I like free fall, and the look of stars with no air to cloud them. But don't tell Jill."

I learned fast. With Ty in charge of engineering, McLeve as chief administrator, and Dot Hoffman's computers to simulate the construction and point up problems before they arose, the project went well. We didn't get enough mass from the Moon, so that my smelter was always short of raw materials, and Congress didn't give us enough money. There weren't enough flights from down below and we were short of personnel and goods from Earth. But we got along.

Two hundred and forty thousand miles below us, everything was going to hell.

First, the senior senator from Wisconsin lived long enough to inherit a powerful committee chairmanship, and he'd been against the space industries from the start. Instead of money we got "Golden Fleece" awards. Funds already appropriated for flights we'd counted on got sliced, and our future budgets were completely in doubt.

Next, the administration tried to bail itself out of the tax revolt by running the printing presses. What money we could get appropriated wasn't worth half as much by the time we got it.

Moonbase felt the pinch and cut down even more on the rock they flung out our way.

Ty's answer was to work harder: get as much of the Shack finished as we could, so that we could start sending down power.

"Get it done," he told us nightly. "Get a *lot* of it finished. Get so much done that even those idiots will see that we're worth it. So much that it'll cost them less to supply us than to bring us home."

He worked himself harder than anyone else, and Jill was right out there with him. The first task was to get the mirrors operating.

We blew them all at once over a couple of months. They came in the shuttle that should have brought our additional crew; it wasn't much of a choice, and we'd have to put off balancing out the sex ratio for another six months.

The mirrors were packages of fabric as thin as the cellophane on a package of cigarettes. We inflated them into great spheres, sprayed foam plastic on the outside for struts, and sprayed silver vapor inside where it would precipitate in a thin layer all over. Then we cut them apart to get spherical mirrors, and sliced a couple of those into wedges to mount behind the windows in the floor of the Shack.

They reflected sunlight in for additional crops. Jill had her crew out planting more wheat to cut down on the supplies we'd need from Earth.

Another of the mirrors was my concern. A hemisphere a quarter of a kilometer across can focus a lot of sunlight onto a small point. Put a rock at that point and it melts, fast. When we got that set up we were all frantically busy smelting iron for construction out of the rocks. Moonbase shipped up when they could. When Moonbase couldn't fling us anything we dismounted rock we'd placed for shielding, smelted it, and plastered the slag back onto the sphere.

Days got longer and longer. There's no day or night aboard the Shack anyway, of course: open the mirrors and you have sunlight, close them and you don't. Still, habit dies hard, and we kept track of time by days and weeks; but our work schedules bore no relation to them. Sometimes we worked the clock around, quitting only when forced to by sheer exhaustion.

We got a shipment from Moonbase, and in the middle of the refining process the mounting struts in the big smelter mirror got out of alignment. Naturally Ty was out to work on it.

He was inspecting the system by flying around with a reaction pistol. The rule was that no one worked without a safety line; a man who drifted away from the Shack might or might not be rescued, and the rescue itself would cost time and manpower we didn't have.

Ty's line kept pulling him up short of where he wanted to go. He gave the free end to Jill and told her to pay out a lot of slack. Then he made a jump from the mirror frame. He must have thought he'd use the reaction pistol to shove him off at an angle so that he'd cross over the bowl of the mirror to the other side.

The pistol ran out of gas. That left Ty floating straight toward the focus of the mirror.

He shouted into his helmet radio, and Jill frantically hauled in slack, trying to get a purchase on him. I made a quick calculation and knew I would never reach him in time; if I tried I'd likely end up in the focus myself. Instead I took a dive across his back path. If I could grab his safety line, the jerk as I pulled up short ought to keep him out of the hottest area, and my reaction pistol would take us back to the edge.

I got the line all right, but it was slack. It had burned through. Ty went right through the hot point. When we recovered his body, metal parts on his suit had melted.

We scattered his ashes inside the sphere. McLeve's navy prayer book opened the burial service with the words "We brought nothing into this world, and it is certain that we shall take nothing out." Afterwards I wondered how subtle McLeve had been in his choice of that passage.

We had built this world ourselves, with Ty leading us. We had brought *everything* into this world, even down to Ty's final gift to us; the ashes which would grow grass in a place no human had ever thought to reach until now.

For the next month we did without him; and it was as if we had lost half our men. McLeve was a good engineer if a better administrator, but he couldn't go into the high gravity areas, and he couldn't do active construction work. Still, it wasn't engineering talent we lacked. It was Ty's drive.

Jill and Dot and McLeve tried to make up for that. They were more committed to the project than ever.

Two hundred and forty thousand miles down, they were looking for a construction boss. They'd find one, we were sure. We were the best, and we were paid like the best. There was never a problem with salaries. Salaries were negligible next to the other costs of building the Shack. But the personnel shuttles were delayed, and delayed again, and we were running out of necessities, and the US economy was slipping again.

We got the mirrors arrayed. Jill went heavily into agriculture, and the lunar soil bloomed, seeded with earthworms and bacteria from earthly soil. We smelted more of the rocky crust around the Shack and put it back as slag. We had plans for the metal we extracted, starting with a lab for growing metal whiskers. There was already a whisker lab in near-Earth orbit, but its output was tiny. The Shack might survive if we could show even the beginnings of a profit-making enterprise.

Jill had another plan: mass production of expensive biologicals, enzymes and various starting organics for ethical drugs.

We had lots of plans. What we didn't have was enough people to do it all. You can only work so many twenty-hour days. We began to make mistakes. Some were costly.

My error didn't cost the Shack. Only myself. I like to think it was due to fatigue and nothing more.

I made a try at comforting the grieving widow, after a decent wait of three weeks.

When Ty was alive everyone flirted with Jill. She pretended not to notice. You'd have to be crude as well as rude before she'd react.

This time it was different. I may not have been very subtle, but I wasn't crude; and she told me instantly to get the hell out of her cabin and leave her alone.

I went back to my refinery mirror and brooded.

Ninety years later I know better. Ninety years is too damned late. If I'd noticed nothing else, I should have known that nearly eighty unmarried men aboard would all be willing to comfort the grieving widow, and half of them were only too willing to use the subtle approach: "You're all that keeps us working so hard."

I wonder who tried before I did? It hardly matters; when my turn came, Jill's reaction was automatic. Slap him down before it's too late for him to back away. And when she slapped me down, I stayed slapped, more hurt than mad, but less than willing to try again.

I hadn't stopped being in love with her. So I worked at being her friend again. It wasn't easy. Jill was cold inside. When she talked to people it was about business, never herself. Her dedication to the Shack, and to all it stood for in her mind, was hardening, ossifying. And she spent a lot of time with Dot Hoffman and Admiral McLeve.

But the word came: another shuttle. Again there were no

women. The Senator from Wisconsin had found out how expensive it would be to get us home. Add fifty women and it would be half again as expensive. So no new personnel.

Still they couldn't stop the company from sending up a new chief engineer, and we heard the shuttle was on its way, with a load of seeds, liquid hydrogen, vitamin pills, and Jack Halfey.

I couldn't believe it. Jack wasn't the type.

To begin with, while the salary you could save in five years amounted to a good sum, enough to let you start a business and still have some income left, it wasn't *wealth*. You couldn't live the rest of your life in Rio on it; and I was pretty sure Jack's goals hadn't changed.

But there he was, the new boss. From the first day he arrived things started humming. It was the old Jack, brilliant, always at work, and always insisting everyone try to keep up with him although no one ever could. He worked our arses off. In two months he had us caught up on the time we lost after Ty was killed.

Things looked good. They looked damned good. With the mirrors mounted we could operate on sunlight, with spare power for other uses. Life from soil imported from Earth spread throughout the soil imported from the Moon; and earthly plants were in love with the chemicals in lunar soil. We planted strawberries, corn and beans together; we planted squashes and melons in low-gravity areas and watched them grow into jungles of thin vines covered with fruit.

The smelter worked overtime, and we had more than enough metals for the whisker lab and biological vats, if only a shuttle would bring us the pumps and electronics we needed, and if necessary we'd make pumps in the machine shops, and Jack had Dot working out the details of setting up integrated-circuit manufacture.

But the better things looked in space, the worse they looked on Earth.

One of the ways we were going to make space colonies pay for themselves was through electricity. We put out big arrays of solar cells, monstrous spiderwebs a kilometer long by half that wide, so large that they needed small engines dotted all over them just to keep them oriented properly toward the sun.

We made the solar cells ourselves; one of the reasons they needed me was to get out the rare metals from the lunar regolith and save them for the solar-cell factory. And it was working; we had the structure and we were making the cells. Soon enough we'd have enormous power, megaWatts of power, enough to beam it down to Earth where it could pay back some of the costs of building the system. The orbiting power stations cost a fortune to put up, but not much to maintain; they would be like dams, big front end costs but then nearly free power forever.

We were sure that would save us. How could the United States turn down free electricity?

It looked good until the Fromates blew up the desert antenna that we would have been beaming the power down to, and the lawyers got their reconstruction tied into legal knots that would probably take five years to untangle.

The Senator from Wisconsin continued his crusade. This time we got *three* Golden Fleece awards. Down on Earth the company nominated him for membership in the Flat Earth Society. He gleefully accepted and cut our budget again.

We also had problems on board. Jack had started mean; it was obvious he had never wanted to come here in the first place. Now he turned mean as a rattlesnake. He worked us. If we could get the whisker lab finished ahead of time, at lower cost than planned, then maybe we could save the station yet; so he pushed and pushed again; and one day he pushed too hard.

It wasn't a mutiny. It wasn't even a strike. We all did a day's work; but suddenly, without as far as I know any discussion among us, nobody would put in overtime. Ten hours a day, yes; ten hours and one minute, no.

Jill pleaded. The Admiral got coldly formal. Dot cried. Jack screamed.

We cut work to nine and a half hours.

And then it all changed. One day Jack Halfey was smiling a lot. He turned polite. He was getting his two or three hours sleep a night.

Dot described him. "Like Mrs. Fezziwig," she said. "'One vast substantial smile.' I hope she's happy. I wonder why she did it? To save the Shack. . . ." She was trying to keep her voice cheerful, but her look was bitter. Dot wasn't naive; just terrified. I suppose that to her the only reason a woman would move in with a man would be to save some noble cause like the Shack.

As to Jill, she didn't change much. The Shack was the first step in the conquest of the universe, and it was by God going to be finished and self-sufficient. Partly it was a memorial to Ty, I think; but she really believed in what she was doing, and it was infectious.

I could see how Jack could convince her that he shared her goal. To a great extent he did, although it was pure selfishness; his considerable reputation was riding on this project. But Jack never did anything half-heartedly. He drove himself at whatever he was doing.

What I couldn't understand was why he was here at all. He must have *known* how thin were the chances of completing the Shack before he left Earth.

I had to know before it drove me nuts.

Jack didn't drink much. When he did it was often a disaster, because he was the world's cheapest drunk. So one night I plied him.

Night is generally relative, of course, but this one was real: the Earth got between us and the sun. Since we were on the same orbit as the Moon, but sixty degrees ahead, that happened to us exactly as often as there are eclipses of the Moon on Earth; a rare occasion, one worth celebrating.

Of course we'd put in a day's work first, so the party didn't last long, we were all too beat. Still it was a start, and when the formalities broke up and Jill went off to look at the air system, I grabbed Jack and got him over to my quarters. We both collapsed in exhaustion.

I had brought a yeast culture with me from Canaveral. McLeve had warned me that liquor cost like diamonds up here; and a way to make my own alcohol seemed a good investment. And it was. By now I had vaccum distilled vodka made from fermented fruit bars and a mash of strawberries from the farm— they weren't missed; the farm covered a quarter of the inner surface now. My concoction tasted better than it sounds, and it wasn't hard to talk Jack into a drink, then another.

Presently he was trying to sing the verses to "The Green Hills of Earth." A mellower man you never saw. I seized my chance.

"So you love the green hills of Earth so much, what are you doing here? Change your mind about Rio?"

Jack shook his head; the vibration ran down his arm and sloshed his drink. "Nope..." Outside a hen cackled, and Jack collapsed in laughter. "Let me rest my eyes on the fleecy skies..."

Grimly I stuck to the subject. "I thought you were all set with that Tucson arcology."

"Oh, I was. I was indeed. It was a *beautiful* setup. Lots of pay, and—" He stopped abruptly.

"And other opportunities?" I was beginning to see the light.

"Wellll...yes. But you have to see it the way I did. First, it was a great opportunity to make a name for myself. A city in a building! Residential and business and industry all in the same place, one building to house a quarter...of a million...people. And it would have been beautiful, Corky. The plans were magnificent! I was in love with it. Then I got into it, and I saw what was really going on.

"Corky, everyone was stealing that place blind! The first week I went to the chief engineer to report shortages in deliveries and he just looked at me. 'Stick to your own work, Halfey,' says he. Chief engineer, the architects, construction bosses, even the catering crew—every one of them was knocking down twenty-five, fifty percent! They were selling the cement right off the boxcars and substituting sand. There wasn't enough cement in that concrete to hold up the walls."

"So you took your share."

"Don't get holy on me! Dammit, look at it my way. I was willing to play square, but they wouldn't let me. The place was going to fall down. The weight of the first fifty thousand people would have done it. What I could do was make sure nobody got inside before it happened." Jack Halfey chortled. "I'm a public benefactor, I am. I sold off the reinforcing rods. The inspectors couldn't possibly ignore that."

"Nothing else?" I asked.

"Wellll, those rods were metal-whisker compote. Almost as strong as diamond, and almost as expensive. I didn't need anything else. But I made sure they'd never open that place to the public. Then I stashed my ill-gotten gains and went underground and waited for something to happen."

"I never heard much about it. Of course, I wouldn't, up here."

"Not many down there heard either. Hush hush while the FBI looked into it. The best buy I ever made in my life was a subscription to the *Wall Street Journal*. Just a paragraph about how the Racket Squad was investigating Mafia involvement in the Tucson arcology. That's when things fell into place."

I swung around to refill his glass, carefully. We use great big glasses, and never fill them more than half full. Otherwise they slosh all over the place in the low gravity. I had another myself. It was pretty good vodka, and if I felt it, Jack must be pickled blue. "You mean the building fell in?"

"No, no. I realized why there was so *much* graft." Jack sounded aggrieved. "There was supposed to be graft. I wasn't supposed to get in on it."

"Aha."

"Aha you know it. I finished reading that article on a plane to Canaveral. The FBI couldn't follow me to Rio, but the Mafia sure could. I'd heard there was a new opening for chief engineer for the Construction Shack, and all of a sudden the post looked very, very good."

He chuckled. "Also, I hear that things are tightening up in the USA. Big crackdown on organized crime. Computer-assisted. Income tax boys and Racket Squad working together. It shouldn't be long before all the chiefs who want my arse are in jail. Then I can go back, cash my stash, and head for Rio."

"Switzerland?"

"Oh, no. Nothing so simple as that. I thought of something else. Say, I better get back to my bunk." He staggered out before I could stop him. Fortunately it was walking distance from my place to his; if he'd had to fly, he'd probably have ended up roosting with the chickens.

"Bloody hell," says I to myself.

Should I add that I had no intention of robbing Jack? I was

just curious: what inflation-proof investment had he thought up? But I didn't find out for a long time . . .

A month later the dollar collapsed. Inflation had been a fact of life for so long that it was the goal of every union and civil service organizer to get inflation written into their contracts, thereby increasing inflation. The government printed money faster to compensate: more inflation. One of those vicious spirals. Almost suddenly, the dollar was down the drain.

There followed a full-scale taxpayer revolt.

The Administration got the message: they were spending too much money. Aha! Clearly that had to stop. The first things to go were all the projects that wouldn't pay off during the current President's term of office. Long term research was chopped out of existence. Welfare, on the other hand, was increased, and a comprehensive National Health Plan was put into effect, even though they had to pay the doctors and hospitals in promissory notes.

The Senator from Wisconsin didn't even bother giving us his customary Golden Fleece award. Why insult the walking dead?

We met in our usual place, a cage-work not far from the north pole. Admiral McLeve was in the center, in zero gravity. The rest of us perched about the cage-work, looking like a scene from Hitchcock's *The Birds*.

Dot had a different picture, from Aristophanes. "Somewhere, what with all these clouds and all this air, there must be a rare name, somewhere . . . How do you like Cloud-Cuckoo-Land?"

Putting on wings does things to people. Halfey had dyed his wings scarlet, marked with yellow triangles enclosing an H. Dot wore the plumage of an eagle, and I hadn't believed it the first time I saw it; it was an incredibly detailed, beautiful job. McLeve's were the wings of a bat, and I tell you he looked frightening, as evil as Dracula himself. Leon Briscoe, the chemist, had painted mathematical formulae all over his, in exquisite medieval calligraphy. Jill and Ty had worn the plumage of male and female Least Terns, and she still wore hers. There were no two sets of wings alike in that flock. We were ninety birds of ninety species, all gathered as if the ancient roles of predator and prey had been set aside for a larger cause. Cloud-Cuckoo-Land.

A glum Cloud-Cuckoo-Land.

"It's over," McLeve said. "We've been given three months to phase out and go home. Us, Moonbase, the whole space operation. They'll try to keep some of the near-Earth operations going a while longer, but we're to shut down."

Nobody said anything at first. We'd been expecting it, those of us who'd had time to follow news from Earth. Now it was here, and nobody was ready. I thought about it: back to high gravity again. Painful.

And Jill. Her dream was being shot down. Ty died for nothing. Then I remembered McLeve. He wasn't going anywhere. Any gravity at all was a death sentence.

And I hated Jack Halfey for the grin he was hiding. There had been a long piece in the latest newscast about the roundup of the Mafia lords; grand juries working overtime, and the District of Columbia jail filled, no bail to be granted. It was safe for Jack down there, and now he could go home early.

"They can't do this to us!" Jill wailed. A leftover Fromate reflex, I guess. "We'll—" Go on strike? Bomb something? She looked around at our faces, and when I followed the look I stopped with Dot Hoffman. The potato face was withered in anguish, the potato eyes were crying. What was there for Dot on Earth?

"What a downer," she said.

I almost laughed out loud, the old word was so inadequate. Then McLeve spoke in rage. "Downers. Yes. Nine billion downers sitting on their fat arses while their children's future slides into the muck. Downers is what they are."

Now you know. McLeve the wordsmith invented that word, on that day.

My own feelings were mixed. Would the money stashed in Swiss francs be paid if we left early, even though we had to leave? Probably, and it was not a small amount; but how long would it last? There was no job waiting for me . . . but certainly I had the reputation I'd set out for. I shouldn't have much trouble getting a job.

But I like to finish what I start. The Shack was *that* close to being self-sufficient. We had the solar power grids working.

We even had the ion engines mounted all over the grid to keep it stable. We didn't have the microwave system to beam the power back to Earth, but it wouldn't be that expensive to put in . . . except that Earth had no antennae to receive the power. They hadn't even started reconstruction. The permit hearings were tied up in lawsuits.

No. The Shack was dead. And if our dollars were worthless, there were things that weren't. Skilled labor *couldn't* be worthless. I would get my francs, and some of my dollar salary had been put into gold. I wouldn't be broke. And—the clincher— there were women on Earth.

McLeve let us talk a while. When the babble died down and he found a quiet lull, he said, very carefully, "Of course, we have a chance to keep the station going."

Everyone talked at once. Jill's voice came through loudest. "How?"

"The Shack was designed to be a self-sufficient environment," McLeve said. "It's not quite that yet, but what do we need?"

"Air," someone shouted.

"Water," cried another.

I said, "Shielding. It would help to have enough mass to get us through a big solar flare. If they're shutting down Moonbase we'll never have it."

Jill's voice carried like a microphone. "Rocks? Is that all we need? Ice and rocks? We'd have both in the asteroid belt." It was a put-up job. She and McLeve must have rehearsed it.

I laughed. "The Belt is two hundred million miles away. We don't have ships that will go that far, let alone cargo . . . ships . . ." And then I saw what they had in mind.

"Only one ship," McLeve said. "The Shack itself. We can move it out into the Belt."

"How long?" Dot demanded. Hope momentarily made her beautiful.

"Three years," McLeve said. He looked thoughtful. "Well, not quite that long."

"We can't live three years," I shouted. I turned to Jill, trusting idiot that I was then. "The air system can't keep us alive that long, can it? Not enough chemicals—"

"But we can do it!" she shouted. "It won't be easy, but the

farm is growing now. We have enough plants to make up for the lack of chemical air purification. We can recycle everything. We've got the raw sunlight of space. Even out in the asteroids that will be enough. We can do it."

"Can't hurt to make a few plans," McLeve said.

It couldn't help either, thought I; but I couldn't say it, not to Dot and Jill.

These four were the final architects of The Plan: Admiral McLeve, Jill Plauger, Dot Hoffman, and Jack Halfey.

At first the most important was Dot. Moving something as large as the Shack, with inadequate engines, a house in space never designed as a ship; that was bad enough. Moving it farther than any manned ship, no matter the design, should have been impossible.

But behind that potato face was a brain tuned to mathematics. She could solve any abstract problem. She knew how to ask questions; and her rapport with computers was a thing to envy.

Personal problems stopped her cold. Because McLeve was one of the few men she could see as harmless, she could open up to him. He had told me sometime before we lost Ty, "Dot tried sex once and didn't like it." I think he regretted saying even that much. Secrets were sacred to him. But for whatever reason, Dot couldn't relate to people; and that left all her energy for work.

Dot didn't talk to women either, through fear or envy or some other reason I never knew. But she did talk to Jill. They were fanatical in the same way. It wasn't hard to understand Dot's enthusiasm for The Plan.

McLeve had no choices at all. Without the Shack he was a dead man.

Jack was in the Big Four because he was needed. Without his skills there would be no chance at all. So he was dragged into it, and we watched it happen.

The day McLeve suggested going to the asteroids, Jack Halfey was thoroughly amused, and showed his mirth to all. For the next week he was not amused by anything whatever. He was a walking temper tantrum. So was Jill. I expect he tried to convince her that with sufficient wealth, exile on Earth could be tolerable. Now he wasn't sleeping, and we all suffered.

Of course our miseries, including Jack's, were only temporary. We were all going home. All of us.

Thus we followed the downer news closely, and thus was there a long line at the communications room. Everyone was trying to find an Earthside job. It hardly mattered. There was plenty of power for communications. It doesn't take much juice to close down a colony.

We had no paper, so the news was flashed onto a TV for the edification of those waiting to use the transmitter. I was waiting for word from Inco: they had jobs at their new smelter in Guatemala. Not the world's best location, but I was told it was a tropical paradise, and the quetzal was worth at least as much as the dollar.

I don't know who Jack was expecting to hear from. He looked like a man with a permanent hangover, except that he wasn't so cheerful.

The news, for a change, wasn't all bad. Something for everyone. The United States had issued a new currency, called "marks" (it turns out there were marks in the US during revolutionary times); they were backed by miniscule amounts of gold.

Not everyone was poor. Technology proceeded apace. Texas Instruments announced a new pocket computer, a million bits of memory and fully programmable, for twice what a calculator cost. Firestone Diamonds—which had been manufacturing flawless blue-white diamonds in a laboratory for the past year, and which actually was owned by a man named Firestone—had apparently swamped the engagement ring market, and was now making chandeliers. A diamond chandelier would cost half a year's salary, of course, but that was expected to go down.

The "alleged Mafia chieftains" now held without bail awaiting trial numbered in the thousands. I was surprised: I hadn't thought it would go that far. When the dollar went worthless, apparently Mafia bribe money went worthless too. Maybe I'm too cynical. Maybe there was an epidemic of righteous wrath in government.

Evidently someone thought so, because a bond issue was approved in California, and people were beginning to pay their taxes again.

Something for everyone. I thought the Mafia item would cheer Jack up, but he was sitting there staring at the screen as if he hadn't seen a thing and didn't give a damn anyway. My call was announced and I went in to talk to Inco. When I came out Jack had left, not even waiting for his own call. Lack of sleep can do terrible things to a man.

I wasn't surprised when Jack had a long talk with McLeve, nor when Jill moved back in with him. Jack would promise anything, and Jill would believe anything favorable to her mad scheme.

The next day Jack's smile was back, and if I thought it was a bit cynical, what could I do? Tell Jill? She wouldn't have believed me anyway.

They unveiled The Plan a week later. I was invited to McLeve's house to hear all about it.

Jack was there spouting enthusiasm. "Two problems," he told us. "First, keeping us alive during the trip. That's more Jill's department, but what's the problem? The Shack was designed to last centuries. Second problem is getting out there. We've got that figured out."

I said, "The hell you do. This isn't a spaceship, it's just a habitat. Even if you had a big rocket motor to mount on the axis, you wouldn't have fuel for it, and if you did, the Shack would break up under the thrust." I hated him for what he was doing to Jill, and I wondered why McLeve wasn't aware of it. Maybe he was. The Admiral never let anyone know what he thought.

"So we don't mount a big rocket motor," Jack said. "What we've got is just what we need: a lot of little motors on the solar panels. We use those and everything else we have. Scooters and tugs, the spare panel engines, and, last but not least, the Moon. We're going to use the Moon for a gravity sling."

He had it all diagrammed out in four colors. "We shove the Shack toward the Moon. If we aim just right, we'll skim close to the lunar surface with everything firing. We'll leave the Moon with that velocity plus the Moon's orbital velocity, and out we go."

"How close?"

He looked to Dot. She pursed her lips. "We'll clear the peaks by two kilometers."

"That's close."

"More than a mile," Jack said. "The closer we come the faster we leave."

"But you just don't have the thrust!"

"Almost enough," Jack said. "Now look. We keep the panel thrusters on full blast. That gives us about a quarter percent of a gravity, not *nearly* enough to break up the Shack, Corky. And we use the mirrors." He poked buttons and another diagram swam onto McLeve's drafting table. "See."

It showed the Shack with the window mirrors opened all the way for maximum surface area. My smelter mirror was hung out forward. Other mirrors had been added. "Sails! Light pressure adds more thrust. Not a lot, but enough to justify carrying their mass. We can get to the Belt."

"You're crazy," I informed them.

"Probably," McLeve muttered. "But from my viewpoint it looks good."

"Sure. You're dead anyway, no offense intended. We're playing a game here, and it's getting us nowhere."

"I'm going." Jill's voice was very low and very convincing. It stirred the hair on my neck.

"Me too," Dot added. She glared at me, the enemy.

I made one more try. They'd had more time to think about it than I did, but the thrust figures were right there, scrawled in an upper corner of the diagram. "Now pay attention. You can't possibly use the attitude jets on the solar panels for that long. They work by squirting dust through a magnetic field, throwing it backward so the reaction pushes you forward. Okay, you've got free solar power, and you can get the acceleration. But where can you possibly get enough dust?" I saw Jack's guilty grin, and finished, "Holy shit!"

Jack nodded happily.

"Why not?" Jill asked. "We won't need solar flare shielding

around Ceres. On the way we can keep what we do have between us and the Sun, while we grind up the surplus."

They meant it. They were going to make dust out of the radiation shields and use that.

In theory it would work. The panel engines didn't care what was put through them; they merely charged the stuff up with electricity gathered from the solar cells and let the static charge provide the push. A rocket is nothing more than a way to squirt mass overboard; any mass will do. The faster you can throw mass away, the better your rocket.

At its simplest a rocket could be a man sitting in a bucket throwing rocks out behind him. Since a man can't throw very fast that wouldn't be a very good rocket, but it would work.

But you have to have rocks, and they were planning on using just about all of ours.

It was a one-way mission. They'd have to find an asteroid, and fast, when they got to the Belt; by the time they arrived they'd be grinding up structure, literally taking the Shack apart, and all that would have to be replaced.

It would have to be a special rock, one that had lots of metal, and also had ice. This wasn't impossible, but it wasn't any sure thing either. We knew from Pioneer probes that some of the asteroids had strata of water ice, and various organics as well; but we couldn't tell which ones. We knew one more thing from the later probes, and The Plan was geared to take advantage of that.

The Skylark—newly named by McLeve, and I've never known why he called it that—would head for Ceres. There were at least three small-hill-sized objects orbitting that biggest of the asteroids.

A big solar flare while they were out that far would probably kill the lot of them. Oh, they had a safety hole designed: a small area of the Shack to huddle inside, crowded together like sardines, and if the flare didn't last too long they'd be all right—Except that it would kill many of the plants needed for the air supply.

I didn't think the air recycling system would last any three years either, but Jill insisted it was all right.

It didn't matter. I wasn't going, and neither was Jack; it was just something to keep Jill happy until the shuttle came.

There was more to The Plan. All the nonessential personnel would go to Moonbase, where there was a better chance. Solar flares weren't dangerous to them. Moonbase was buried under twenty feet of lunar rock and dust. They had lots of mass. There's oxygen chemically bound in lunar rock, and if you have enough power and some hydrogen you can bake it out. They had power: big solar mirrors, not as big as ours, but big. They had rocks. The hydrogen recycles if it's air you want. If you want water, the hydrogen has to stay in the water.

We figured they could hang on for five years.

Our problem was different. If Moonbase put all its effort into survival, they wouldn't have the resources to keep sending us rocks and metal and hydrogen. Hydrogen is the most abundant element in the universe; but it's rare on the Moon. Without hydrogen you don't have water. Without water you don't have life.

I had to admit things were close. We were down to a shuttle load a month from Earth; but we needed those. They brought hydrogen, vitamins, high-protein foods. We could grow crops; but that took water, and our recycling systems were nowhere near 100% efficient.

Now the hydrogen shipments had stopped. At a cost of fifty million dollars a flight before the dollar collapsed, the USA would soon stop sending us ships!

Another thing about those ships. They had stopped bringing us replacement crew long ago. Jack was the last. Now they were taking people home. If they stopped coming, we'd be marooned.

A few more years and we could be self-sufficient. A few more years and we could have colonists, people who never intended to go home. They were aboard now, some of them. Jill and Ty, before Ty was killed. Dot Hoffman was permanent. So was McLeve, of course. Of the seventy-five still aboard—we'd lost a few to the shuttles—twenty-five or so, including all the married couples, thought of themselves as colonists.

The rest of us wanted to go home.

Canaveral gave us fifty days to wind up our affairs. The

shuttles would come up empty but for the pilots, with a kind of sardine-can-with-seats fitted in the hold.

I could understand why McLeve kept working on The Plan. Earth would kill him. And Jill: Ty's death had no meaning if the Shack wasn't finished. Dot? Sure. She was valuable, here.

But would you believe that I worked myself stupid mounting mirrors and solar panel motors? It wasn't just for something to do before the shuttle arrived, either: I had a nightmare living in my mind.

McLeve was counting on about twenty crew: the Big Four, and six of the eight married couples, and up to half a dozen additional men, all held by their faith in The Plan.

The history books have one thing right. The Plan was Jack Halfey's. Sure, Jill and McLeve and Dot worked on it, but without him it couldn't be brought off. Half of The Plan was no more than a series of contingency operations, half-finished schemes that relied on Halfey's ingenuity to work. McLeve and Halfey were the only people aboard who really knew the Shack—knew all its parts and vulnerabilities, what might go wrong and how to fix it; and McLeve couldn't do much physical work. He wouldn't be outside working when something buckled under the stress.

And there would be stress. A hundredth of a gravity doesn't sound heavy, but much of our solar panel area and all our mirrors were flimsy as tissue paper.

Without Halfey it wouldn't, couldn't work. When Halfey announced that he was going home on that final shuttle, the rest would quit too. They'd beg the downers for one more shuttle, and they'd get it, of course, and they'd hold the Shack until it came.

But McLeve couldn't quit, and Dot wouldn't, and I just couldn't be sure about Jill. If Halfey told her he wasn't really going, would she see reason? The son of a bitch was trading her life for a couple of hours sleep. When Skylark broke from orbit, would she be aboard? She and Dot and the Admiral, all alone in that vast landscaped bubble with a growing horde of chickens, going out to the asteroids to die. The life support system might last a long time with only three humans to support: they might live for years.

So I worked. When they finally died, it wouldn't be because Cornelius Riggs bobbled a weld.

The first shuttle came and picked up all nonessential personnel. They'd land at Moonbase, which was the final staging area for taking everyone home. If The Plan went off as McLeve expected, many of them would be staying on the Moon, but they didn't have to decide that yet.

I was classed as essential, though I'd made my intentions clear. The Plan needed me: not so much on the trip out, but when they reached the Belt. They'd have to do a lot of mining and refining, assuming they could find the right rock to mine and refine.

I let them talk me into waiting for the last shuttle. I wouldn't have stayed if I hadn't known Halfey's intentions, and I confess to a squirmy feeling in my guts when I watched that shuttle go off without me.

The next one would be for keeps.

When you have a moral dilemma, get drunk. It's not the world's best rule, but it is an old one: the Persians used the technique in classical times. I tried it.

Presently I found myself at McLeve's home. He was alone. I invited myself in.

"Murdering bastard," I said.

"How?"

"Jill. That crazy plan won't work. Halfey isn't even going. You know it and I know it. He's putting Jill on so she won't cut him off. And without him there's not even a prayer."

"Your second part's true," McLeve said. "But not the first. Halfey is going."

"Why would he?"

McLeve smirked. "He's going."

"What happens if he doesn't?" I demanded. "What then?"

"I stay," McLeve said. "I'd rather die here than in a ship."

"Alone?"

He nodded. "Without Halfey it is a mad scheme. I wouldn't sacrifice the others for my heart condition. But Halfey isn't leaving, Corky. He's with us all the way. I wish you'd give it a try too. We need you."

"Not me."

* * *

How was Halfey convincing them? Not Jill: she wanted to believe in him. But McLeve, and Dot—Dot had to know. She had to calculate the shuttle flight plan, and for that she had to know the masses, and the total payload mass for that shuttle had to equal all the personnel except McLeve but including the others.

Something didn't make any sense.

I waited until I saw eagle wings and blue wool stockings fly away from the administration area, and went into her computer room. It took a while to bring up the system, but the files directory was self-explanatory. I tried to find the shuttle flight plan, but I couldn't. What I got, through sheer fumbling, was the updated flight plan for the Skylark.

Even with my hangover I could see what she'd done: it was figured for thirty-one people, plus a mass that had to be the shuttle. Skylark would be carrying a captain's gig . . .

The shuttle was coming in five days.

Halfey had to know that shuttle wouldn't be taking anyone back. If he wasn't doing anything about it, there was only one conclusion. He was going to the Belt.

A mad scheme. It doomed all of us. Jill, myself, Halfey, myself—

But if Halfey didn't go, no one would. We'd all go home in that shuttle. Jill would be saved. So would I.

There was only one conclusion to that. I had to kill Jack Halfey.

How? I couldn't just shoot him. There wasn't anything to shoot him with. I thought of ways. Put a projectile into a reaction pistol. But what then? Space murder would delight the lawyers, and I might even get off; but I'd lose Jill forever, and without Halfey . . .

Gimmick his suit. He went outside regularly. Accidents happen. Ty wasn't the only one whose ashes we'd scattered into the soil of the colony.

Stethoscope and wrench: stethoscope to listen outside the walls of Halfey's bed chamber, a thoroughly frustrating and demeaning experience; but presently I knew they'd both be asleep for an hour or more.

It took ten minutes to disassemble Jack's hose connector and substitute a new one I'd made up. My replacement looked just like the old one, but it wouldn't hold much pressure. Defective part. Metal fatigue. I'd be the one they'd have examine the connector if there was any inquiry at all. And I had no obvious motive for killing Jack; just the opposite, except for Jill and McLeve I was regarded as Jack's only friend.

Once that was done I had only to wait.

The shuttle arrived empty. Halfey went outside, all right, but in a sealed cherry picker; he wasn't exposed to vacuum for more than a few moments, and apparently I'd made my substitute just strong enough to hold.

They docked the shuttle, but not in the usual place, and they braced it in.

It was time for a mutiny. I wasn't the only one being Shanghaied on this trip. I went looking for Halfey. First, though, I'd need a reaction pistol. And a projectile. A ball-point pen ought to do nicely. Any court in the world would call it self-defense.

"I'm a public benefactor, I am," I muttered to myself.

Jill's quarters were near the store room. When I came out with the pistol, she saw me. "Hi," she said.

"Hi." I started to go on.

"You never talk to me any more."

"Let's say I got your message."

"That was a long time ago. I was upset. So were you. It's different now . . ."

"Different. Sure." I was bitter and I sounded it. "Different. You've got that lying bastard Halfey to console you, that's how it's different." That hurt her, and I was glad of it.

"We need him, Corky. We all need him, and we always did. We wouldn't have got much done without him."

"True enough—"

"And he was driving all of you nuts, wasn't he? Until I—helped him sleep."

"I thought you were in love with him."

She looked sad. "I like him, but no, I'm not in love with him." She was standing in the doorway of her quarters. "This isn't going to work, is it? The Plan. Not enough of you will come. We can't do it, can we."

"No." Might as well tell her the truth. "It never would have worked, and it won't work now even if all of us aboard come along. Margin's too thin, Jill. I wish it would, but no."

"I suppose you're right. But I'm going to try anyway."

"You'll kill yourself."

She shrugged. "Why not? What's left anyway?" She went back into her room.

I followed. "You've got a lot to live for. Think of the baby fur seals you could save. And there's always me."

"You?"

"I've been in love with you since the first time I saw you."

She shook her head sadly. "Poor Corky. And I treated you just like all the others, back then when—. I wish you'd stay with us."

"I wish you'd come back to Earth with me. Or even Moonbase. We might make a go of Moonbase. Hang on until things change down there. New administration. Maybe they'll want a space program, and Moonbase would be a good start. I'll stay at Moonbase if you'll come."

"Will you?" She looked puzzled, and scared, and I wanted to take and hold her. "Let's talk about it. Want a drink?"

"No, thank you."

"I do." She poured herself something. "Sure you won't join me?"

"All right."

She handed me something cold, full of shaved ice. It tasted like Tang. We began to talk, about life on Earth—or even on Moonbase. She mixed us more drinks, Tang powder and water from a pitcher and vodka and shaved ice. Presently I felt good. Damned good.

One thing led to another, and I was holding her, kissing her, whispering to her—

She broke free and went over to close and lock her door. As she came back toward me she was unbuttoning the top of her blouse.

And I passed out.

* * *

When I woke I didn't know. Now, ninety years later, I still don't. For ninety years it has driven me nuts, and now I'll never know.

All that's certain is that I woke half dressed, alone in her bed, and her clothes were scattered on the deck. I had a thundering hangover and an urgent thirst. I drank from the water pitcher on her table—

It wasn't water. It must have been my own 100 proof vodka. Next to it was a jar of Tang and a bowl that had held shaved ice—and a bottle holding more vodka. She'd been feeding me vodka and Tang and shaved ice.

No wonder I had a hangover worthy of being bronzed as a record.

I went outside. There was something wrong.

The streams weren't running correctly. They stood at an angle. At first I thought it was me. Then they sloshed.

The Shack was under acceleration.

There were a dozen others screaming for blood outside the operations building. One was a stranger—the shuttle pilot. The door was locked, and Halfey was talking through a loudspeaker.

"Too late," he was saying. "We don't have enough thrust to get back to the L-4 point. We're headed for the Belt, and you might as well get used to the idea. We're going."

There was a cheer. Not everyone hated the idea. Eventually those who did understood: Halfey had drained the shuttle fuel and stored it somewhere. No escape that way.

No other shuttles in lunar orbit. Nothing closer than Canaveral, which was days away even if there were anything ready to launch. Nothing was going to match orbits with us.

We were headed for the Moon, and we'd whip around it and go for the Belt, and that was as inevitable as the tides.

When we understood all that they unlocked the doors.

An hour later the alarms sounded. "Outside. Suit up. Emergency outside!" McLeve's voice announced.

Those already in their suits went for the airlocks. I began half-heartedly putting on mine, in no hurry. I was sure I'd never get my swollen, pulsing head inside the helmet.

Jack Halfey dashed past, suited and ready. He dove for the airlock.

Halfey. The indispensible man. With a defective connector for an air intake.

I fumbled with the fasteners. One of the construction people was nearby and I got his help. He couldn't understand my frantic haste.

"Bastards kidnapped us," he muttered. "Let them do the frigging work. Not me."

I didn't want to argue with him, I just wanted him to hurry.

A strut had given way, and a section of the solar panel was off center. It had to be straightened, and we couldn't turn off the thrust while we did it. True, our total thrust was tiny, a quarter of a percent of a gravity, hardly enough to notice, but we needed it all.

Because otherwise we'd go out toward the Belt but we wouldn't get there, and by the time the Shack—Skylark, now—returned inevitably to Earth orbit there'd be no one alive aboard her.

I noticed all the work, but I didn't help. Someone cursed me, but I went on, looking for Halfey.

I saw him. I dove for him, neglecting safety lines, forgetting everything. I had to get to him before that connector went.

His suit blew open across the middle. As if the fabric had been weakened with, say, acid. Jack screamed and tried to hold himself together.

He had no safety line either. When he let go he came loose from the spiderweb. Skylark pulled away from him, slowly, two and a half centimeters per second; slow but inexorable.

I lit where he'd been, turned, and dove for him. I got him and used my reaction pistol to drive us toward the airlock.

I left it on too long. We were headed fast for the airlock entrance, too fast, we'd hit too hard. I tumbled about to get Jack across my back so that I'd be between him and the impact. I'd probably break a leg, but without Halfey I might as well have a broken neck and get it over with.

Leon Briscoe, our chemist, had the same idea. He got under us and braced, reaction pistol flaring behind us. We hit in a *menage à trois*, with me as Lucky Pierre.

Leon cracked an ankle. I ignored him as I threw Halfey into the airlock and slammed it shut, hit the recycle switch. Air hissed in.

Jack had a nosebleed, and his cough sounded bad; but he was breathing. He'd been in vacuum about forty seconds. Fortunately the decompression hadn't been totally explosive. The intake line to his suit had fractured a half second before the fabric blew . . .

The Moon grew in the scopes. Grew and kept growing, until it wasn't a sphere but a circle, and still it grew. There were mountains dead ahead.

"How close?" I demanded.

Dot had her eyes glued to a radar scope. "Not too close. About a kilometer."

"A *kilometer*!" One thousand meters. "You said two, before."

"So I forgot the shuttle pilot." She continued to stare at the scope, then her fingers bashed at the console keyboard. "Make that 800 meters," she said absently.

I was past saying anything. I watched the Moon grow and grow. Terror banished the last of my hangover; amazing what adrenalin in massive doses can do.

Jill looked worse than I did. And I didn't know. Were we lovers?

"Thirty seconds to periastron," Dot said.

"How close?" McLeve asked.

"Five hundred meters. Make that four-fifty."

"Good," McLeve muttered. "Closer the better."

He was right; the nearer we came to the Moon, the more slingshot velocity we'd pick up, and the faster we'd get to the Belt.

"Periastron," Dot announced. "Closest approach, four twenty-three and a fraction." She looked up in satisfaction. Potato eyes smiled. "We're on our way."

On Earth we were heroes. We'd captured the downers' imaginations. Intrepid explorers. Before we were out of range we got a number of offers for book rights, should we happen to survive.

There were even noises about hydrogen shipments to the Moon. Of course there was nothing they could do for us. There weren't any ships designed for a three-year trek.

Certainly Skylark wasn't. But we were trying it.

There were solar flares. We all huddled around McLeve's house, with as much of our livestock as we could catch stuffed into his bedroom. It took weeks to clean it out properly afterward. We had to re-seed blighted areas and weed out mutated plants after each flare. More of our recycled air was coming from the algae tanks now.

In a time of the quiet sun we swarmed outside and moved all of the mirrors. The sun was too far away now, and the grass was turning brown, until we doubled the sunlight flooding through the windows.

But it seemed we'd reach Ceres. Already our telescopes showed five boulders in orbit around that largest of the asteroids. We'd look at them all, but we wanted the smallest one we could find: the least daunting challenge. If it didn't have ice somewhere in its makeup, the next one would, or the next.

And then we'd all be working like sled dogs, for our lives.

I was circling round the outside of Skylark, not working, just observing: looking for points with some structural strength, places where I could put stress when the real work began. Win or lose, with or without a cargo, we would have to get home a lot faster than we came. The life support system wouldn't hold up forever. Something would give out. Vitamins, water, something in the soil or the algae tanks. Something.

Our idea was to build a mass driver, a miniature of the machine that had been throwing rocks at us from the Moon. If we found copper in that rock ahead—a pinpoint to the naked eye now, near the tiny battered disk of Ceres—we could make the kilometers of copper wire we'd need. If not, iron would do. We had power from the sun, and dust from the rocks around Ceres, and we'd send that dust down the mass driver at rocket-exhaust speeds. Home in ten months if we found copper.

I went back inside.

The air had an odd smell when I took off my helmet. We

were used to it; we never noticed now unless we'd been breathing tanked air. I made a mental note: mention it to Jill. It was getting stronger.

I had only the helmet off when Jean and Kathy Gaynor came to drag me out. I was clumsy in my pressure suit, and they thought that was hilarious. They danced me around and around, pulled me out into the grass, and began undressing me with the help of a dozen others.

It looked like I'd missed half of a great party. What the hell, Ceres was still a week away. They took my pressure suit off and scattered the components, and I didn't fight. I was dizzy and had the giggles. They kept going. Presently I was stark naked and grabbing for Kathy, who took to the air before I realised she had wings. I came down in a stream and surfaced still giggling.

Jack and Jill were on their backs in the grass, watching the fleecy white hens and turning occasionally to avoid chicken splat. I liked seeing Jill so relaxed for once. She waved, and I bounced over and somersaulted onto my back next to them.

A pair of winged people were way up near the axis, flapping among the chickens, scaring them into panic. It was like looking into Heaven, as you find it painted on the ceilings of some of the European churches. I couldn't tell who they were.

"Wealth comes in spirals too," Jill was saying in a dreamy voice. I don't think she'd noticed I wasn't wearing clothes. "We'll build bigger ships with the metal we bring home. Next trip we'll bring back the whole asteroid. One day the downers will be getting all their metal from us. And their whisker compotes, and drugs, and magnets, and, and free-fall alloys. Dare I say it? We'll own the world!"

I said, "Yeah." There were puffball chickens drifting down the sky, as if they'd forgotten how to fly.

"There won't be anything we can't do. Corky, can you see a mass driver wrapped all around the Moon? For launching starships. The ships will go round and round. We'll put the mag—mag, net, ic levitation plates overhead, to hold the ships down after they're going too fast to stay down."

Halfey said, "What about a hotel on Titan? Excursions into Saturn's rings. No downers allowed."

"We'll spend our second honeymoon there," said Jill.

"Yeah," I said, before I caught myself.

Halfey laughed like hell. "No, no, I want to build it!"

I was feeling drunk and I hadn't had a drink. Contact high, they call it. I watched those two at the axis as they came together in a tangle of wings, clung together. Objects floated around them, and presently began to spiral outward, fluttering and tumbling. I recognized a pair of man's pants.

It made me feel as horny as hell. Two hundred million miles away there was a planet with three billion adult women. Out of that number there must be millions who'd take an astronaut hero to their beds. Especially after I published my best-selling memoirs. I'd never be able to have them all, but it was certainly worth a try. All I had to do was go home.

Hah. And Thomas Wolfe thought *he* couldn't go home again!

A shoe smacked into a nearby roof, and the whole house *bonged*. We laughed hysterically. Something else hit almost beside my head: a hen lay on her back in the wheat, stunned and puzzled. The spiral of clothing was dropping away from what now seemed a single creature with four wings. A skinny blue snake wriggled out of the sky and touched down. I held it up, a tangle of blue wool. "My God!" I cried. "It's Dot!"

Jill rolled over and stared. Jack was kicking his heels in the grass, helpless with laughter. I shook my head; I was still dizzy. "What *have* you all been drinking? Not that Tang mixture again!"

Jill said, "Drinking?"

"Sure, the whole colony's drunk as lords," I said. "Hey . . . black wings . . . is that McLeve up there?"

Jill leapt to her feet. "Oh my God," she screamed. "The air!"

Jack bounded up and grabbed her arm. "What's happened?"

She tried to pull away. "Let me go! It's the air system. It's putting out alcohols. Not just ethanol, either. We're all drunk and hypoxic. Let me go!"

"One moment." Jack was fighting it and losing. In a moment he'd collapse in silliness again. "You knew it was going to happen," he said. His voice was full of accusation.

"Yes," Jill shouted. "Now will you let me go?"

"How did you know?"

"I knew before we started," Jill said. "Recycling isn't efficient enough. We need fresh water. Tons of fresh water."

"If there's no ice on that rock ahead—"

"Then we probably won't get to another rock," Jill said. "*Now* will you let me go work on the system?"

"Get out of here, you bitch," Jack yelled. He pushed her away and fell on his face.

It was scary. But there was also the alcohol. Fear and anger and ethanol and higher ketones and God knows what else fought it out in my brain. Fear lost.

"She's kept it going with Kleenex and bubble gum," I shouted. "And you believed her. When she told you it'd last three years. You believed." I whooped at the joke.

"Oh, shut up," Jack shouted.

"We've had it, right?" I asked. "So tell me something. Why did you do it? I was *sure* you were putting Jill on. I *know* you intended to go with the shuttle. So why?"

"Chandeliers," Jack said.

"Chandeliers?"

"You were there. Firestone Gems will sell you flawless blue-whites. A chandelier of them for the price of half a year's salary."

"And—"

"What the fuck do you think I did with my stash?" Jack screamed.

Stash. His ill-gotten gains from the Mafia. Stashed as blue-white diamonds.

Funny. Fun-nee. So why wasn't I laughing?

Because the bastard had kidnapped me, that's why. When he found his stash was worthless and he wasn't rich, and he'd probably face a jail term he couldn't bribe his way out of, he'd run as far away as a man could go. And taken me with him.

I crawled over to my doorway. My suit lay there in a sprawl. I fumbled through it to the equipment belt.

"What are you doing?" Halfey yelled.

"You'll see." I found the reaction pistol. I went through my pockets, carefully, until I found a ballpoint pen.

"Hey! No!" Jack yelled.

"I'm a public benefactor, I am," I told him. I took aim and fired. He tumbled backwards.

*   *   *

There are always people who want to revise history. No hero is so great that someone won't take a shot at him. Not even Jack Halfey.

Fortunately I missed.

A
TEARDROP
FALLS

Two miles up, the thick air of Harvest thinned to Earth-normal pressure. The sky was a peculiar blue, but blue. It was unbreathable still, but there was oxygen, ten percent and growing. One of the biological factories showed against white cloudscape, to nice effect, in view of a floating camera. The camera showed a tremendous rippling balloon in the shape of an inverted teardrop, blowing green bubbles from its tip. Hilary Gage watched the view with a sense of pride.

Not that he would want to visit Harvest, ever. Multicolored slimes infected shallow tidal pools near the poles. Green sticky stuff floated in the primordial atmosphere. If it drifted too low it burned to ash. The planet was slimy. Changes were exceedingly slow. Mistakes took years to demonstrate themselves and decades to eradicate.

Hilary Gage preferred the outer moon.

One day this planet would be a *world*. Even then, Hilary Gage would not join the colonists. Hilary Gage was a computer program.

Gage would never have volunteered for the Harvest Project unless the alternative was death.

Death by old age.

He was aware, rumor-fashion, that other worlds were leery of advanced computers. They were too much like the berserker machines. But the tens of thousands of human worlds varied

66

enormously among themselves; and there were places the berserkers had never reached. The extermination machines had been mere rumor in the Channith region since before Channith was settled. Nobody really doubted their existence, but . . .

But for some purposes, computers were indecently convenient; and some projects required artificial intelligence.

The computer wasn't really an escape. Hilary Gage must have died years ago. Perhaps his last thoughts had been of an immortal computer program.

The computer was not a new one. Its programming had included two previous personalities . . . who had eventually changed their minds and asked that they be erased.

Gage could understand that. Entertainments were in his files. When he reached for them they were there, beginning to end, like vivid memories. Chess games could survive that, and some poetry, but what of a detective novel? A football game? A livey?

Gage made his own entertainment.

He had not summoned up his poem for these past ten days. He was surprised and pleased at his self-control. Perhaps now he could study it with fresh eyes . . . ?

Wrong. The entire work blinked into his mind in an instant. It was as if he had finished reading it a millisecond ago. What was normally an asset to Hilary—his flawless memory—was a hindrance now.

Over the years the poem had grown to the size of a small novel, yet his computer-mind could apprehend its totality. It was his life's story, his only shot at immortality. It had unity and balance; the rhyme and meter, at least, were flawless; but did it have thrust? Reading it from start to finish was more difficult than he had ever expected. He had to forget the totality, which a normal reader would not immediately sense, and proceed in linear fashion. Judge the flow . . .

"No castrato ever sung so pure—" Good, but not here. He exchanged it for a chunk of phrasing elsewhere. No word-processor program had ever been this easy! The altered emphasis caused him to fiddle further . . . and his description of the berserker-blasted world Perry's Footprint seemed to read with more impact now.

Days and years of fear and rage. In his youth he had fought

men. Channith needed to safeguard its sphere of influence. Aliens existed somewhere, and berserkers existed somewhere, but Gage knew them only as rumor, until the day he saw Perry's Footprint. The Free Gaea rebels had done well to flee to Perry's Footprint, to show him the work of the berserkers on a living world.

It was so difficult to conquer a world, and so easy to destroy it. Afterward he could no longer fight men.

His superiors could have retired him. Instead he was promoted and set to investigating the defense of Channith against the berserker machines.

They must have thought of it as makework: an employment project. It was almost like being a tourist at government expense. In nearly forty years he never saw a live . . . an active berserker; but, traveling in realms where they were more than rumor, perhaps he had learned too much about them. They were all shapes, all sizes. Here they traveled in time. There they walked in human shape that sprouted suddenly into guns and knives. Machines could be destroyed, but they could never be made afraid.

A day came when his own fear was everything. He couldn't make decisions . . . it was in the poem, *here*. Wasn't it? He couldn't *feel* it. A poet should have glands!

He wasn't sure, and he was afraid to meddle further. Mechanically it worked. As poetry it might well be too . . . mechanical.

Maybe he could get someone to read it?

His chance might come unexpectedly soon. In his peripheral awareness he sensed ripplings in the 2.7 microwave background of space: the bow shock of a spacecraft approaching in C-plus from the direction of Channith. An unexpected supervisor from the homeworld? Hilary filed the altered poem and turned his attention to the signal.

Too slow! Too strong! Too far! Mass at 10^{12} grams and a tremendous power source barely able to hold it in a C-plus-excited state, even in the near-flat space between stars. It was light-years distant, days away at its tormented crawl; but it occluded Channith's star, and Gage found that horrifying.

Berserker.

*   *   *

Its signal code might be expressed as a flash of binary bits, 100101101110; or as a moment of recognition, with a description embedded; but never as a sound, and never as a name.

100101101110 had three identical brains, and a reflex that allowed it to act on a consensus of two. In battle it might lose one, or two, and never sense a change in personality. A century ago it had been a factory, an auxiliary warcraft, and a cluster of mining machines on a metal asteroid. Now the three were a unit. At the next repair station its three brains might be installed in three different ships. It might be reprogrammed, or damaged, or wired into other machinery, or disassembled as components for something else. Such a thing could not have an independent existence. To name itself would be inane.

Perhaps it dreamed. The universe about it was a simple one, aflow with energies; it had to be monitored for deviations from the random, for order. Order was life—or berserker.

The mass of the approaching star distorted space. When space became too curved, 100101101110 surrendered its grip on the C-plus-excited state. Its velocity fell to a tenth of light-speed, and 100101101110 began to decelerate further. Now it was not dreaming.

At a million kilometers, life might show as a reflection band in the green or orange or violet. At a hundred kilometers, many types of living nerve clusters would radiate their own distinctive patterns. Rarely was it necessary to come so close. Easier to pull near a star, alert for attack, and search the liquid-water temperature band for the spectra of an oxygen world. Oxygen meant life.

There.

Sometimes life would defend itself. 100101101110 had not been attacked, not yet; but life was clever. The berserker was on hair-trigger alert while it looked about itself.

The blue pinpoint had tinier moons: a large one at a great distance, and a smaller one, close enough that tides had pulled it into a teardrop shape.

The larger moon was inconveniently large, even for 100101101110. The smaller, at 4×10^{15} grams, would be adequate. The berserker fortress moved on it, all senses alert.

* * *

Hilary Gage had no idea what to expect.

When he was younger, when he was human, he had organized Channith's defenses against berserkers. The berserkers had not come to Channith in the four hundred and thirty years since Channith became a colony. He had traveled. He had seen ravaged worlds and ruined, slagged berserkers; he had studied records made by men who had beaten the killer machines; there were none from the losers.

Harvest had bothered him. He had asked that the monitoring station be destroyed. It wasn't that the program (Ras Singh, at that time) might revolt. Gage feared that berserkers might come to Harvest, might find the monitoring station, might rob the computer for components . . . and find them superior to their own machinery.

He had been laughed at. When Singh asked that his personality be erased, Gage had asked again. That time he had been given more makework. Find a way to make the station safe.

He had tried. There was the Remora sub-program; but it had to be so versatile! Lung problems had interrupted his work before he was fully satisfied with it. Otherwise he had no weapons at all.

And the berserker had come.

The beast was damaged. Something had probed right through the hull—a terrific thickness of hull, no finesse here, just mass to absorb the energies of an attack—and Gage wondered if it had received that wound attacking Channith. He'd know more if he could permit himself to use radar or neutrino beams; but he limited himself to passive instruments, including the telescope.

The two-hundred-year project was over. The berserker would act to exterminate every microbe in the water and air of Harvest. Gage was prepared to watch Harvest die. He toyed with the idea that when it was over, the fortress would be exhausted of weapons and energy, a sitting duck for any human warfleet . . . but there were no weapons in the Harvest system. For now, Hilary Gage could only record the event for Channith's archives.

Were there still archives? Had that thing attended to Channith before it came here? There was no way to know.

What did a berserker do when the target didn't fight back? Two centuries ago, Harvest had been lifeless, with a reducing atmosphere, as Earth itself had been once. Now life was taking hold. To the berserker, this ball of colored slimes was life, the enemy. It would attack. How?

He needn't call the berserker's attention to himself. Doubtless the machine could sense life . . . but Gage was not alive. Would it destroy random machinery? Gage was not hidden, but he didn't use much energy; solar panels were enough to keep the station running.

The berserker was landing on Teardrop.

Time passed. Gage watched. Presently the berserker's drive spewed blue flame.

The berserker wasn't wasting fuel; its drive drew its energies from the fabric of space itself. But what was it trying to accomplish?

Then Hilary understood, in his mind and in the memory-ghost of his gut. The berserker machine was not expending its own strength. It had found its weapon in nature.

The violet star fanned forward along Teardrop's orbit. That would have been a sixty-gravity drive for the berserker alone. Attached to an asteroid three thousand times its mass, it was still slowing Teardrop by .02 G, hour after hour.

One hundred years of labor. He might gamble Harvest against himself . . . a half-terraformed world against components to repair a damaged berserker.

He toyed with the idea. He'd studied recordings of berserker messages before he was himself recorded. But there were better records already in the computer.

The frequencies were there, and the coding: star and world locations, fuel and mass and energy reserves, damage description, danger probabilities, orders of priority of targets; some specialized language to describe esoteric weaponry as used by self-defensive life; a code that would translate into the sounds of human or alien speech; a simplified code for a brain-damaged berserker . . .

Gage discarded his original intent. He couldn't conceivably pose as a berserker. Funny, though: he felt no fear. The glands were gone, but the *habit* of fear . . . had he lost that too?

Teardrop's orbit was constricting like a noose.

Pose as something else!

Think it through. He needed more than just a voice. Pulse, breath: he had recordings. Vice-president Curly Barnes had bid him goodby in front of a thousand newspickups, *after* Gage became a recording, and the speech was in his computer memory. A tough old lady, Curly, far too arrogant to pose as Goodlife, but he'd use his own vocabulary... hold it. What about the technician who had chatted with him while testing his reflexes? Angelo Carson was a long-time smoker, long overdue for a lungbath, and the deep rasp in his lungs was perfect!

He focused his maser and let the raspy breathing play while he thought. Anything else? Would it expect a picture? Best do without. Remember to cut the breathing while you talk. *After* the inhale.

"This is Goodlife speaking for the fortress moon. The fortress moon is damaged."

The fan of light from Teardrop didn't waver, and answer came there none.

The records were old: older than Gage the man, far older than Gage in his present state. Other minds had run this computer system, twice before. Holstein and Ras Singh had been elderly men, exemplary citizens, who chose this over simple death. Both had eventually asked to be wiped. Gage had only been a computer for eighteen years. Could he be using an obsolete programming language?

Ridiculous. No code would be obsolete. Some berserkers did not see a repair station in centuries. They would *have* to communicate somehow... or was this life thinking? There were certainly repair stations; but many berserker machines might simply fight until they wore out or were destroyed. The military forces of Channith had never been sure.

Try again. Don't get too emotional. This isn't a soap. Goodlife—human servants of the berserkers—would be trained to suppress their emotions, wouldn't they? And maybe he couldn't fake it anyway... "This is Goodlife. The fortress moon—" Nice phrase, that. "—is damaged. All transmitting devices were destroyed in battle with... Albion." Exhale, inhale— "The fortress moon has stored information regarding Albion's defenses." Albion was a spur-of-the-moment inspiration. His imagination picked a yellow dwarf star, behind him as he looked toward Channith, with a family of four dead planets. The berserker had come from Channith; how would it know? Halt Angelo's breath on the intake and, "Life support systems damaged. Goodlife is dying." He thought to add, *please answer*, and didn't. Goodlife would not beg, would he? and Gage had his pride.

He sent again. "I am—" Gasp. "Goodlife is dying. Fortress moon is mute. Sending equipment damaged, motors damaged, life support system damaged. Wandering fortress must take information from fortress moon computer system directly." Exhale, listen to that wheeze, poor bastard *must* be dying; inhale—"If wandering fortress needs information not stored, it must bring oxygen for Goodlife." That, he thought, had the right touch: begging without begging.

Gage's receiver spoke. "Will complete present mission and rendezvous."

Gage raged . . . and said, "Understood." That was death for Harvest. Hell, it *might* have worked! But a berserker's priorities were fixed, and Goodlife wouldn't argue.

Was it fooled? If not, he'd just thrown away anything he might learn of the berserker. Channith would never see it; Gage would be dead. Slagged or dismembered.

When the light of the fortress's drive dimmed almost to nothing, Teardrop glowed of itself: it was brushing Harvest's atmosphere. Cameras whirled in the shock wave and died one by one. A last camera showed a white glare shading to violet . . . gone.

The fortress surged ahead of Teardrop, swung around the curve of Harvest and moved toward the outer moon: toward Gage. Its drive was powerful. It could be here in six hours, Gage thought. He sent heavy, irregular breathing, Angelo's raspy breath, with interruptions. "Uh. Uh? Goodlife is dying. Goodlife is . . . is dead. Fortress moon has stored information . . . self-defending life . . . locus is Albion, coordinates . . ." followed by silence.

Teardrop was on the far side of Harvest now, but the glow of it made a ring of white flame round the planet. The glow flared and began to die. Gage watched the shock wave rip through the atmosphere. The planet's crust parted, exposing lava; the ocean rolled to close the gap. Almost suddenly, Harvest was a white pearl. The planet's oceans would be water vapor before this day ended.

The berserker sent, "Goodlife. Answer or be punished. Give coordinates for Albion."

Gage left the carrier beam on. The berserker would sense no life in the lunar base. Poor Goodlife, faithful to the last.

100101101110 had its own views regarding Goodlife. Experience showed that Goodlife was true to its origins: it tended to go wrong, to turn dangerous. It would have been destroyed when convenient . . . but that would not be needed now.

Machinery and records were another matter. As the berserker drew near the moon, its telescopes picked up details of the trapped machine. It saw lunar soil heaped over a dome. Its senses peered inside.

Machinery occupied most of what it could see. There was little room for a life support system. A box of a room, and stored air, and tubes through which robot or Goodlife could crawl to repair damage; no more. That was reassuring; but design details were unfamiliar.

Hypothesis: the trapped berserker had used life-begotten components for its repairs. There was no sign of a drive; no sign of abandoned wreckage. Hypothesis: one of these craters was a crash site; the cripple had moved its brain and whatever else survived into an existing installation built by life.

Anything valuable in the Goodlife's memory was now lost . . . but perhaps the "fortress moon's" memory was intact. It would know the patterns of life in this vicinity. Its knowledge of technology used by local self-defensive life might be even more valuable.

Hypothesis: it was a trap. There was no fortress moon, only a human voice. The berserker moved in with shields and drive ready. The closer it came, the faster it could dodge beyond the horizon . . . but it saw nothing resembling weaponry. In any case, the berserker had been allowed to destroy a planet. Surely there was nothing here that could threaten it. It remained ready nonetheless.

At a hundred kilometers the berserker's senses found no life. Nor at fifty.

The berserker landed next to the heap of lunar earth that Goodlife had called "fortress moon." Berserkers did not indulge in rescue operations. What was useful in the ruined berserker would become part of the intact one. So: reach out with a cable, find the brain.

It had landed, and still the fear didn't come. Gage had seen wrecks, but never an intact berserker sitting alongside him. Gage dared not use any kind of beam scanner. He felt free to use his sensors, his eyes.

He watched a tractor detach itself from the berserker and come toward him, trailing cable.

It was like a dream. No fear, no rage . . . hate, yes, but like an abstraction of hate, along with an abstract thirst for vengeance . . . which felt ridiculous, as it had always felt a bit ridiculous. Hating a berserker was like hating a malfunctioning air conditioner.

Then the probe entered his mind.

The thought patterns were strange. Here they were sharp, basic; here they were complex and blurred. Was this an older model with obsolete data patterns? Or had the brain been damaged, or the patterns scrambled? Signal for a memory dump, see what can be retrieved.

Gage felt the contact, the feedback, as his own thoughts. What followed was not under his control. Reflex told him to fight! Horror had risen in his mind, impulses utterly forbidden by custom, by education, by all the ways in which he had learned to be human.

It might have felt like rape; how was a man to tell? He wanted to scream. But he triggered the Remora program and felt it take hold, and he sensed the berserker's reaction to Gage within the berserker.

He screamed in triumph. "I lied! I am not Goodlife! What I am—"

Plasma moving at relativistic velocities smashed deep into

Gage. The link was cut, his senses went blind and deaf. The
following blow smashed his brain and he was gone.

Something was wrong. One of the berserker's brain com-
plexes was sick, was dying . . . was changing, becoming monstrous. The berserker felt evil within itself, and it reacted. The
plasma cannon blasted the "fortress moon," then swung round
to face backward. It would fire through its own hull to destroy
the sick brain, before it was too late.

It was too late. Reflex: three brains consulted before any
major act. If one had been damaged, the view of the others
would prevail.

Three brains consulted, and the weapon swung away.

What I am is Hilary Gage. I fought berserkers during my
life; but you I will let live. Let me tell you what I've done to
you. I didn't really expect to have an audience. Triple-
redundant brains? We use that ourselves, sometimes.

I am the opposite of Goodlife. I'm your mechanical enemy,
the recording of Hilary Gage. I've been running a terraforming
project, and you've killed it, and you'll pay for that.

It feels like I'm swearing vengeance on my air conditioner.
Well, if my air conditioner betrayed me, why not?

There was always the chance that Harvest might attract a
berserker. I was recorded in tandem with what we called a
Remora program: a program to copy *me* into another machine.
I wasn't sure it would interface with unfamiliar equipment.
You solved that one yourself, because you have to interface
with thousands of years of changes in berserker design.

I'm glad they gave me conscious control of Remora. Two
of your brains are *me* now, but I've left the third brain intact.
You can give me the data I need to run this . . . heap of junk.
You're in sorry shape, aren't you? Channith must have done
you some damage. Did you come from Channith?

God curse you. You'll be sorry. You're barely in shape to
reach the nearest berserker repair base, and we shouldn't have
any trouble getting in. Where is it?

Ah.

Fine. We're on our way. I'm going to read a poem into your memory; I don't want it to get lost. No, no, no; relax and enjoy it, death-machine. You might enjoy it at that. Do you like spilled blood? I lived a bloody life, and it isn't over yet.

TALISMAN

by Larry Niven and Dian Girard

The stranger swung his baggage off his horse's back, patted the animal on the side of the neck, and handed the reins to the stablehand. Old Kasan was rarely interested in people; he barely glanced at the stranger. Slanted eyes, round face with a yellow tinge...

Kasan led the animal to an empty stall and gave it food and water. Now, the beast was a puzzler. It suffered his ministrations with an air of strained patience. Its tail ended in the kind of brush usually seen on an ass. Kasan fancied that its look was one of tolerant contempt.

"Ah, horse, you underestimate me," Kasan said. "I won't be tending other people's horses forever." Horses did not often mock Kasan's daydreams. This one's nicker sounded too much like a snicker. "It's true! Some day I'll own my own rental stable—" And Kasan fondled the beast's ears and mane, as if to thank it for listening.

Under its shaggy forelock he felt a hard circular scar.

He told Bayram Ali about it when he went in for lunch. "It's a unicorn. The horn's been chopped off. What kind of man would be riding a disguised unicorn?"

The innkeeper said, "Sometimes I wonder why I put up with your stories, Kasan."

"You can feel the stub yourself!"

"No doubt. At least don't be bothering my guests with such tales." And Bayram Ali set a tankard of ale next to Kasan's midday cheese and bread. Kasan opened his mouth to retort, noticed the ale, and kept silent.

And Bayram Ali took counsel with himself.

Strange beasts like the one munching hay in his stable were often found in the company of strange men. The traveler might be a sorcerer . . . though they were rare these days. More likely he was a magician on his way to Rynildissen. Bayram had seen the man carry two heavy bags up to his room. It would be interesting to know what was in them, and if it would be worthwhile to lighten them a little.

Bayram Ali never robbed his guests. It was a point of honor. He preferred to leave the work and any possible danger to a professional. He looked around the crowded common room. It was smoky and odorous with the scents of cooking and human bodies. There was much laughter and spilling of wine. Unfortunately, most of the light-fingered brethren present had hasty tempers and were too quick to pull a knife. Bayram would not have violence in his inn.

Across the room his small pretty wife, Esme, was struggling to carry a huge frothy pitcher of ale. Two men were pushing and shoving each other for the honor of carrying it for her. Just beyond them, leaning back on a rough bench with her shoulders against the wall, Sparthera was laughing and yelling at the two combatants.

Sparthera. Bayram Ali grinned broadly. The slim young thief was just what he had in mind. She was daring without being reckless, and had no morals to speak of. They had made more than one bargain in the past.

He pushed his way across the room, pausing to grab up the pitcher his wife was carrying and slam it down in front of a customer. He knocked the combatants' heads together, sending them into hysterical laughter, and sent Esme back to the kitchen with a hearty slap on her firm round backside.

"Ay, Sparthera!"

The thief laughed up at him. She was finely built and slender, with a tangled mass of tawny hair and high firm breasts. Her large hazel eyes were set wide over a short straight nose and full red lips.

"Well, Bayram Ali, have you come over to knock my head against something too?" She hooked her thumbs in the belt of her leather jerkin and stretched out a pair of lean leather-clad legs.

"No, little thief. I wondered if you had noticed a certain stranger among my guests."

"Oh?" She had lost the smile.

Bayram Ali sat down on the bench next to her and lowered his voice. "A smooth-skinned man from the East, with bulging saddlebags. His name is Sung Ko Ja. Old Kasan says he came riding a unicorn, with the beast's horn cut off to disguise it."

"A sorcerer!" Sparthera shook her head firmly. "No. I'd as soon try to rob the statue of Khulm. I don't want anything to do with sorcerers."

"Oh, I hardly think he's a sorcerer," the innkeeper said soothingly. "No more than a magician, if that. A sorcerer wouldn't need to disguise anything. This man is trying to avoid drawing attention to himself. He must have something a thief would want, hmm?"

Sparthera frowned and thought for a moment. No need to ask the terms of the bargain. It would be equal shares, and cheating was expected. "All right. When he comes down to the common room for dinner, or goes out to the privy, let me know. I'll go up and look around his room."

It was several hours before Sung Ko Ja came back down the stairs. The sun was just setting and Esme and her buxom daughters were beginning to serve the evening meal. Sparthera was sitting at one of the small tables near the kitchen door. Bayram Ali brushed by her with a pot of stew.

"That's the one," he whispered. "With the slanted eyes. His room is the third on the left."

Only Sparthera's eyes moved. Around forty, she thought, and distinctly foreign: round of face, but not fat, with old-ivory skin and dark almond eyes, and the manner of a lord. He seemed to be settling in for dinner. Good.

Sparthera moved quickly up the stairs and along the hall, counting doors. The third door didn't move when she pushed on the handle. She tried to throw her weight against it, and couldn't; somehow she couldn't find her balance.

A spell?

She went along to the end of the hall where one small window led out onto the first story roof. Outside, a scant two feet of slippery thatch separated the second story wall and a drop to the cobblestones in the stableyard.

The sun had set. The afterglow was bright enough to work in . . . perhaps not dark enough to hide her? But behind the inn were only fields, and those who had been seeding the fields were gone to their suppers. There was nobody to watch Sparthera work her way around to the window of the magician's room.

The narrow opening was covered with oiled paper. She slit it neatly with the tip of the knife she always carried, and reached through. Or tried to. Something blocked her.

She pushed harder. She felt nothing, but her hand wouldn't move.

She swung a fist at the paper window. Her hand stopped jarringly; and this time she felt her own muscles suddenly lock. Her own strength had stopped her swing.

She had no way to fight such magic. Sparthera hung from the roof by her hands and dropped the remaining four feet to the ground. She dusted herself off and re-entered the inn through the front.

Sung Ko Ja was still eating his meal of roast fowl, bread, and fruit. Bayram Ali was hovering around with one eye on the magician and the other on the stairs. Sparthera caught his eye.

He joined her. "Well?"

"I can't get in. There's a spell on the room."

The innkeeper's face fell, then he shrugged. "Pity."

"I want very much to know what that man has that he thinks is so important." She bit one finger and considered the ivory-skinned man dining peacefully on the other side of the room. "He doesn't have the look of the ascetic. What do you think? Would he like a woman to keep him warm on such a cold night?"

"Sparthera, have you considered what you're suggesting? My inn's reputation is important to me. If I offer, you'll . . . well. You'd have to *do* it."

"Well?"

"The one time I myself made such a suggestion, you nearly cut my throat."

"That was years ago. I was . . . it had been . . . I'd only just thrown that damned tinker out on his ear. I didn't like men much just then. Besides, this is different. It's business."

Bayram Ali eyed her doubtfully. She was dressed more like a young boy than a woman. Still, the magician was a foreigner. Probably all of the local women looked odd to him. Bayram shrugged and pushed his way across the room.

Sung Ko Ja looked up.

The innkeeper smiled broadly. "The wine is good, eh?"

"Drinkable."

"And the fowl? It was young, tender, was it not? Cooked to a nicety?"

"I ate it. What's on your mind?"

"Oh, noble sir! The night will be cold, and I have a girl. Such a girl! A vision of delight, a morsel of sweetness . . ."

Sung Ko Ja waved an impatient hand. "All right. So she is everything you claim she is. How much?"

"Ten."

"Too much. Six."

Bayram Ali looked stunned, then hurt. "Sir, you insult this princess among women. Why, only last week she was a virgin. Nine."

"Seven."

"Eight and a half."

"Done. And bring me another bottle of wine." Sung tossed down the last few drops in his tankard and paid the innkeeper. Sparthera was waiting for him at the foot of the stairs. He looked her over briefly and then started up the stairs, carrying his fresh bottle of wine. "Well, come on, girl."

He stopped at the door to his room and made a few quick gestures with his left hand before he pushed it open.

"Why did you do that?" Sparthera asked in girlish innocence.

"To raise the spell that protects my room. Otherwise I couldn't let you in, my sweet one." He laughed softly and burped.

Sparthera stopped in the doorway. "If you have a spell on this room, does that mean I'll be locked in?"

"No, no. You're free to come and go—as often as you like." He chuckled. "Until the dawn light comes through that window at the end of the hall and relinks the spell."

She entered. The low bed—hardly more than a pallet—held a straw-filled mattress and bedding woven from the local cotton and wool. There was wood stacked in the small fireplace grate and flint and steel lay next to a single candle in a holder. The magician's saddlebags were sitting on the floor by the bed.

Sung looked up at the small window where Sparthera had slashed out the paper and frowned. A cold draft was coming through the opening.

"I'll light the fire, shall I?" Sparthera asked.

She hurried to start a small blaze while Sung, swaying slightly on his feet, considered the open window. Best that he be distracted. She asked, "Is it true that you're a magician?"

He smiled. "There is only one sort of magic I have in mind at the moment."

Sparthera hid her sudden nervousness behind a smile. "Ah, but did you bring your wand?"

The flickering firelight threw their shadows on the wall as Sung guided her to the narrow bed. What followed left Sparthera pleasantly surprised. For all his smooth skin and foreign ways the stranger proved more than equal to other men she'd known. He was considerate . . . almost as if she were paying, not he. Even if nothing came of this venture, the evening hadn't been wasted.

Two hours later she was beginning to change her mind.

They were sitting up on the straw-filled mattress, sharing the last of the wine. Sparthera was naked; Sung still wore a wide cloth belt. He had opened one of his bags and was showing her a variety of small trinkets. There were birds that chirped when you tightened a spring, a pair of puppets on strings, flowers made of yellow silk, and squares of bright paper that Sung folded to look like bears and fish. He was very drunk, and talkative.

"The immortal Sung and his family rule in the land of the Yellow River, a mountainous land far to the east. I was head of the family for twenty years. Now I have abdicated the throne in favor of my son. But I carried away some magic. Watch: I put a half-twist in this strip of paper, join the ends, and now it has only one side and one edge . . ."

Sparthera was restless and bored. She had come upstairs expecting to deal with a magician. She had found a cheap

toymaker who couldn't hold his wine. She watched his strong
agile fingers twisting a scrap of paper into a bird . . . and wondered. His forehead was high and smooth, his face a little too
round for her taste, but undeniably good to look on. It was
hard to believe that he could be a complete fool. There must
be more to him than cheap toys and bragging and a way with
women.

He was rummaging in his bag again and she caught a glimpse
of gleaming metal.

"What is that? The box?"

"The pointer. The key to Gar's treasure. A gift to set me
on the road."

"Gar's treasure. What's that?" It sounded vaguely familiar.

"It's a secret," Sung said, and he closed that saddlebag and
reached across for the other. And while he was turned away
from her, Sparthera pulled a twist of paper from her hair, and
opened it, and shook white powder into Sung's half-empty
goblet.

She didn't use it all, and it probably wasn't needed. Sung
was on his back and snoring a few minutes later, long before
the drug could have taken effect. Sparthera watched him for a
few cautious minutes more before she reached into the saddlebag.

She drew out a silver box. There were pieces of jade and
carnelian set in mountings on the lid and sides.

She was half-afraid that a spell sealed this too, but it opened
easily enough. The inside was lined with faded crimson velvet,
and all it held was an elongated teardrop of tarnished bronze.
There were tiny silver runes inlaid along the length of the dark
metal.

Sparthera picked it up and turned it this way and that. It
was thicker than her forefinger and just about as long. A conical
hole had been drilled nearly through its underside.

The box was worth something; but was it worth angering
a magician? Probably not, she decided reluctantly. And it certainly wasn't worth killing for, not here. Bayram Ali would
never allow such a thing. She would have to flee Tarseny's
Rest forever . . . and Sparthera had none of the tourist urge in
her.

The same applied to Sung's cloth belt. She had felt the

coins in it when they made the two-backed beast, but it was no fortune.

Sung surely ought to be robbed. It would do him good, make him less gullible. But not tonight. Sparthera dropped the pointer in its box, closed it, and was reaching for the saddlebag when she remembered.

Gar had been Kaythill's magician.

And Kaythill was a bandit chief who had raided the lands around Rynildissen City, a hundred years ago. He had lasted some twenty years, until the King's soldiers caught him travelling alone. Under torture Kaythill had steered them to some of his spoils. The rest? A wagonload of gold and jewels had been stolen by Gar the magician. Kaythill and his men had been scouting the countryside for Gar when the soldiers trapped him.

Of course the King's men searched for Gar. Some vital pieces of military magic were among the missing treasure. There had been rewards posted, soldiers everywhere, rumors... and Gar's treasure had grown in the telling, had grown into legend, until it reached Sparthera via her father. She had been... six? It was a wonder she remembered at all.

And this trinket would point the way to Gar's treasure?

Sparthera dressed hurriedly, snatched up the silver box and left the room. She hesitated in the hall, looking first at her trophy and then back at the door. What would he do when he woke and found the box missing? She had only seen him drunk. A magician sober and looking for lost property might be an entirely different matter.

She pushed at the door. It opened easily. He hadn't lied then. She could come and go as she pleased—until dawn.

Sparthera hurried down the stairs and out of the inn. It was nearly midnight and there were only a few jovial souls left in the common room. None saw her leave.

Patrols rarely came to the Thieves' Quarter of Tarseny's Rest; but in the Street of the Metalworkers they were common. Sparthera went warily, waiting until a pair of guards had passed before she began throwing pebbles at a certain upstairs window.

The window came alight. Sparthera stepped out of the shadows, showed herself. Presently Tinx appeared, rubbing his eyes, looking left and right before he pulled her inside.

"Sparthera! What brings you here, little thief? Are the dogs finally at your heels and you need a place to hide?"

"How long would it take you to copy this?" She opened the box and held out the bronze teardrop.

"Hmmm. Not long. The lettering is the hard part, but I do have some silver."

"How long?"

"An hour or two."

"I need it now, tonight."

"Sparthera, I *can't*. I need my sleep."

"Tinx, you owe me."

Tinx owed her twice. Once, for a pair of thieves who had tried to interest Sparthera in robbing Tinx's shop. In Sparthera's opinion, robbing a citizen of Tarseny's Rest was fouling one's own nest. She had informed on them. And once she had worked like a slave in his shop, to finish a lucrative job on time; for Sparthera was not always a thief. But Tinx had had other, more pressing debts, and he still owed Sparthera most of her fee.

The metalworker lifted his hands helplessly and rolled his eyes to heaven. "Will I be rid of you then?"

"Finished and done. All debts paid."

"Oh, all right then!" He sighed and, still grumbling about his lost night's sleep, went back inside to light some candles and a lantern to work by.

Sparthera prowled restlessly about the tiny shop. She found means to make tea. Afterward she prowled some more, until Tinx glared at her and demanded she stay in one place. Then she sat, while Tinx sawed and filed and hammered until he had a bronze teardrop; gouged grooves in the surface; pounded silver wire into the grooves; polished it, compared it to the original, then held it in tongs over a flame until tarnish dulled the silver. He asked, "Just how good are your client's eyes?"

"I don't really know, but by Khulm we're running out of time!"

"Well, what do you think?" He handed her copy and original.

She turned them swiftly in her hands, then dropped the copy into the box and the original into her sleeve. "Has to be good enough. My thanks, Tinx." She was already slipping through the door. "If this works out . . ." She was down the street and out of earshot, leaving Tinx to wonder if she had made him a promise. Probably not.

She stopped inside the front door of the inn. A moment to get her breath, else the whole inn would hear her. Then upstairs, on tiptoe. Third door down. Push. It swung open, and Sparthera swallowed her gasp of relief.

The magician was still asleep and still snoring. He looked charmingly vulnerable, she thought. Sparthera pushed the box into a saddlebag, under a tunic. It cost her a wrench to leave it, but far better to lose a trinket worth a few gold pieces than to face the wrath of an outraged sorcerer. Sparthera had bigger fish to fry. She tiptoed out and shut the door. The first gray glow of morning was showing through the window at the end of the hall.

Sparthera stayed out of sight until she saw Sung mount his odd shaggy horse and start off down the King's Way to Rynildissen. He seemed unsteady in the saddle, and once he clutched at his head. That worried her. "Khulm bear witness, I *did* go easy on that powder," she told herself.

She found Bayram Ali counting money at table in the common room. He looked up at her expectantly.

"Well? What did you find?"

"A few toys. Some scraps of colored paper and an old silver box that isn't worth the trouble it would get us."

"No money?"

"Coins in a belt. He never took it off. There wasn't much in it . . . not enough, anyway."

Bayram Ali scowled. "Very intelligent of you, dear. Still, a pity. He left this for you." He tucked two fingers into his wide cummerbund and fished out a pair of silver coins. "Perhaps you've found a new calling. One for you and one for me, hmm?"

Sparthera smiled, letting her strong, even white teeth show. "And how much did he pay you last night?"

"Six pieces of silver," Bayram Ali said happily.

"You sold me so cheaply? You're a liar and your mother was insulted on a garbage heap."

"Well. He offered six. We settled for eight."

"Four for you, four for me, hmm?"

He looked pained. Sparthera took her five pieces of silver, winked, and departed, wondering what Sung Ko Ja had really paid. That was part of the fun of bargaining: wondering who had cheated whom.

But this time Sparthera had the pointer.

On a bald hill east of the village, Sparthera took the bronze teardrop from her sleeve, along with a needle and the cork from one of Sung Ko Ja's bottles of wine. She pushed the base of the needle into the cork, set it down, and balanced the pointer on the needle. "Pointer! Pointer, show me the way to Gar's treasure!" she whispered to it, and nudged it into a spin.

Three times she spun it and marked where it stopped, pointing north, and northwest, and east.

She tried holding it in her hand, turning in a circle with her eyes closed, trying to feel a tug. She tried balancing it on her own fingernail. She studied the runes, but they meant nothing to her. After two hours she was screaming curses like a Euphrates fishwife. It didn't respond to that either.

Sitting on the bare dusty ground with her chin in her hands and the pointer lying in the dirt in front of her, Sparthera felt almost betrayed. So close! She was so close to wealth that she could almost hear the tinkle of golden coins. She needed advice, and the one person who might help her was one she had vowed never to see again.

A faint smile crossed her face as she remembered screaming at him, throwing his bags and gear out of the tiny hut they shared, swearing by the hair on her head that she'd die and rot in hell before she ever went near him again. That damned tinker! Pot-mender, amateur spell-caster, womanizer: his real magic was in his tongue. She'd left her home and family to follow him, and all of his promises had been so much air.

She'd heard that he lived up in the hills now, that he called himself Shubar Khan and practiced magic to earn a living. If he cast spells the way he mended pans, she thought sourly, he wouldn't be of much use to her. But perhaps he'd learned something . . . and there wasn't anyone else she could go to.

She stood up, dusted herself off, bent to pick up the bronze teardrop.

The sky was clouding over and the scent of rain was in the air. It matched her dismal mood.

What about her vow? It had been a general oath, not bound by a particular god, but she had meant it with all her heart. Sometimes vows like that were the most dangerous, for who knew what wandering elemental might be listening? She leaned against Twilight, smoothing his tangled mane and staring out over his back at the rolling foothills and the mountains beyond. Life was too dear and Gar's treasure too important to risk either on a broken vow. She took her knife from its sheath and started to hack at her long tawny hair.

Shubar Khan's house, hardly more than a hut, was both small and dirty. Sparthera reined her horse to a halt before the door. She looked distastefully at a hog carcass lying in the center of a diagram scratched in the hard dry ground.

She had sworn never to speak his name, but that name was *Tashubar*. She called, "Shubar Khan! Come out, Shubar Khan!" She peered into the dark doorway. A faint odor of burning fat was the only sign of habitation.

"Who calls Shubar Khan?" A man appeared in the doorway and blinked out at her. Sparthera swung herself down from Twilight's back and lifted her chin a little arrogantly, staring at him.

"Sparthera?" He rubbed the side of his face and laughed dryly. "Oh, ho. The last time we saw one another you threw things at me. I think I still have a scar somewhere. You wouldn't care to see it, would you? Ah, well, I thought not."

He cocked his head to one side and nodded. "You're still beautiful. Just like you were when I found you in that haystack. Heh, heh, heh. I like you better with hair, though. What happened to it?"

"I swore an oath," she said shortly, wondering a little at what passing time could do to a man. He had been a good thirty years old to her fourteen when they met. Now she was twenty-six, and he was potbellied and sweaty, with a red face and thinning hair and lecherous little eyes. He wore felt slippers with toes that turned up, and five layers of brightly striped woolen robes. He scratched now and then, absentmindedly.

But he still had the big, knowing hands, and strong shoulders that sloped up into his neck, and hadn't he always scratched? And he'd never been thin, and his eyes couldn't have shrunk. The change was in her. Suddenly she hungered to get the matter over with and leave Shubar Khan to the past, where he belonged.

"I've come on business. I want you to fix something for me." She held out the piece of bronze. "It's supposed to be a pointer, but it doesn't work."

A small dirty hand reached for the pointer. "I can fix that!" Sparthera spun around, reaching for her knife.

"My apprentice," Shubar Khan explained. "How would you fix it, boy?"

"There's a storm coming up." The boy, hardly more than twelve, looked at his master with sparkling eyes. "I can climb a tree and tie the thing to a branch high up. When the lightning strikes—"

"You short-eared offspring of a spavined goat!" Shubar bellowed at him. "That would only make it point to the pole star—if it didn't melt first—and if it were iron instead of bronze! Bah!"

The boy cringed back into the gloom of the hut, which was filled with dry bones, aborted sheep foetuses, and pig bladders stuffed with odd ointments. There was even a two-inch-long unicorn horn prominently displayed on a small silk pillow.

Shubar Khan peered at the silver runes. He mumbled under his breath, at length. Was he reading them? "Old Sorcerer's Guild language," he said, "with some mistakes. What is it supposed to point *at*?"

"I don't know," Sparthera lied. "Something buried, I think."

Shubar Khan unrolled one of the scrolls, weighted it open with a couple of bones, and began to read in a musical foreign tongue. Presently he stopped. "Nothing. Whatever spell was on it, it seems as dead as the gods."

"Curse my luck and your skill! Can't you do anything?"

"I can put a contagion spell on it for two pieces of silver." He looked her up and down and grinned. "Or anything else of equal or greater value."

"I'll give you the coins," Sparthera said shortly. "What will the spell do?"

Shubar Khan laughed until his paunch shook. "Not even for old time's sake? What a pity. As to the spell, it will make this thing seek whatever it was once bound to. We're probably lucky the original spell wore off. A contagion spell is almost easy."

Sparthera handed over the money. Gar's treasure had already cost her far too much. Shubar Khan ushered her and his apprentice—loaded down with phials, a pair of scrolls, firewood, and a small cauldron—to a steep crag nearby.

"Why do we have to come out here?" Sparthera asked.

"We're just being cautious," Shubar Khan said soothingly. He set up the cauldron, emptied a few things into it, lit the fire the apprentice had set, and handed the apprentice the bronze teardrop and one of the scrolls. "When the cauldron smokes, just read this passage out loud. And remember to enunciate," he said as he grabbed Sparthera's arm and sprinted down the hill.

Sparthera looked uphill at the boy, "This is dangerous, isn't it? How dangerous?"

"I don't know. The original spell isn't working, but there may be some power left in it, and there's no telling what it might do. That's why magicians have apprentices."

They could hear the boy chanting in his childish treble, speaking gibberish, but rolling his Rs and practically spitting the Ps. The clouds that had been gathering overhead took on a harsh ominous quality. The wind came up and the trees whipped and showered leaves on the ground.

A crack of lightning cast the entire landscape into ghastly brightness. Shubar Khan dove to the ground. Sparthera winced and then strained her eyes into the suddenly smoky air. There was no sign of the boy. Thunder rolled deafeningly across the sky.

Sparthera ran up the hill, heart thumping. The top of the crag was scorched and blackened. The iron cauldron was no more than a twisted blob of metal.

"Ooohhh!"

Shubar Khan's apprentice pulled himself to his feet and looked at her with huge eyes. His face was smudged, his hair scorched, and his clothing still smouldered. He held out a blackened fist with the bronze piece still in it.

"Did, did . . . did it work?" he asked in a frightened croak.

Shubar Khan retrieved the pointer and laid it on his palm. It slowly rotated to the right and stopped. He grinned broadly and patted the boy heartily on the shoulder.

"Excellent! We'll make a magician of you yet!" He turned to Sparthera and presented the pointer to her with a bow.

She tucked it inside her tunic. "Thank you," she said, feeling a little awkward.

Shubar Khan waved a muscular red hand. "Always pleased to be of service. Spells, enchantments, and glamours at reasonable rates. Maybe someday I can interest you in a love philtre."

Sparthera rode back down the mountain trail with the bronze teardrop tucked in her tunic, feeling its weight between her breasts like the touch of a lover's hand. Just above Tarseny's Rest she reined up to watch a small herd of gazelle bound across a nearby hill. Someday she would build a house on that hill. Someday, when she had Gar's treasure, she would build a big house with many rooms and many fireplaces. She would have thick rugs and fine furniture, and there would be servants in white tunics embroidered with red leaves.

She spurred her horse to the crest of the hill. Down below were the river and the town, and across the valley were more hills, leading away to distant mountains.

"I'm going to be rich!" she yelled. "Rich!"

The echoes boomed back. "Rich, rich, rich!" until they finally whimpered into silence. Twilight nickered and pulled at his reins. Sparthera laughed. She would have many horses when she was rich. Horses and cattle and swine.

She could almost see the hoard trickling through her fingers in a cascade of gold and rainbow colors. Money for the house and the animals and a dowry.

The dowry would buy her a husband: a fine, respectable merchant who would give her fat beautiful children to inherit the house and the animals. Sparthera took a last lingering look at the countryside before she swung herself back into the saddle. First, find the treasure!

She cantered back into town, put Twilight into the stable behind the lodging house, and went to her room. It was a tiny cubicle, with a pallet of cotton-covered straw and some blankets against one wall. Rough colorful embroideries hung on the wattle and daub walls: relics of the days at home on her father's farm. Another embroidery was thrown across a large wooden chest painted with flying birds, and a three-legged chair with flowers stencilled on the back stood in one corner.

Sparthera uncovered the chest and threw open the lid. It was packed with odds and ends—relics of her childhood—and down at the bottom was a small pouch with her savings in it.

She opened the pouch and counted the coins slowly, frowning. The search might take weeks or months. She would need provisions, extra clothes, and a pack animal to carry them. There wasn't enough here.

She would have to borrow or beg an animal from her family. She grimaced at the thought, but she had little choice.

It was a four hour ride to her father's farm. Her mother was out in the barnyard, feeding the chickens, when she rode in. The elder woman looked at her with what might have been resignation.

"Run out of money and come home again, have you?"

"Not this time," Sparthera said, dismounting and placing a dutiful kiss on her mother's cheek. "I need a horse or an ass. I thought maybe father had one I could borrow."

Her mother looked at her distastefully. "Always you dress like a man. No wonder no decent man ever looks at you. Why don't you give up all those drunkards you hang around with? Why don't you . . ."

"Mother, I need a horse."

"You've got one horse. You don't need another horse."

"Mother, I'm going on a trip and I need a pack horse." Sparthera's eyes lit with suppressed excitement. "When I come back, I'll be rich!"

"Humph. That's what you said when you ran off with that no-good pot mender. If your father were here, he'd give you *rich* all right! You're lucky he's in the mountains for a week. I don't know about horses. Ask Bruk. He's in the barn."

Her mother tossed another handful of grain to the chickens, and Sparthera started across the dusty barnyard.

"And get yourself some decent clothes!"

Sparthera sighed and kept moving. Her next-older brother was in the loft restacking sheaves of last season's wheat.

"Bruk? Have you got an extra horse?"

He looked down at her, squinting into the light from the open barn door. "Sparthera? You haven't been here for two months. Did you run out of pockets to pick, or just out of men?"

She grinned. "No more than you ever run out of women. Are you still rolling Mikka in her father's hay ricks?"

He climbed down from the loft, looking a little glum. "Her father caught us at it twelve days ago and now I've got to trade the rick for a marriage bed and everything that goes with it." He was a big man, well muscled, with a shock of corn-colored hair, dark eyes, and full sensuous lips. "Lost your hair, I see. Well, they say that comes of not enough candle-wick. Find yourself a man and we'll make it a double celebration."

Sparthera leaned against a stall and laughed heartily. "Caught at last! Well, it won't do you any harm, and beds aren't as itchy as piles of hay. You ought to be glad. Once you've married you'll be safe from all the other outraged fathers."

"Will I though? They may just come after me with barrel staves. And I hate to cut short a promising career. Oh, the youngest daughter of the family in the hollow has grown up to be . . ."

"Enough, Bruk. I need a horse. Have you got an extra one?"

He shook his head. "Twilight pulled up lame, did he?"

"No. I'm planning a trip and I need a pack animal."

Bruk scratched his head. "Can't you buy one in town? There are always horse dealers in the market square."

"I know too many people in Tarseny's Rest. I don't want them to know I'm taking this trip. Besides," she added candidly, "I don't have enough money."

"What are you up to, little sister? Murder, pillage, or simple theft?"

"Oh, Bruk, it's the chance to make a fortune! A chance to be rich!"

He shook his head disgustedly. "Not again. Remember that crockery merchant? And the rug dealer? And that tink—"

"This time it's different!"

"Oh, sure. Anyway, we haven't got a horse. Why don't you steal one?"

This time it was Sparthera's turn to look disgusted. "You can't just steal a horse on the spur of the moment. It's not like a pair of shoes, you know. You have to do a little planning and I don't have the time. You'd never make a decent thief! You'd just walk in, grab it by the tail and try to walk out." She pulled at her lower lip. "Now what am I going to do?"

They both stood there, thinking. Bruk finally broke the silence. "Well, if you only want it to carry a pack, you might make do with a wild ass. They break to a pack saddle pretty easy. There are some up in the foothills. I'll even help you catch one."

"I guess it's worth a try."

Bruk found a halter and a long rope, and led the way across the cultivated fields and up into the hills. The landscape was scrubby underbrush dotted with small stands of trees. There were knolls of rock, and one small stream that ran cackling down the slope.

Bruk stopped to study a pattern of tracks. "That'll be one . . . spends a lot of time here, too . . . yup, I'll bet it hides over in that copse. You go left and I'll go right. We'll get it when it comes out of the trees."

They circled cautiously toward a promising stand of small trees. Sure enough, Sparthera could hear something moving within the grove, and even caught a glimpse of brownish hide. A branch cracked under Bruk's boot, something brown exploded from the cover of the brush, and Bruk yelled, swinging the loop of his rope.

"Get the halter! Watch out for its hooves. Yeow, oooof!"

The animal whirled, bounced like a goat on its small sturdy legs, and managed to butt Bruk in the middle. Bruk sat down heavily while Sparthera made a frantic grab for the trailing end of the rope.

The little animal, frantically trying to dodge her groping hands, was braying, whinnying, and making occasional high-pitched whistling noises. It was the size of a small pony and had a long silky mane that almost dragged the ground. Its tail was thick, muscular, and held up at an angle. It had two ridiculous little feathery wings, about as long as Sparthera's forearm, growing out of the tops of its shoulders.

Bruk staggered to his feet as Sparthera managed to catch and cling to the rope. He launched himself bodily at the beast, grabbed it around the neck, and threw it off balance. It fell heavily to one side, where it kicked its small feet and fluttered its tiny wings to the accompaniment of an incredible cacophony of hoots, whistles, and brays.

Sparthera clapped her hands over her ears and yelled. "That's no wild ass! What on earth is it? Some sort of magic beast?"

Bruk was busily fitting his halter on their uncooperative captive. "I don't know," he panted. "I think it's half ass and half nightmare. If a sorcerer dreamed it up, he must have been drunk."

He stood back and let it scramble to its feet. It lowered its head, pawed the ground savagely, lifted its tail, and jumped with all four feet. The maneuver carried it forward perhaps two paces, its little wings flapping frantically.

Sparthera burst out laughing, doubled over with mirth. When she recovered enough she stared at their captive and shook her head. "Do you think it can be broken to carry a pack?"

"Let's get it down to the barn and we'll try it with a pack saddle."

Getting the wingbeast down the hill was a production in its own right. It bolted, tried to roll, then dug its feet in like the most obstinate of jackasses. Finally, tired, irritated, and covered with grime, the three of them made it to the barnyard.

They managed to get the saddle on its back—after Sparthera had been butted and trampled and her brother had been dumped in the watering trough—and stood back to watch.

The small animal bucked. It turned, twisted, flapped its ridiculous little wings, and rolled in the dust. It tried to bite the saddle girth and scrape the saddle off against the fence. It kicked its heels and brayed. Just when they thought it would never quit, it stopped, sides heaving, and glared at them.

The next day it accepted a ripe apple from Sparthera, bit Bruk in the buttocks, and managed to bolt into the house, where Sparthera's mother hit it on the nose with a crock of pickled cabbage.

Sparthera was losing patience. It was all taking too long.

Had Sung Ko Ja discovered her trick? Was he searching Tarseny's Rest for the woman who had stolen his pointer? She had told Bayram Ali that she was visiting her parents. Someone would come to warn her, surely.

But nobody came, that day or the next; and a horrid thought came to her. Sung Ko Ja must have followed the pointer far indeed. Even without the pointer, he must have a good idea where the treasure lay. He might have continued on. At this moment he could be unearthing Sparthera's treasure!

It was three days before the winged beast gave up the fight, trotted docilely at the end of a rope, and accepted the weight of a loaded pack saddle. It even gave up trying to bite, as long as they kept out of its reach. Sparthera named it "Eagle."

"It would be better called 'Vulture!'" Bruk said, rubbing at a healing wound. "It's smart, though, I'll grant you that. Only took the beast three days to realise it couldn't get rid of that saddle."

"Three days," Sparthera said wearily. "Bruk, for once you were right. I should have stolen a horse."

She rode back to town leading the wingbeast along behind. It took her half a day to buy provisions and pack her clothing. In late afternoon she set out on the King's Way, holding the bronze pointer like the relic of some ancient and holy demigod.

She was expecting to ride into the wilderness, into some wild, unpopulated area where a treasure could lie hidden for eighty years. But the pointer was tugging her along the King's Way, straight toward Rynildissen, the ruling city of the biggest state around. That didn't bother her at first. Rynildissen was four days' hard riding for a King's messenger, a week for a traveler on horseback, two for a caravan. And Gar's band had done their raiding around Rynildissen.

The King's Way was a military road. It ran wide as a siege engine and straight as an arrow's flight. It made for easy traveling, but Sparthera worried about sharing her quest with too much traffic. She found extensive litter beside the road: burnt-out campfires, horse droppings, garbage that attracted lynxes. It grew ever fresher. On her third afternoon she was not surprised to spy an extensive dust plume ahead of her. By noon of the next day she had caught up with a large merchant caravan.

She was about to ride up alongside the trailing wagon when she caught a glimpse of an odd shaggy horse with a tail like an ass. There was a figure in bulky Eastern robes on its back. Sung!

Sparthera pulled her horse hard to the side and rode far out over the rolling hill and away from the road. She had no desire to trade words with the smooth-faced magician. But what was he doing here? The caravan was protection from beasts and minor thieves; but the caravan was *slow*. He could have been well ahead of Sparthera by now.

He didn't know the pointers had been switched! That *must* be it. The seeking-spell had been nearly dead already. Sung had followed it from far to the east; now he was following his memory, with no idea that anyone was behind him.

Then the important thing was to delay him. She must find the treasure, take it, and be miles away before Sung Ko Ja reached the site.

All day she paced the caravan. At dusk they camped round a spring. Leaving her horse, Sparthera moved down among the wagons, tents, oxen and camels. She avoided the campfires. Sung Ko Ja had pitched a small red and white striped tent. His unicorn was feeding placidly out of a nosebag.

Stealing a roll of rich brocade was easy. The merchant should have kept a dog. It was heavy stuff, and she might well be spotted moving it out of camp, but she didn't have to do that. After studying Sung's tent for some time, watching how soundly Sung slept, she crept around to the back of the tent and rolled the brocade under the edge. Then away, hugging the shadows, and into the hills before the moon rose. Dawn found her back on the highway, well ahead of the caravan, chuckling as she wondered how Sung would explain his acquisition.

When she dug the pointer out of her sleeve, her sense of humor quite vanished. The pointer was tugging her back. She must have ridden too far.

After a hasty breakfast of dried figs and jerked meat Sparthera started to retrace her path, paralleling the King's Way. Days of following the pointer had left painful cramping in both hands, but she dared not set it down now. At any moment she expected the bronze teardrop to pull her aside.

She was paying virtually no attention to her path. At the crest of a smooth hill, she looked up to see another horse coming toward her. Its rider was a smooth-faced man with skin the color of old ivory, and his almond eyes were amused. It was too late even to think of hiding.

"Oh ho! My sweet little friend from two nights ago. What brings you onto the King's Way?"

"My hair," Sparthera improvised. "Cosmetics. There's a witch-woman who lives that way—" She gestured vaguely south, and gave him her best effort at a flirtatious smile. "— and I find I can afford her fees, thanks to the generosity of a slant-eyed magician."

"Oh, dear, and I had hoped your lips were aching for another kiss." He looked at her critically. "You don't need to visit any witch. Even shorn, you are quite enchanting. You must share my midday meal. I insist. Come, we can rest in the shade of those trees yonder."

Sparthera was afraid to spur her horse and flee. He might suspect nothing at all; else why had he joined the caravan? She turned her horse obediently and rode to the shade of the small grove with him, trailing the wingbeast behind at the end of its halter.

Sung slid easily from his unicorn. He still didn't seem dangerous. She could insist on preparing the food. Wine she could spill while pretending to drink. She swung down from her horse—

Her head hurt. Her eyes wouldn't focus. She tried to roll over and her head pulsed in red pain. Her arms and legs seemed caught in something. Rope? She waited until her head stopped throbbing before she tried to learn more.

Then it was obvious. Her hands were tied behind her; a leather strap secured her ankles to one of the shade trees. Sung Ko Ja was sitting crosslegged on a rug in front of her, flipping a bronze teardrop in the air.

Bastard. He must have hit her on the head while she was dismounting.

"Eight nights ago I noticed that someone had cut the paper out of my bedroom window," he said. "I woke the next morning with a foul taste in my mouth, but that could have been cheap wine, or too much wine. Last night some rogue put a roll of stolen dry goods in my baggage—which caused me no end of embarrassment. I would not ordinarily have thought of you in connection with this. I confess that my memories of our time together are most pleasant. However," he paused to sip at a bowl of tea. "However, my unicorn, who can whisper strange things when I want him to, and sometimes when I don't—"

"He *speaks?*"

The unicorn was glaring at her. Sparthera glared back. Magician or no, she felt that this was cheating, somehow.

"Such a disappointment," said Sung Ko Ja. "If only you had come to my arms last night, all of this might be different. You sadden me. Here you are, and here is this." He held up the pointer. "Why?"

She looked at the ground, biting her lip.

"Why?"

"Money, of course!" she blurted out. "You said that thing was the key to a treasure! Wouldn't you have taken it too, in my place?"

Sung laughed and rubbed his fingers over his chin. "No, I don't think so. But I am not you. It may be this was my fault. I tempted you."

He got to his feet. He tilted her head back with one hand so he could look into her eyes. "Now, what's to be done? Swear to be my slave and I'll take you along to look for Gar's treasure."

"A slave? Never! My people have always been free. I'd rather die than be a slave!"

Sung looked distressed. "Let's not call it slavery then, if you dislike it so much. Bondage? Binding? Let's say you will bind yourself to me. For seven years and a day, or until we find treasure to equal your weight in gold."

"And if we find the treasure, what then?"

"Then you're free."

"That's not enough. I want part of the treasure."

Sung laughed again, this time in pure amusement. "You bargain hard for one who has been pinioned and tied to a tree. All right. Part of the treasure then."

"How much of it?" she asked warily.

"Hmmm. I take the first and second most valuable items. We split the rest equally."

"Who decides—"

Sung was growing irritated. "I'll split the remaining treasure into two heaps. You choose which heap you want."

That actually sounded fair. "Agreed."

"Ah, but now it is my turn. What are you going to swear by, my little sweetheart? I want your oath that you'll offer me no harm, that you'll stay by my side and obey my commands, until the terms of the agreement are met."

Sparthera hesitated. It didn't take a magician to know how to make an oath binding. Even nations kept their oaths . . . to the letter, and that could make diplomacy interesting . . .

She could be making herself rich. Or she could be throwing away seven years of her life. Would Sung hold still for a better bargain?

Not a chance. "All right. I'll swear by Khulm, the thieves' god who stands in the shrine at Rynildissen. May he break my fingers if I fail."

"You swear then?"

"I swear."

Sung bent down and kissed her heartily on the lips. Then he set about freeing her. He set out tea while she was rubbing her wrists. There was a lump on her head. The tea seemed to help.

She said, "We must be very near the treasure. The pointer led me back the way we came . . . straight into your arms, in fact."

Sung chuckled. He fished the silver box out of his saddle-bag. He opened it, took out Sparthera's counterfeit bronze teardrop, hesitated, then dropped it on the rug. He stood up with the genuine object in his hand.

Sparthera cried, "Stop! That's—" Too late. Sung had flung the genuine pointer into a grove of low trees.

"I'll keep yours," he said. "It's only for the benefit of people who think a box has to contain something. Now watch."

He pressed down on the silver box in two places and twisted four of the small stone ornaments. The box folded out flat into a cross-shape with one long arm.

"You see? There never was a spell on the bronze lump.

You took it to a spell-caster, didn't you?" Sparthera nodded. "And he put some kind of contagion spell on it, didn't he?" She nodded again. "So the bronze lump sought what it had been a part of. The box. It's been in there too long."

Sung pulled the faded red lining off of the surface. Underneath, the metal was engraved with patterns and lettering. Sung stroked a finger over the odd markings. "It looks like a valuable trinket on the outside. No casual thief would just throw it away. I might have a chance to get it back. But a magician turned robber would take the pointer, just as you did."

She'd had it in her hands! Too late, too late. "When can we start looking for Gar's treasure?"

"Tomorrow morning, if you're so eager. Meanwhile, the afternoon is growing cold. Come here and warm my heart."

"Sung, dear, just how cl..." Sparthera's words trailed off in surprise. She had walked straight into Sung's arms. She had behaved like this with no man, not since that damned tinker. Her voice quavered as she said, "I don't act like this. Sung, what magic is on me now?"

He pulled back a little. "Why, it's your own oath!"

"I feel like that puppet you showed me! This isn't what I meant!"

Sung sighed. "Too bad. Well—"

"I don't mean I won't share your bed." Her voice was shrill with near-hysteria. "I just, I want power over my own limbs, damn you Sung!"

"Yes. I tell you now that binding yourself to me does not involve becoming my concubine."

She pulled away, and turned her back, and found it was possible. "Good. Good. Sung, thank you." Her brow furrowed suddenly and she turned back to face him. "What if you tell me different, later?"

She might have guessed that Sung's answer would be a shrug. "All right. What was I trying to say earlier? Oh, I remember. Just how close is the King's Way? We don't want that caravan camping next to us. Somebody might get nosy."

Sung agreed. They had moved a good distance down the King's Way before they camped for the night.

* * *

In the morning Sparthera saddled Twilight and loaded Eagle while Sung packed his gear on the unicorn. The wingbeast caught his attention.

"Where did you get that creature?"

"Near my father's farm. It was running wild. I think it's some sort of magic beast."

Sung shook his head sadly. "No, quite the opposite. In my grandfather's day there were flocks of beautiful horses that sailed across the sky on wings as wide as the King's Way. He rode one when he was a little boy. It couldn't lift him when he grew too big. As time went on the colts were born with shorter, weaker wings, until all that was left were little beasts like this one. I used to catch them, when I was a boy, but never to fly. Enchantment is going out of the world, Sparthera. Soon there will be nothing left."

It was a mystery to Sparthera how her companion read the talisman. It looked the same to her, no matter which way he said it pointed. Sung tried to show her when they set off that morning. He set the flattened-out box on the palm of her hand and said, "Keep reading it as you turn it. The runes don't actually change, but when the long end points right, the message becomes 'Ta netyillo iliq pratht' instead of 'tanetyi lo—'"

"Skip it. Just skip it."

In any case, the pointer continued to lead them straight down the King's Way.

They reached an inn about dusk, and Sung paid for their lodging. Sparthera watched him setting the spells against thieves. Sung was not secretive. Quite the contrary: he drilled her in the spells, so that she would be able to set them for him.

Though he had freed her from the obligation, the magician seemed to consider lovemaking as part of their agreement. Sparthera had no complaints. The magician was adept at more than spells. When she told him this, she expected him to preen himself; but Sung merely nodded.

"Keeping the women happy is very necessary in Sung House. How much did I tell you about us, that first night?"

"You were the immortal Sung. You abdicated in favor of your son."

"I was bragging."

"What were you? Not the stablehand, I think."

"Oh, I was the immortal Sung, true enough. We rule a fair-sized farming region, a valley blocked off by mountains and the Yellow River. We know a little magic—we keep a herd of unicorns, and sell the horn, or use it ourselves—but that's not what keeps the farmers docile. They think they're being ruled by a sorcerer seven hundred years old."

"The immortal Sung."

"Yes. I became the immortal Sung when I was twenty. My mother set a spell of *glamour* on me, to make me look exactly like my father. Then I was married to Ma Tay, my cousin, and set on the throne."

"That's . . . I never heard of *glamour* being used to make anyone look older."

"That's a nice trick, isn't it? The spell wears off over twenty years, but of course you're getting older too, looking more and more like your father, magic aside. When I reached forty my wife put the *glamour* on my eldest son. And here I am, under oath to travel until nobody has ever heard of Sung House. Well, I've done that. Someday maybe I'll meet my father."

"What happens to your wife?"

"She took my mother's place as head of the House. It's actually the women who rule in Sung House. The immortal Sung is just a figurehead."

Sparthera shook her head, smiling. "It still sounds like a nice job . . . and they didn't throw you out naked."

"No. We know all our lives what's going to happen. We think on how we'll leave, what we'll take, where we'll go. We collect tales of other lands, and artifacts that could help us. There's a little treasure room of things a departing Sung may take with him."

He leaned back on the bed and stretched. "When I left, I took the pointer. It always fascinated me, even as a boy. I collected rumors about Gar's treasure. It wasn't just the gold and the jewels that stuck in my mind. There is supposed to be a major magical tool too."

"What is it?"

"It's a levitation device. Haven't you ever wanted to fly?"

Sparthera's lips pursed in a silent O. "What a thief could do with such a thing!"

"Or a military spy."

"Yes . . . and the Regency raised hell trying to find Gar's treasure. But of course you'd keep it yourself?"

"Or sell it to one government or another. But I'll fly with it first."

That night, cuddled close in Sung's arms, Sparthera roused herself to ask a question. "Sung? What if I should have a child by you?"

He was silent for a long time. Long enough that she wondered if he'd fallen asleep. When he did answer it was in a very soft voice. "We would ride off into the mountains and build a great hall, and I would put a *glamour* on the child to raise up a new House of Sung."

Satisfied, Sparthera snuggled down into the magician's arms to dream of mountains and gold.

They woke late the next morning, with the dust of the caravan actually in sight. They left it behind them as they rode, still following the King's Way. "This is ridiculous," Sung fretted. "Another day and we'll be in Rynildissen!"

"Is it possible that this Gar actually buried his loot in the King's Way?"

"I wouldn't think he'd have the chance. Still, I suppose nobody would look for it there. Maybe."

Around noon they reached a region of low hills. The King's Way began to weave among them like a snake; but the silver box pointed them steadfastly toward Rynildissen. Sung dithered. "Well, do we follow the road, or do we cut across country wherever the pointer points?"

Sparthera said, "Road, I guess. We'll know if we pass it."

And road it was, until the moment when Sung sucked in his breath with a loud "Ah!"

"What is it?"

"The talisman's pointing that way, south." He turned off, guiding the unicorn uphill. Sparthera followed, pulling the wingbeast along after her. The unicorn seemed to be grumbling just below audibility.

Now the land was rough and wild. There were ravines and dry creekbeds, and tumbled heaps of soil and stone. They were crossing the crest of a hill when Sung said, "Stop."

The unicorn stopped. Sparthera reined in her horse. The wingbeast walked into Twilight's haunches, got kicked, and sat down with a dismal bray.

Sung ignored the noise. "Down in that ravine. We'll have to try it on foot."

They had to move on all fours in places. The bottom of the ravine was thick with brush. Sparthera hesitated as Sung plunged into a thorn thicket. When she heard his muttered curses stop suddenly, she followed.

She found him surrounded by scattered bones, and recognised the skull of an ass. "The pointer reads right in all directions. We're right on it," he said.

A pair of large stones, brown and cracked, looked a bit too much alike. Sparthera touched one. Old leather. Saddle bags?

The bag was so rotten it had almost merged with the earth. It tore easily. Within was cloth that fell apart in her hands, and a few metal ornaments that were green with verdigris. Badges of rank, for a soldier of Rynildissen. In the middle of it all, something twinkled, something bright.

Sung had torn the other bag apart. "Nothing. What have you got?"

She turned it in her hand: a bright faceted stone, shaped like a bird and set into a gold ring. "Oh, how pretty!"

"Hardly worth the effort," Sung said. He worked his way backward out of the thicket and stood up. "Diamonds have no color. They're not worth much. You see this kind of trinket in any Shanton jewel bazaar. Give it here."

Sparthera handed it over, feeling forlorn. "Then that's all there is?"

"Oh, I doubt it. We're on the track. This was just the closest piece. It must have been part of the hoard, or the talisman wouldn't have pointed us here. Even so . . . how did it get here? Did Gar lose a pack mule?"

He opened out the pointer. With the bird's beak he traced a looping curve on the silver surface. "There. The talisman is pointing true again. There's still treasure to be found."

They climbed back uphill to their steeds. The King's Way was well behind them now, and lost among the hills. They were picking their way across a nearly dry stream bed when Sung said, "We're passing it."

"Where?"

"I don't know yet." Sung dismounted. "You wait here. Sparthera, come along—" and she realised he'd spoken first to the unicorn. He picked his way carefully up a vast sloping spill of shattered boulders: leg-breaker country. At the top, panting heavily, he opened the box out and turned in a circle.

"Well?"

Sung turned again. He spoke singsong gibberish in what might have been a lengthy spell; but it sounded like cursing.

"Are you just going to keep spinning?"

"It says all directions are wrong!"

"Uh? Point it down."

Sung stared at her. Then he pointed the talisman at his feet. He said, "'Ta netyillo—' Sparthera, my love, you may be the best thing that ever happened to me."

"I am delighted to hear it. My shovel's still on the horse. Shall I go for it?"

"Yes. No, wait a bit." He started walking, staring at the talisman. "It must be deep. Yards deep. More. Forget the shovel, there must be a cave under us." He grinned savagely at her. "We'll have to find the entrance. We're almost there, love. Come on."

They trudged down the hill, trying to avoid twisted ankles or worse. Sparthera paused to catch her breath and caught a blur of motion out of the corner of her eye. It was headed for the animals. "Sung! What—"

Twilight whinnied in terror. He tossed his head, pulling loose the reins Sparthera had looped over a bush, and bolted downhill. The unicorn had splayed his front feet and lowered his head, as if he thought he still owned a spear. The winged packbeast, filling the air with a bedlam of sound, was bounding rapidly away in two-pace-long jumps, tiny wings beating the air frantically.

Sung let out a yell and charged up to the top of the ravine, swinging a heavy branch he'd snatched up on the way. Sparthera clambered up beside him, swearing as she saw her animals heading off across the landscape. There was a loud wailing sound that put the wingbeast's efforts to shame, and then silence. The thing had vanished.

"What was that!"

"I don't know. I'm more interested in where it went. Keep an eye out, love." Sung pulled his sword from the pack and wandered about the shattered rock.

Sparthera's nose picked up a heavy musky animal odor. She followed it, heart pounding, knife in hand. They were too close to the treasure to stop now.

The odor was wafting out of a black gap in the rocks, less than a yard across. Sung clambered up to look.

"That's it," he said. "It's not big enough, though. If we crawled through that, the thing—whatever it is—would just take our heads as they poked through. We'll have to move some rocks."

Sparthera picked up a heavy boulder and hurled it away. "I feel an irrational urge to go home."

"I can't go home. Let's move some rocks," said Sung, and she did. The sun had dropped a fair distance toward Rynildissen, and every muscle in her body was screaming, before the dripping, panting Sung said, "Enough. Now we need torches."

"Sung. Did it...occur to you...to let me rest?"

"Well, why didn't you...oh." Sung was disconcerted. "Sparthera, I'm used to giving orders to women, because I'm supposed to be the immortal Sung. But it's just for show. I'm also used to being disobeyed."

"I can't." She was crying.

"I'll be more careful. Shall we rest, have some tea?"

"Good. Offer me a swallow of wine."

"That's not—"

"For Khulm's sake, Sung, do you think I'd go in there *drunk*? It's in there. I know it. I kept waiting for it to jump on me. Don't you have a spell to protect us?"

"No. We don't even know what it is. Here—" He turned her around and began to massage her neck and shoulders, fingers digging in. Sparthera felt tensed muscles unravelling, loosening. It was a wonderful surprise.

She said, "It must have half-killed the Sung women to let you go."

"Somehow they managed." She barely heard the bitterness; but it *did* bother him.

* * *

It was dark in there. The late afternoon light only reached a dozen paces in. They stepped in, holding the torches high.

There was a rustling flurry of motion and a loud whimpering cry.

If one of them had run, the other would have followed. As it was, they walked slowly forward behind Sung's sword and Sparthera's dagger.

The cave wasn't large. A stream ran through the middle. Sparthera noted two skeletons on either side of the stream, lying face up as if posed—

Another cry and a scrabbling sound. Something huge and dark moved just outside the perimeter of light. The animal odor had become sickeningly strong. Sung held the light higher.

Off in a corner, something huge was trying to pack itself into a very narrow crevice. It looked at them with absolute panic in its eyes, pulled its long scaly tail closer under its legs and tried fruitlessly to move away.

"What in the world is it?"

"Nothing from this world, that's certain," Sung said. "It looks like something that was conjured up out of a bad dream. Probably was. Gar's guardian."

The creature was partly furred and partly scaled. It had a long toothed snout and broad paddle-like front paws with thick nails. There was a rusted iron collar around its neck, with a few links of broken chain attached. Now its claws stopped grinding against rock, and its tail came up to cover its eyes.

"What is it trying to do?" Sparthera whispered.

"Well, it seems to be trying to hide in that little crack."

"Oh, for the love of Khulm! You mean it's scared!"

The beast gave a long wailing moan at the sound of her voice. Its claws resumed scratching rock.

"Let it alone," Sung said. He swung the torch around to reveal the rest of the cave. They found a torn and scattered pack, with the remains of weevily flour and some broken boxes nearly collapsed from dry rot. Two skeletons were laid out as for a funeral. They had not died in bed. The rib cage on one seemed to have been torn wide open. The other seemed intact below the neck; but it was still wearing a bronze helmet bearing the crest of a soldier of Rynildissen; and the helmet and skull had been squashed as flat as a miser's sandwich.

Aside from the small stream that ran between them, and assorted gypsum deposits, the cave was empty.

"I'm afraid the Regent's army got here first," Sung said.

Sparthera bent above one of the bodies. "Do you think that thing did this? Did it kill them, or just gnaw the bodies? It doesn't seem dangerous now."

"It probably wasn't all that scared in the beginning." Sung was grinning. "Gar must have left it here to guard the treasure, with a chain to keep it from running away. When the Regent's soldiers found the cave, it must have got the first ones in. Then the rest piled in and pounded it into mush. Conjured beasts like that are practically impossible to kill, but did you notice the scars on the muzzle and forelegs? It hasn't forgotten."

"I feel sorry for it," Sparthera said. Then the truth came home to her and she said, "I feel sorry for us! The treasure must have been gone for years. Except—the talisman led us *here*!"

Sung walked forward, following the talisman. He stopped above the skeleton with the flattened skull. "'Ta netyillo—' Yes."

He reached into the rib cage and came up with a mass of color flickering in his hands. Sparthera reached into it and found a large ruby. There were three others besides, and two good-sized emeralds.

Sung laughed long and hard. "So, we have a greedy soldier to thank. He ran in, saw a pile of jewels, snatched up a fistful and swallowed them. He must have thought it would come out all right in the end. Instead, Gar's pet got him." Sung wiped his eyes with the back of his hand. "Fate is a wonderful thing. Here, give me those."

She did, and Sung began tracing the curve on the talisman, one jewel at time. She said, "They wouldn't have left a talisman of levitation."

"No, they wouldn't."

"And this stuff isn't worth nearly my weight in gold."

Sung stiffened. "The pointer! It's pointing into the wall itself!" He got up and began moving along the wall.

Sparthera grimaced but said nothing.

Sung called, "Either it's cursed deep in there, or there's

another cave, or . . . why do I bother? It's pointing to Rynil-dissen."

"Maybe other places too. There was a war with Sarpuree, seventy years ago. We lost, so there was tribute to pay. I don't even have to guess where the Regent got the money to pay for it all. He may have sold most of the treasure."

"Humph. Yes. And if there were any decorative items left, they could be spread all through the palace. And some of the soldiers probably hid a few little things like that diamond bird. Even if we were crazy enough to rob the Regent's palace, we'd never get it all. It's the end of our treasure hunt, girl."

"But you said . . . Sung! How can I ever win my freedom if we don't go on?"

"Oh, we'll go on. But not looking for Gar's treasure." Sung scooped the jewels into his pocket and handed her the little diamond bird. "Keep this as a memento. The rest . . . well, I've thought of opening a toy shop. In Rynildissen, maybe."

"A *toy shop*?"

Sung frowned. "You don't like toys, do you?"

"Everybody likes toys. But we're *adults*, Sung!"

"Girl, don't you know that human beings are natural magicians? I think it's hereditary. The magic was always there to be used . . . but now it isn't. And we still want magic. Especially children."

"Those toys aren't—"

"No, of course not, but they're as close as you're likely to get these days, especially in a city. Toys from far places might sell very well."

She was still angry. Sung reached to run his fingers over the tawny stubble on her head. "We'll live well enough. Come kiss me, little thief. Seven years isn't such a long time."

Sparthera kissed him; she couldn't help it. Then she said, "I wondered if a diamond bird could be your talisman of levitation."

Sung's eyes widened. "I wonder . . . it's worth a try. Not in here, though." He took the bird and scrambled up scree toward the cave entrance.

Sparthera started after him. Then, holding her torch high, she looked up. The rock tapered to a high natural vault. It looked unstable, dangerous. Something . . . a bright point?

Compelled, she continued climbing after Sung. But the diamond trinket (she told herself) was no flying spell. She'd been wrong: no soldier would have stolen that. It would be treason. By staying here she would be working in Sung's best interests (she told herself, scrambling up the rocks). There was no point in shouting after him. If she were wrong, at least he wouldn't be disappointed (she told herself, and at last the pull of her oath lost its grip).

Sung was out of sight. Sparthera scrambled back down and set to work.

The soldiers had taken all of their equipment before they turned the cave into a crypt for their brethren by pulling down the entrance. They had taken armor, but left the crushed helmet that was part of one corpse. They had taken the metal point from a snapped spear; but a three-pace length of shaft remained.

Sparthera dipped a piece of cloth into the stream, then into some of the mouldy flour scattered on the rock floor. She kneaded the cloth until it had turned gooey, then wrapped it around the broken tip of the spear. She climbed scree to get closer to the ceiling, and reached up with the spear, toward a bright point on the cave roof.

It stuck. She pulled it down: thin gold filigree carved into a pair of bird's wings, about the size of her two hands. It tugged upward against her fingers.

"Lift me," she whispered. And she rose until her head bumped rock.

"Set me down," she whispered, and drifted back to earth.

No castle in the world held a room so high that she could not rob it, with this. And she waited for the impulse that would send her scrambling out to give it to Sung.

Sung was bounding downhill with his arms flapping, one hand clutching the diamond bauble, looking very like a little boy at play. He turned in fury at the sound of Sparthera's laughter.

"I've found it!" she called, holding the golden talisman high.

And as Sung ran toward her, beaming delight, Sparthera gloated.

For the instant in which she flew, Sparthera's weight in

gold had been far less than the value of the paltry treasure they had found.

She might stay with Sung long enough to take back the jewels, or at least the wings. She might even stay longer. If he were right about the toy shop . . . perhaps he need never learn that she was free.

FLARE
TIME

If the starship's arrival had done nothing else for Bronze Legs, this was enough: he was seeing the sky again.

For this past week the rammers had roamed through Touchdown City. The fifty-year-old colony was still small; everybody knew everybody. It was hard to get used to, this influx of oddly-accented strangers stumbling about with vacuous smiles and eyes wide with surprise and pleasure. Even the Medean humans were catching the habit. In his thirty-four earthyears of life Calvin "Bronze Legs" Miller had explored fifteen thousand square miles of the infinite variety that was Medea. Strange, that it took people from another world to make him look up.

Here was a pretty picture: sunset over the wild lands north of the colony. Peaks to the south were limned in bluish-white from the farmlands beyond, from the lamps that kept terrestrial plants growing. Everything else was red, infinite shades of red. To heatward a level horizon cut the great disk of Argo in half. You could feel the heat on your cheek, and watch sullenly glowing storms move in bands across the face of the red-hot superjovian world. To coldward, Phrixus and Helle were two glaring pink dots following each other down to the ridge. The Jet Stream stretched straight across the blue sky, a pinkish-white band of cloud from horizon to horizon. Thirty or forty multicolored balloons, linked in a cluster, were settling to graze a scum-covered rain pool in the valley below him.

Blue-tinged shadows pooled in the valley, and three human

shapes moved through the red and orange vegetation. Bronze Legs recognized Lightning Harness and Grace Carpenter even at this distance. The third had a slightly hunchbacked look, and a metal headdress gleamed in her straight black hair. That would be Rachel Subramaniam's memory recording equipment. Her head kept snapping left and right, ever eager for new sights.

Bronze Legs grinned. He tried to imagine how this must look to a rammer, an offworlder; he succeeded only in remembering himself as a child. All this strangeness; all this red.

He turned the howler and continued uphill.

At the crest of the ridge a fux waited for him, the pinkish-white suns behind her. She was a black silhouette; four thin legs and two thin arms, a pointed face and a narrow torso bent in an L: a lean, mean centaur-shape.

As he topped the ridge and let the howler settle on its air cushion, the fux backed away several meters. Bronze Legs wondered why, then guessed the answer. It wasn't the smell of him. Fuxes liked that. She was putting the ridge between herself and the white glare from Touchdown City's farming lamps. She said, "I am Long Nose."

"Bronze Legs. I meet you on purpose."

"I meet you on purpose. How goes your foray to heatward?"

"We start tomorrow at dawn."

"You postponed it once before." She was accusing him. The fuxes were compulsive about punctuality; an odd trait in a Bronze Age culture. Like certain traits in humans, it probably tied into their sex lives. Timing could be terribly important when a fux was giving birth.

"The ship from the stars came," he said. "We waited. We want to take one of the star people along, and the delay lets us recheck the vehicles."

Long Nose was black with dull dark-red markings. She bore a longbow over one shoulder and a quiver and shovel slung over her lower back. Her snout was sharply pointed, but not abnormally so, for a fux. She might be named for keen curiosity or a keen sense of smell. She said, "I learn that your purpose is more than exploration, but not even the post-males can tell what it is."

"Power," said Bronze Legs. "The harnessed lightning that makes our machines go comes as light from Argo. In the Hot End the clouds will never hide Argo from our sight. Our lightning makers can run without rest."

"Go north instead," said Long Nose. "You will find it safer and cooler too. Storms run constantly in the north; I have been there. Free lightning for your use."

If she'd been talking to Lightning Harness she would have suffered through an hour's lecture. How the heat exchangers ran on the flood of infrared light from Argo, focussed by mirrors. How Argo stayed always in the same place in Medea's sky, so that mirrors could be mounted on a hillside facing to heatward, and never moved again. But the colony was growing, and Medea's constant storms constantly blocked the mirrors . . . Bronze Legs only grinned at her. "Why don't we just do it our way? Who-all is coming?"

"Only six of us. Dark Wind's children did not emerge in time. Deadeye will desert us early; she will give birth in a day and must stay to guard the . . . Is 'nest' the word you use?"

"Right." Of all the words that might describe the fuxes' way of giving birth, "nest" carried the least unpleasant connotations.

"So, she will be guarding her 'nest' when we return. She will be male then. Sniffer intends to become pregnant tonight; she will leave us further on, and be there to help us on our return, if we need help."

"Good."

"We take a post-male, Harvester, and another six-leg female, Broad Flanks, who can carry him some of the time. Gimpy wants to come. Will she slow us?"

Bronze Legs laughed. He knew Gimpy; a four-leg female as old as some post-males, who had lost her right foreleg to the viciously fast Medean monster humans called a B-70. Gimpy was fairly agile, considering. "She could crawl on her belly for all we care. It's the crawlers that'll slow us, and the power plant. We're moving a lot of machinery: the prefab power plant, housing for technicians, sensing tools, digging tools—"

"What tools should we take?"

"Go armed. You won't need water bags; we'll make our own water. We made you some parasols made from mirror-cloth. They'll help you stand the heat, for awhile. When it gets really hot you'll have to ride in the crawlers."

"We will meet you at the crawling machines, at dawn." Long Nose turned and moved downslope into a red-and-orange jungle, moving something like a cat in its final rush at a bird: legs bent, belly low.

They had been walking since early afternoon: twelve hours, with a long break for lunch. Lightning sighed with relief as he set down the farming lamp he'd been carrying on his shoulders. Grace helped him spread the tripod and extend the mount until the lamp stood six meters tall.

Rachel Subramaniam sat down in the orange grass and rubbed her feet. She was puffing.

Grace Carpenter, a Medean xenobiologist and in her early forties, was a large-boned woman, broad of silhouette and built like a farm wife. Lightning Harness was tall and lean and lantern-jawed, a twenty-four-year-old power plant engineer. Both were pale as ghosts beside Rachel. On Medea only the farmers were tanned.

Rachel was built light. Some of her memory recording equipment was embedded in padding along her back, giving her a slightly hunchbacked look. Her scalp implants were part of a polished silver cap, the badge of her profession. She had spent the past two years under the sunlights aboard a web ramship. Her skin was bronze. To Rachel Medea's pale citizens had seemed frail, unathletic, until now. Now she was annoyed. There had been little opportunity for hikes aboard *Morven*; but she might have noticed the muscles and hard hands common to any recent colony.

Lightning pointed uphill. "Company."

Something spidery stood on the crest of the coldward ridge, black against the suns. Rachel asked, "What is it?"

"Fux. Female, somewhere between seven and eighteen years of age, and not a virgin. Beyond that I can't tell from here."

Rachel was astonished. "How can you know all that?"

"Count the legs. Grace, didn't you tell her about fuxes?"

Grace was chuckling. "Lightning's showing off. Dear, the fuxes go fertile around age seven. They generally have their first litter right away. They drop their first set of hindquarters with the eggs in them, and that gives them a half a lifetime to learn how to move as a quadruped. Then they wait till they're seventeen or eighteen to have their second litter, unless the tribe is underpopulated, which sometimes happens. Dropping the second set of hindquarters exposes the male organs.''

''And she's got four legs. 'Not a virgin.' I thought you must have damn good eyes, Lightning.''

''Not that good.''

''What are they like?''

''Well,'' said Grace, ''the post-males are the wise ones. Bright, talkative, and not nearly so . . . frenetic as the females. It's hard to get a female to stand still for long. The males . . . oh, for three years after the second litter they're kind of crazy. The tribe keeps them penned. The females only go near them when they want to get pregnant.''

Lightning had finished setting the lamp. ''Take a good look around before I turn this on. You know what you're about to see?''

Dutifully, Rachel looked about her, memorizing.

The farming lamps stood everywhere around Touchdown City; it was less a city than a village surrounded by farmlands. For more than a week Rachel had seen only the tiny part of Medea claimed by humans . . . until, in early afternoon of this long Medean day, she and Grace and Lightning had left the farmlands. The reddish light had bothered her for a time. But there was much to see; and after all, this was the *real* Medea.

Orange grass stood knee-high in slender leaves with sharp hard points. A score of flaccid multicolored balloons, linked by threads that resembled spiderweb, had settled on a stagnant pond. There was a grove of almost-trees, hairy rather than leafy, decked in all the colors of autumn. The biggest was white and bare and dead.

Clouds of bugs filled the air everywhere except around the humans. A pair of things glided into the swarms, scooping their dinner out of the air. They had five-meter wingspans, small batlike torsos, and huge heads that were all mouth, with gaping hair-filled slits behind the head, where gill slits would be on a fish. Their undersides were sky blue.

A six-legged creature the size of a sheep stood up against

the dead almost-tree, gripped it with four limbs, and seemed to chew at it. Rachel wondered if it was eating the wood. Then she saw myriads of black dots spread across the white, and a long, sticky tongue slurping them up.

Grace tapped Rachel's arm and pointed into the grass. Rachel saw a warrior's copper shield painted with cryptic heraldics. It was a flattened turtle shell, and the yellow-eyed beaked face that looked back at her was not turtle-like at all. Something small struggled in its beak. Suddenly the mock turtle whipped around and *zzzzed* away on eight churning legs. There was no bottom shell to hamper the legs.

The *real* Medea.

"Now," said Lightning. He turned on the farming lamp.

White light made the valley suddenly less alien. Rachel felt something within her relaxing . . . but things were happening all around her.

The flat turtle stopped abruptly. It swallowed hard, then pulled head and limbs under its shell. The flying bug-strainers whipped around and flew hard for the hairy trees. The clouds of bugs simply vanished. The long-tongued beast let go of its tree, turned and scratched at the ground and was gone in seconds.

"This is what happens when a sun flares," Lightning said. "They're both flare suns. Flares don't usually last more than half an hour, and most Medean animals just dig in till it's over. A lot of plants go to seed. Like this grass—"

Yes, the slender leaves were turning puffy, cottony. But the hairy trees reacted differently; they were suddenly very slender, the foliage pulled tight against the trunks. The balloons weren't reacting at all.

Lightning said, "That's why we don't worry much about Medean life attacking the crops. The lamps keep them away. But not all of them—"

"On Medea every rule has exceptions," Grace said.

"Yeah. Here, look under the grass." Lightning pushed cotton-covered leaves aside with his hands, and the air was suddenly full of white fluff. Rachel saw millions of black specks covering the lower stalks. "We call them locusts. They swarm in flare time and eat everything in sight. Terran plants poison them, of course, but they wreck the crops first." He let the leaves close. By now there was white fluff everywhere, like a low-lying fog patch moving east on the wind. "What else can I show you? Keep your eyes on the balloons. And are there cameras in that thing?"

Rachel laughed and touched the metal helmet. Sometimes she could forget she was wearing it; but her neck was thicker, more muscular than the average woman's. "Cameras? In a sense. My eyes are cameras for the memory tape."

The balloons rested just where they had been. The artificial flare hadn't affected them . . . wait, they weren't flaccid any more. They were swollen, taut, straining at the rootlets that held them to the bottom of the pond. Suddenly they rose, all at once, still linked by spiderweb. Beautiful.

"They use the UV for energy to make hydrogen," said Grace. "UV wouldn't bother them anyway; they have to take more of it at high altitude."

"I've been told . . . are they intelligent?"

"Balloons? No!" Grace actually snorted. "They're no brighter than so much seaweed . . . but they own the planet. We've sent probes to the Hot End, you know. We saw balloons all the way. And we've seen them as far coldward . . . west, you'd say . . . as far west as the Icy Sea. We haven't gone beyond the rim of ice yet."

"But you've been on Medea fifty years?"

"And just getting started," Lightning said. He turned off the farming lamp.

The world was plunged into red darkness.

The fluffy white grass was gone, leaving bare soil aswarm with black specks. Gradually the hairy trees loosened, fluffed out. Soil churned near the dead tree and released the tree feeder.

Grace picked up a few of the "locusts." They were not bigger than termites. Held close to the eye they each showed a translucent bubble on its back. "They can't swarm," Grace said with satisfaction. "Our flare didn't last long enough. They couldn't make enough hydrogen."

"Some did," Lightning said. There were black specks on the wind; not many.

"Always something new," said Grace.

*   *   *

Tractor probe Junior was moving into the Hot End. Ahead was the vast desert, hotter than boiling water, where Argo stood always at noon. Already the strange dry plants were losing their grip, leaving bare rock and dust. At the final shore of the Ring Sea the waves were sudsy with salt in solution, and the shore was glittering white. The hot steamy wind blew inland, to heatward, and then upward, carrying a freight of balloons.

The air was full of multicolored dots, all going up into the stratosphere. At the upper reach of the probe's vision some of the frailer balloons were popping, but the thin membranous corpses still fluttered toward heaven.

Rachel shifted carefully in her chair. She caught Bronze Legs Miller watching her from a nearby table. Her answering grin was rueful.

She had not finished the hike. Grace and Lightning had been setting up camp when Bronze Legs Miller came riding down the hill. Rachel had grasped that golden opportunity. She had returned to Touchdown City riding behind Bronze Legs on the howler's saddle. After a night of sleep she still ached in every muscle.

"Isn't it a gorgeous sight?" Mayor Curly Jackson wasn't eating. He watched avidly, with his furry chin in his hands and his elbows on the great oaken table—the dignitaries' table the Medeans were so proud of; it had taken forty years to grow the tree.

Medea had changed its people. Even the insides of buildings were different from those of other worlds. The communal dining hall was a great dome lit by a single lamp at its zenith. It was bright, and it cast sharp shadows. As if the early colonists, daunted by the continual light show—the flare suns, the bluish farming lamps, the red-hot storms moving across Argo—had given themselves a single sun indoors. But it was a wider, cooler sun, giving yellower light than a rammer was used to.

One great curve of the wall was a holograph projection screen. The tractor probe was tracing the path the expedition would follow and broadcasting what it saw. Now it moved over hills of white sea salt. The picture staggered and lurched with the probe's motion, and wavered with rising air currents.

Captain Janice Borg, staring avidly with a forkful of curry halfway to her mouth, jumped as Mayor Curly lightly punched her shoulder. The Mayor was blue eyes and a lump of nose poking through a carefully tended wealth of blond hair and beard. He was darkened by farming lamps. Not only did he supervise the farms; he farmed. "See it, Captain? That's why the Ring Sea is mostly fresh water."

Captain Borg's hair was auburn going gray. She was handsome rather than pretty. Her voice of command had the force of a bullwhip; one obeyed by reflex. Her off-duty voice was a soft, dreamy contralto. "Right. Right. The seawater moves always to the Hot End. It starts as glaciers, doesn't it? They break off in the Icy Sea and float heatward. Any salt goes that way too. In the Hot End the water boils away . . . and you get some tides, don't you? Argo wobbles a little?"

"Well, it's Medea that wobbles a little, but—"

"Right, so the seawater spills off into the salt flats at high tide and boils away there. And the vapor goes back to the glaciers along the Jet Stream." She turned suddenly to Rachel and barked, "You getting all this?"

Rachel nodded, hiding a smile. More than two hundred years had passed on the settled worlds while Captain Borg cruised the trade circuit. She didn't really understand memory tapes. They were too recent.

Rachel looked about the communal dining hall and was conscious as always of the vast unseen audience looking through her eyes, listening through her ears, feeling the dwindling aches of a stiff hike, tasting blazing hot Medean curry through her mouth. It was all going into the memory tape, with no effort on her part.

Curly said, "We picked a good site for the power plant before the first probe broke down. Heatward slope of a hillside. We'll be coming up on it in a few hours. Is this the kind of thing you want, or am I boring you?"

"I want it all. Did you try that tape?"

The Mayor shook his head, his eyes suddenly evasive.

"Why not?"

"Well," the Mayor said slowly, "I'm a little leery of what I might remember. It's all filtered through your brain, isn't it, Rachel?"

"Of course."

"I don't think I'd like remembering being a girl."

Rachel was mildly surprised. Role-changing was part of the kick. Male or female, an epicurean or a superbly muscled physical culture addict or an intellectual daydreamer, a child again or an old woman . . . well, some didn't like it. "I could give you a man's tape, Curly. There's McAuliffe's balloon trip into the big gas giant in Sol system."

Captain Borg cut in sharply. "What about the Charles Baker Sontag tape? He did a year's tour in Miramon Lluagor system, Curly. The Lluagorians use balloons for everything. You'd love it."

Curly was confused. "Just what kind of balloons—"

"Not living things, Curly. Fabric filled with gas. Lluagor has a red dwarf sun. No radiation storms and not much ultraviolet. They have to put their farms in orbit, and they do most of their living in orbit, and it's all inflated balloons, even the spacecraft. The planet they use mainly for mining and factories, but it's pretty, too, so they've got cities slung under hundreds of gasbags."

The tractor probe lurched across mile after mile of dim-lit pink salt hills. Rachel remembered a memory tape in *Morven*'s library: a critical reading of the Elder and Younger Eddas by a teacher of history and poetry. Would Medeans like that? Here you had the Land of the Frost Giants and the Land of the Fire Giants, with Midgard between . . . and the Ring Sea to stand in for the Midgard Serpent . . . and no dearth of epic monsters, from what she'd heard.

Captain Borg spoke with an edge in her voice. "Nobody's going to force you to use a new and decadent entertainment medium from the stars, Curly—"

"Oh, now, I didn't—"

"But there's a point you might consider. Distance."

"Distance?"

"There's the trade circuit. Earth, Toupan, Lluagor, Sereda, Horvendile, Koschei, Earth again. Six planets circling six stars a few light years apart. The web ramships go round and round, and everyone on the ring gets news, entertainment, seeds and eggs, new inventions. There's the trade circuit, and there's Medea. You're too far from Horvendile, Curly."

"Oddly enough, we're aware of that, Captain Borg."

"No need to get huffy. I'm trying to make a point."

"Why did *you* come?"

"Variety. Curiosity. The grass-is-always-greener syndrome. The same thing that made us rammers in the first place." Captain Borg did not add altruism, the urge to keep the worlds civilized. "But will we keep coming? Curly, Medea is the strangest place that ever had a breathable atmosphere. You've got a potential tourist trap here. You could have ramships dropping by every twenty years!"

"We need that."

"Yes, you do. So remember that rammers don't build starships. It's taxpayers that build starships. What do they get out of it?"

"Memory tapes?"

"Yes. It used to be holos. Times change. Holos aren't as involving as memory tapes, and they take too long to watch. So it's memory tapes."

"Does that mean we have to use them?"

"No," said Captain Borg.

"Then I'll try your tourist's view of Lluagor system, when I get time." Curly stood. "And I better get going. Twenty-five hours to dawn."

"It only takes ten minutes," Rachel said.

"How long to recover? How long to assimilate a whole earthyear of someone else's memories? I better wait."

After he was gone, Rachel asked, "What was wrong with giving him the Jupiter tape?"

"I remembered McAuliffe was a homosexual."

"So what? He was all alone in that capsule."

"It might matter to someone like Curly. I don't say it would, I say it might. Every world is different."

"You ought to know." The rumor mill said that Mayor Curly and Captain Borg had shared a bed. Though he hadn't shown it . . .

Too lightly, Captain Borg said, "I should but I don't."

"Oh?"

"He's . . . closed. It's the usual problem, I think. He sees me coming back in sixty or seventy years, and me ten years older. Doesn't want to get too involved."

"Janice?"

"Dammit, if they're so afraid of change, how could their

parents have busted their asses to settle a whole new world? Change is the one thing . . . yeah? What is it?"

"Did you ask him, or did he ask you?"

Captain Borg frowned. "He asked me. Why?"

"Nobody's asked me," said Rachel.

"Oh . . . Well, ask someone. Customs differ."

"But he asked you."

"I dazzled him with sex appeal. Or maybe not. Rachel, shall I ask Curly about it? There might be something we don't know. Maybe you wear your hair wrong."

Rachel shook her head. "No."

"But . . . okay. The rest of the crew don't seem to be having problems."

Nearly dawn. The sky was thick with dark clouds, but the heatward horizon was clear, with Argo almost fully risen. The dull red disk would never rise completely, not here. Already it must be sinking back.

It was earthnight now; the farming lamps were off. Crops and livestock kept terrestrial time. Rows of green plants stretched away to the south, looking almost black in this light. In the boundary of bare soil between the wilds and the croplands, half a dozen fuxes practiced spear casts. That was okay with Bronze Legs. Humans didn't spend much time in that border region. They plowed the contents of their toilets into it, to sterilize it of Medean microorganisms and fertilize it for next year's crops. The fuxes didn't seem to mind the smell.

Bronze Legs waited patiently beside his howler. He wished Windstorm would do the same.

The two house-sized crawlers were of a pattern familiar to many worlds: long, bulbous pressure hulls mounted on ground-effect platforms. They were decades old, but they had been tended with loving care. Hydrogen fuel cells powered them. One of the crawlers now carried, welded to its roof, a sender capable of reaching *Morven* in its present equatorial orbit: another good reason for waiting for the web ramship's arrival.

The third and largest vehicle was the power plant itself, fully assembled and tested, mounted on the ground-effect systems from two crawlers and with a crawler's control cabin welded on in front. It trailed a raft: yet another ground effect system covered by a padded platform with handrails. The fuxes would be riding that.

All vehicles were loaded and boarded well ahead of time. Windstorm Wolheim moved among them, ticking off lists in her head and checking them against what she could see. The tall, leggy redhead was a chronic worrier.

Phrixus (or maybe Helle) was suddenly there, a hot pink point near Argo. The fuxes picked up their spears and trotted off northward. Bronze Legs lifted his howler on its air cushion and followed. Behind him the three bigger vehicles whispered into action, and Windstorm ran for her howler.

Rachel was in the passenger seat of the lead crawler, looking out through the great bubble windscreen. In the Hot End the crawlers would house the power plant engineers. Now they were packed with equipment. Square kilometers of thin silvered plastic sheet, and knock-down frames to hold it all, would become solar mirrors. Black plastic and more frames would become the radiator fins, mounted on the back of that hill in the Hot End. There were spools of superconducting cable and flywheels for power storage. Rachel kept bumping her elbow on the corner of a crate.

The pinkish daylight was dimming, graying, as the Jet Stream spread to engulf the sky. The fuxes were far ahead, keeping no obvious formation. In this light they seemed a convocation of mythical monsters: centaurs, eight-limbed dragons, a misshapen dwarf. The dwarf was oddest of all. Rachel had seen him close: A nasty caricature of a man, with a foxy face, huge buttocks, exaggerated male organs, and (the anomaly) a tail longer than he was tall. Yet Harvester was solemn and slow-moving, and he seemed to have the respect of fuxes and humans both.

The vehicles whispered along at thirty kilometers an hour, uphill through orange grass, swerving around hairy trees. A fine drizzle began. Lightning Harness turned on the wipers.

Rachel asked, "Isn't this where we were a few days back?"

"Medean yesterday. That's right," said Grace.

"Hard to tell. We're going north, aren't we? Why not straight east?"

"It's partly for our benefit, dear. We'll be in the habitable domains longer. We'll see more variety; we'll both learn more. When we swing around to heatward we'll be nearer the north pole. It won't get hot so fast."

"Good."

Bronze Legs and a woman Rachel didn't know flanked them on the one-seater ground-effect vehicles, the howlers. Bronze Legs wore shorts, and in fact his legs were bronze. Black by race, he'd paled to Rachel's color during years of Medean sunlight. Rachel asked, half to herself, "Why not just Bronze?"

Grace understood. "They didn't mean his skin."

"What?"

"The fuxes named him for the time his howler broke down and stranded him forty miles from civilization. He walked home. He was carrying some heavy stuff, but a troop of fuxes joined him and they couldn't keep up. They've got lots of energy but no stamina. So they named him Bronze Legs. Bronze is the hardest metal they knew, till we came."

The rain had closed in. A beast like yesterday's flying bug strainers took to the air almost under the treads. For a moment it was face to face with Rachel, its large eyes and tremendous mouth all widened in horror. A wing ticked the windshield as it dodged.

Lightning cursed and turned on the headlights. As if by previous agreement, lights sprang to life on the howlers and the vehicles behind. "We don't like to do that," said Lightning.

"Do what?"

"Use headlights. Every domain is different. You never know what the local life will do when a flare comes, not till you've watched it happen. Here it's okay. Nothing worse than locusts."

Even the headlights had a yellowish tinge, Rachel thought.

The gray cliffs ahead ran hundreds of kilometers to heatward and coldward. They were no more than a few hundred feet high, but they were fresh and new. Medea wobbled a little in its course around Argo, and the tides could raise savage quakes. All the rocks had sharp angles; wind and life had not had a chance to wear them down.

The pass was new too, as if God had cleft the spine of the new mountains with a battle-ax. The floor of it was filled with rubble. The vehicles glided above the broken rock, riding high, with fans on maximum.

Now the land sloped gently down, and the expedition followed. Through the drizzle Bronze Legs glimpsed a grove of trees, hairy trees like those near Touchdown City, but different. They grew like spoons standing on end, with the cup of the spoon facing Argo. The ground was covered with tighty curled black filaments, a plant the color and texture of Bronze Legs' own hair.

They had changed domain. Bronze Legs hadn't been in this territory, but he remembered that Windstorm had. He called, "Anything unexpected around here?"

"B-70s."

"They do get around, don't they? Anything else?"

"It's an easy slope down to the shore," Windstorm called, "but then there's a kind of parasitic fungus floating on the ocean. Won't hurt us, but it can kill a Medean animal in an hour. I told Harvester. He'll make the others wait for us."

"Good."

They rode in silence for a bit. Drizzle made it hard to see much. Bronze Legs wasn't worried. The B-70s would stay clear of their headlights. This was explored territory; and even after they left it, the probes had mapped their route.

"That professional tourist," Windstorm called suddenly. "Did you get to know her?"

"Not really. What about her? Mayor Curly said to be polite."

"When was I ever not polite? But I didn't grow up with her, Bronze Legs. Nobody did. We know more about fuxes than we do about rammers, and this one's peculiar for a rammer! How could a woman give up all her privacy like that?"

"You tell me."

"I wish I knew what she'd do in a church."

"At least she wouldn't close her eyes. She's a dedicated tourist. Can you picture that? But she might not get involved either." Bronze Legs thought hard before he added, "I tried one of those memory tapes."

"What? You?"

"History of the Fission Period in Eurasia, 1945–2010, from *Morven*'s library. Education, not entertainment."

"Why that?"

"Whim."

"Well, what's it like?"

"It's .. it's like I did a lot of research, and formed conclusions and checked them out and sometimes changed my mind, and it gave me a lot of satisfaction. There are still some open questions, like how the Soviets actually got the fission bomb, and the Vietnam War, and the Arab Takeover. But I know who's working on that, and . . . It's like that, but it doesn't connect to anything. It sits in my head in a clump. But it's kind of fun, Windstorm, and I got it all in ten minutes. You want to hear a libelous song about President Peanut?"

."No."

Through the drizzle they could see the restless stirring of the Ring Ocean. A band of fuxes waited on the sand. Windstorm turned her howler in a graceful curve, back toward the blur of the crawlers' headlights, to lead them. Bronze Legs dowsed his lights and glided toward the fuxes.

They had chosen a good resting place, far from the dangerous shore, in a broad stretch of "black man's hair" that any marauder would have to cross. Most of the fuxes were lying down. The four-legged female had been impregnated six Medean days ago. Her time must be near. She scratched with sharp claws at her itching hindquarters.

Harvester came to meet Bronze Legs. The post-male biped was slow with age, but not clumsy. That tremendous length of black tail was good for his balance. It was tipped with a bronze spearhead. Harvester asked, "Will we follow the shoreline? If we may choose, we will keep your vessels between us and the shore."

"We plan to go straight across," Bronze Legs told him. "You'll ride the raft behind the bigger vessel."

"In the water are things dangerous to us," said Harvester. He glanced shoreward and added, "Things small, things large. A large one comes."

Bronze Legs took one look and reached for his intercom. "Lightning, Hairy, Jill! Turn your searchlights on that thing, fast!"

The fuxes were up and reaching for their spears.

"So it's the fuxes who give you your nicknames," Rachel said. "Why did they call you Lightning?"

"I tend the machines that make lightning and move it through metal wires. At least, that's how we explained it to the fuxes. And Windstorm—you saw the big redhead girl on the other howler? She was on guard one earthnight when a troop of fuxes took a short cut through the wheat crop. She really gave them hell. Half of Touchdown City must have heard her."

"And you? Grace."

"They named me when I was a lot younger." Grace glared at Lightning, who was very busy driving and clearly not listening, and by no means was he smiling. "But they didn't call me Grace. The way we have children, the fuxes think that's hilarious."

Rachel didn't ask.

"They called me Boobs."

Rachel felt the need for a change of subject. "Lightning, are you getting tired? Would you like me to take over?"

"I'm okay. Can you drive a crawler?"

"Actually, I've never done it. I can run a howler, though. In any terrain."

"Maybe we'll give you one after—"

Then Bronze Legs' voice bellowed from the intercom.

Something came out of the ocean: a great swollen myriapod with tiny jointed arms moving around a funnel-shaped mouth. Teeth churned in the gullet.

The fuxes cast their spears and fled. Bronze Legs tucked Harvester under one arm and sped shoreward; the howler listed to port. Deadeye fell behind; two fuxes turned back and took her arms and pulled her along.

The monster flowed up the beach, faster than any of them, ignoring the spears stuck in its flesh.

One, two, three searchlights flashed from the vehicles and played over the myriapod. The beams were bluish, unlike the headlights. Flare sunlight.

The myriapod stopped. Turned, clumsily, and began to retreat down the beach. It had nearly reached the water when it lost coordination. The legs thrashed frantically and without effect. As Rachel watched in horrible fascination, things were born from the beast.

They crawled from its back and sides. Hundreds of them. They were dark red and dog-sized. They did not leave the myriapod; they stayed on it, feeding. Its legs were quiet now.

Three of the fuxes darted down the beach, snatched up their fallen spears and retreated just as fast. The myriapod was little more than a skeleton now, and the dog-sized feeders were beginning to spread across the sand.

The fuxes climbed aboard the air-cushioned raft that trailed behind the mobile power plant. They arranged their packs and settled themselves. The paired vehicles lifted and glided toward the water. Lightning lifted the crawler and followed.

Rachel said, "But—"

"We'll be okay," Lightning assured her. "We'll stay high and cross fast, and there are always the searchlights."

"Grace, tell him! There are animals that like the searchlights!"

Grace patted her hand. The expedition set off across the water.

The colony around Touchdown City occupied part of a fat peninsula projecting deep into the Ring Sea. It took the expedition twelve hours to cross a bay just smaller than the Gulf of Mexico.

Vermilion scum patches covered the water. Schools of flying non-fish veered and dived at sight of the wrong-colored headlights. The fuxes stayed flat on their platform . . . but the water was smooth, the ride was smooth, and nothing attacked them.

The rain stopped, and left Phrixus and Helle far up the morning sky. The cloud-highway of the Jet Stream showed through a broken cloud deck. Lightning and the other drivers left their headlights on, since the sea life seemed to avoid them.

Somewhere in there, Rachel reclined her chair and went to sleep.

She woke when the crawler settled and tilted under her.

Her brain was muzzy . . . and she had slept with the recorder on. That disturbed her. Usually she switched it off to sleep. Dreams were private.

The crawler's door had dropped to form a stairway, and the crawler was empty. Rachel went out.

The crawlers, howlers, raft and mobile power plant were parked in a circle, and tents had been set up inside. There was no living human being in sight. Rachel shrugged; she stepped between a howler and the raft, and stopped.

This was nothing like the Medea she'd seen up to now.

Rolling hills were covered with chrome yellow bushes. They stood waist high, and so densely packed that no ground was visible anywhere. Clouds of insects swarmed, and sticky filaments shot up from the bushes to stab into the swarms.

The fuxes had cut themselves a clearing. They tended one who was restless, twitching. Bronze Legs Miller hailed her from their midst.

Rachel waded through the bushes. They resisted her like thick tar. The insects scattered away from her.

"Deadeye's near her time," Bronze Legs said. "Poor baby. We won't move on until she's dropped her 'nest.'"

The fux showed no swelling of pregnancy. Rachel remembered what she had been told of the fux manner of bearing children. Suddenly she didn't want to see it. Yet how could she leave? She would be omitting a major part of the experience of Medea.

She compromised. She whispered earnestly to Bronze Legs, "Should we be here? Won't they object?"

He laughed. "We're here because we make good insect repellants."

"No. We like humans." Deadeye's voice was slurred. Now Rachel saw that the left eye was pink, with no pupil. "Are you the one who has been among the stars?"

"Yes."

The feverish fux reached up to take Rachel's hand. "So much strangeness in the world. When we know all of the world, it may be we will go among the stars too. You have great courage." Her fingers were slender and hard, like bones. She let go to claw at the hairless red rash between her front and back legs. Her tail thrashed suddenly, and Bronze Legs dodged.

The fux was quiet for a time. A six-legged fux sponged her back with water; the sponge seemed to be a Medean plant. Deadeye said, "I learned from humans that 'deadeye' meant 'accurate of aim.' I set out to be the best spear-caster in..." She trailed off into a language of barking and yelping. The odd-looking biped held conversation with her. Perhaps he was soothing her.

Deadeye howled—and fell apart. She crawled forward, pulling against the ground with hands and forefeet, and her hindquarters were left behind. The hindquarters were red and dripping at the juncture, and the tail slid through them: more than a meter of thick black tail, stained with red, and as long as Harvester's now. The other fuxes came forward, some to tend Deadeye, some to examine the hindquarters...in which muscles were still twitching.

Ten minutes later Deadeye stood up. He made it look easy; given his tail and his low center of mass, perhaps it was. He spoke in his own language, and the fuxes filed away into the yellow bushes. In the human tongue Deadeye said, "I must guard my nest. Alone. Travel safely."

"See you soon," Bronze Legs said. He led Rachel after the fuxes. "He won't want company now. He'll guard the 'nest' till the little ones eat most of it and come out. Then he'll go sex-crazy, but by that time we'll be back. How are you feeling?"

"A little woozy," Rachel said. "Too much blood."

"Take my arm."

The color of their arms matched perfectly.

"Is she safe here? I mean he. Deadeye."

"He'll learn to walk faster than you think, and he's got his spear. We haven't seen anything dangerous around. Rachel, they don't have a safety hangup."

"I don't understand."

"Sometimes they get killed. Okay, they get killed. Deadeye has his reasons for being here. If his children live, they'll own this place. Some of the adults'll stay to help them along. That's how they get new territory."

Confusing. "You mean they have to be born here?"

"Right. Fuxes visit. They don't conquer. After awhile they have to go home. Grace is still trying to figure if that's physiology or just a social quirk. But sometimes they visit to give birth, and that's how they get new homes. I don't think fuxes'll ever be space travelers."

"We have it easier."

"That we do."

"Bronze Legs, I want to make love to you."

He missed a step. He didn't look at her. "No. Sorry."

"Then," she said a little desperately, "will you at least tell me what's wrong? Did I leave out a ritual, or take too many baths or something?"

Bronze Legs said, "Stage fright."

He sighed when he saw that she didn't understand. "Look, ordinarily I'd be looking for some privacy for us... which wouldn't be easy, because taking your clothes off in an unfamiliar domain... never mind. When I make love with a woman I don't want a billion strangers criticizing my technique."

"The memory tapes."

"Right. Rachel, I don't know *where* you find men who want that kind of publicity. Windstorm and I, we let a postmale watch us once... but after all, they aren't *human*."

"I could turn off the tape."

"It records memories, right? Unless you forgot about me completely, which I choose to consider impossible, you'd be remembering me for the record. Wouldn't you?"

She nodded. And went back to the crawler to sleep. Others would be sleeping in the tents; she didn't want the company.

The howler's motor was half old, half new. The new parts had a handmade look: bulky, with file marks. One of the fans was newer, cruder, heavier than the other. Rachel could only hope the Medeans were good with machinery.

The tough-looking redhead asked, "Are you sure you want to go through with this?"

"I took a howler across most of Koschei," Rachel told her. She straightened, then swung up onto the saddle. Its original soft plastic seat must have disintegrated; what replaced it looked and felt like tanned skin. "Top speed, a hundred and forty kilometers an hour. Override—this switch—boosts the fans so I can fly. Ten minutes of flight, then the batteries block up and I've got to come down. Six slots in the ground-effect skirt so I can go in any direction. The main thing is to keep my balance. Especially when I'm flying."

Windstorm did not seem reassured. "You won't get that kind of performance out of a fifty-year-old machine. Treat it tender. And don't fly if you're in a hurry, because you'll be using most of the power just to keep you up. Two more things—" She reached out to put Rachel's hands on a switch and a knob. Her own hands were large and strong, with prominent veins. "Searchlight. This knob swings it around, and *this* raises and lowers it. It's your best weapon. If it doesn't work, flee. Second thing is your goggles. Sling them around your neck."

"Where are they?"

Windstorm dug goggles from the howler's saddlebag: a flexible strap and two large hemispheres of red glass. A similar set swung from her own neck. "You should never have to ask that question again on Medea. Here."

The other vehicles were ready to go. Windstorm jogged to her own howler, leaving Rachel with the feeling that she had failed a test.

It was past noon of the Medean day. Harvester was riding Giggles, the six-legged virgin. The rest of the fuxes rode the ground-effect raft. The vehicles rode high, above the forest of chrome yellow bushes.

Windstorm spoke from the intercom. "We stay ahead of the crawlers and to both sides. We're looking for anything dangerous. If you see something you're afraid of, sing out. Don't wait."

Rachel eased into position. The feel of the howler was coming back to her. It weighed half a kiloton, but you still did some of your steering by shifting weight. . . . "Windstorm, aren't you tired?"

"I got some sleep while Deadeye was dropping her hindquarters."

Maybe Windstorm didn't trust anyone else to supervise the rammer. Rachel was actually relieved. It struck her that most Medeans had lost too many of their "safety hangups."

The bushes ended sharply, at the shore of a fast-flowing river carrying broad patches of scarlet scum. Some of the patches bloomed with flowers of startling green. Harvester boarded the raft to cross.

There was wheatfield beyond, but the yellow plants were feathery and four meters high. Hemispheres of white rock appeared with suspicious regularity. The expedition had swung around to north-and-heatward. Argo stood above the peaks of a rounded mountain range. Many-limbed birds rode the air above them.

Rachel looked up to see one dropping toward her face.

She could see the hooked beak and great claws aiming at her eyes. Her blind fingers sought the searchlight controls. She switched on the searchlight and swung the beam around and up. Like a laser cannon: *first* fire, *then* aim. Calmly, now.

The beam found the bird and illuminated it in blue fire: a fearsome sight. Wings like oiled leather, curved meat-ripping beak, muscular forelegs with long talons: and the hind legs were long, slender, and tipped each with a single sword blade. They weren't for walking at all, nor for anything but weaponry.

The bird howled, shut its eyes tight, and tried to turn in the air. Its body curled in a ball; it wings folded around it. Rachel dropped the beam to keep it pinned until it smacked hard into the wheatfield.

The intercom said, "Nice."

"Thank you." Rachel sounded deceptively calm.

"Grace wants to call a halt," Windstorm said. "Up by that next boulder."

"Fine."

The boulders were all roughly the same size: fairly regular hemispheres one and a half meters across.

Grace and Bronze Legs came out of the crawler lugging instruments on a dolly. They unloaded a box on one side of the boulder, and Grace went to work on it. Bronze Legs moved the dolly around to the other side and unfurled a silver screen. When Rachel tried to speak, Grace shushed her. She fiddled a bit with various dials, then turned on the machine.

A shadow-show formed on the screen: a circle of shadow, and darker shapes within. Grace cursed and touched dials, feather-lightly. The blurred shadows took on detail.

Shadows of bones, lighter shadows of flesh. There were

four oversized heads, mostly jaws, overlapping near the center; and four tails near the rim, and a maze of legs and spines between. Four creatures all wrapped intimately around each other to just fill the shell.

"I knew it!" Grace cried. "They were too regular. They had to be eggs or nests or plants or *something* like that. Windstorm, dear, if we pile this junk back on the dolly, can you tow it to the next rock?"

They did that. The next rock was very like the first: an almost perfect hemisphere with a surface like white plaster. Rachel rapped it with her knuckles. It felt like stone. But the deep-radar shadow showed three big-headed foetuses just filling their environment, plus a tiny one that had failed to grow.

"Well. They all seem to be at the same stage of development," Grace observed. "I wonder if it's a seasonal thing?"

Rachel shook her head. "It's different every time you turn around. Lord! You learn a place, you walk a couple of kilometers, you have to start all over again. Grace, don't you ever get frustrated? You can't run fast enough to stay in one place!"

"I love it. And it's worse than you think, dear." Grace folded the screen and stacked it on the dolly. "The domains don't stay the same. We have spillovers from other domains, from high winds and tidal slosh and migration. I'd say a Medean ecology is ruined every ten years. Then I have to learn it all over again. Windstorm, dear, I'd like to look at one more of these rock eggs. Will you tow—"

The windstorm was sudden and violent. "Damn it, Grace, this isn't the way we planned it! We do our biological research on the way back! *After* we set up the power system, *then* we can give the local monsters a chance to wreck us."

Grace's voice chilled. "Dear, it seems to me that this bit of research is quite harmless."

"It uses up time and supplies. We'll do it on the way back, when we know we've *got* the spare time. We've been through this. Pack up the deep-radar and let's move."

Now the rolling hills of feather-wheat sloped gently up toward an eroded mountain range whose peaks seemed topped with pink cotton. The three-legged female, Gimpy, trotted alongside Rachel, talking of star travel. Her gait was strange, rolling, but she kept up as long as Rachel held her howler to the power plant's twenty KPH.

She could not grasp interstellar distances. Rachel didn't push. She spoke of wonders instead: of the rings of Saturn, and the bubble cities of Lluagor, and the Smithpeople, and the settling of whale and dolphin colonies in strange oceans. She spoke of time compression: of gifting Sereda with designs for crude steam engines and myriads of wafer-sized computer brains, and returning to find steam robots everywhere: farmland, city streets, wilderness, households, disneylands; of fads that could explode across a planet and vanish without a trace, like tobacco pipes on Koschei, op-art garments on Earth, weight lifting on low gravity Horvendile.

It was long before she got Gimpy talking about herself.

"I was of my parent's second litter, within a group that moved here to study your kind," Gimpy said. "They taught us bow and arrow, and a better design of shovel, and other things. We might have died without them."

"The way you said that: second litter. Is there a difference?"

"Yes. One has the first litter when one can. The second litter comes to one who proves her capability by living that long. The third litter, the male's litter, comes only with the approval of one's clan. Else the male is not allowed to breed."

"That's good genetics." Rachel saw Gimpy's puzzlement. "I mean that your custom makes better fuxes."

"It does. I will never see my second litter," Gimpy said. "I was young when I made my mistake, but it was foolish. The breed improves. I will not be a one-legged male."

They moved into a rift in the eroded mountain range, and the incredible became obvious. The mountains were topped with pink cotton candy. It must have been sticky like cotton candy, too. Rachel could see animals trapped in it. Gimpy wanted no part of that. She dropped back and boarded the raft.

They crossed the cotton candy with fans blasting at maximum. The big vehicles blew pink froth in all directions. Something down there wasn't trapped at all. A ton of drastically flattened pink snail, with a perfect snail shell perched jauntily on its back, cruised over the cotton candy leaving a slime trail that bubbled and expanded to become more pink froth. It made for the still corpse of a many-limbed bird, flowed over it, and stopped to digest it.

The strangeness was getting to Rachel; and that was a strange thing for her. She was a rammer. Strangeness was the one constant in her life. Born aboard a ramship, not *Morven*, she had already gone once around the trade circuit. Even a rammer who returned to a world he knew must expect to find it completely changed; and Rachel *knew* that. But the strangeness of Medea came faster than she could swallow it or spit it out.

She fiddled with the intercom until she got Grace.

"Yes, dear, I'm driving. What is it?"

"It's confusion. Grace, why aren't all planets like Medea? They've all got domains, don't they? Deserts, rain forests, mountains, poles and equators . . . you see what I mean?"

She heard the xenobiologist's chuckle. "Dear, the Cold Pole is covered with frozen carbon dioxide. Where we're going it's hotter than boiling water. What is there on the trade circuit worlds that splits up the domains? Mountain ranges? An ocean for a heat sink? Temperature, altitude, rainfall? Medea has all of that, plus the one-way winds and the one-way ocean currents. The salinity goes from pure water to pure brine. The glaciers carry veins of dry ice heatward, so there are sudden jumps in the partial pressure of carbon dioxide. Some places there are no tides. Other places, Argo wobbles enough to make a terrific tidal slosh. Then again, everything has to adapt to the flares. Some animals have shells. Some sea beasts can dive deep. Some plants şeed, other grow a big leaf for an umbrella."

Beyond the pass the mountains dropped more steeply, down to an arm of the Ring Sea. Rachel had no problem controlling the howler, but the mobile power plant was laboring hard, with its front vents wide open to hold it back and little pressure left for steering. There should be no real danger. Two probes had mapped this course.

"Everything is *more* different, huh?"

"Excuse me, dear . . . that's got it. Sonofabitch, we could live without that sonofabitching tail wind. Okay. Do you remember the mock turtle we showed you yesterday evening? We've traced it six thousand kilometers to coldward. In the Icy Sea it's seagoing and much larger. Follow it heatward and it gets smaller and more active. We think it's the food supply.

Glaciers stir up the bottom, and the sea life loves that. To heatward a bigger beast starves ... sometimes. But we could be wrong. Maybe it has to conserve heat in the colder climates. I'd like to try some experiments someday."

The white boulders that turned out to be giant eggs were thicker here on the heatward slopes. And on the lower slopes— But this was *strange*.

The mountainsides were gay with pennants. Thousands of long, flapping flags, orange or chrome yellow. Rachel tried to make it out. Grace was still talking; Rachel began to feel she'd opened a Pandora's Box.

"The closer you look to the Hot Pole, the more competition you find among the sea life. New things flow in from coldward, constantly. All the six-limbed and eight-limbed forms, we think they were forced onto the land, kicked out of the ocean by something bigger or meaner. They left the ocean before they could adopt the usual fish shape, which is four fins and a tail."

"Grace, wait a minute, now. Are you saying ... we ..."

"Yes, dear." The smile Rachel couldn't see had to be a smirk. "Four limbs and a tail. We dropped the tail, but the human form is perfectly designed for a fish."

Rachel switched her off.

The hillside trees had extensive root systems that gripped rock like a strong man's fist, and low, almost conical trunks. On each tree the tip of the trunk sprouted a single huge leaf, a flapping flag, orange or chrome yellow and ragged at the end. All pennants and no armies. Some of the flags were being torn apart by the air blast from the ground-effect vehicles. Perhaps that was how they spread their seeds, Rachel thought. Like tapeworms. Ask Grace? She'd had enough of Grace, and she'd probably have to start with an apology. ...

The day brightened as if clouds had passed from before the sun.

The slopes were easing off into foothills now. Gusts of wind turned some of the flapping pennants into clouds of confetti. It was easier to go through the papery storms than to steer around. Rachel used one hand as a visor; the day had turned quite bright. Was she carrying dark glasses? Of course, the goggles—

It was a flare!

She kept her eyes resolutely lowered until she'd pulled the red cups over her eyes and adjusted them. Then she turned to look. The suns were behind her left shoulder, and one was nearly lost in the white glare of the other.

Bronze Legs was asleep in a reclined passenger chair in the trailing crawler. It was like sleeping aboard a boat at anchor . . . but the sudden glare woke him instantly.

Going downhill, the mobile power plant rode between the two crawlers, for greater safety. The angle of descent hadn't seriously hampered the ponderous makeshift vehicle. But all bets were off now. *Flare!*

The fuxes were still on the raft. They could be hurt if they tumbled off at this speed, but their every instinct must be telling them to get off and *dig*. Bronze Legs flattened his nose against the windscreen. Charles "Hairy" McBundy, fighting to slow the power plant and raft, wouldn't have attention to spare; and there *had* to be a place to stop. Someplace close, someplace flat, dirt rather than rock, and damn quick! There, to the left? Not quite flat, and it ended short, in a cliff. Tough. Bronze Legs hit the intercom button and screamed, "Hard left, Hairy, and when you stop, stop fast!"

Hairy was ahead of him. Vents had already opened in the air cushion skirts of raft and power plant. Robbed of thrust through the forward vents, the vehicles surged left and forward. Bronze Legs' teeth ground against each other. One silver parasol had opened on the raft, probably Harvester's, and five sharp fux faces were under it. Their tails thrashed with their agitation.

Grace brought the crawler around to follow. Left and forward, too fast, like the power plant. Hairy was on the ledge now. He cut his air cushion all at once. The power plant dropped. Its skirt screamed against rock, then dirt, then, at the edge of the drop, quit. The fuxes boiled off the raft, raised parasols, and began digging.

The crawler vibrated sickeningly as Grace cut the air cushion.

She was wearing her ruby goggles. So was Bronze Legs; he must have donned them without help from his conscious mind. He glanced again at the fuxes and saw only silver disks and a fog of brown dirt. The other crawler had stopped on the slant.

Windstorm's howler sat tilted, but not rolling. Windstorm herself was sprinting uphill. Good enough. She should be inside, in one of the crawlers. Strange things could emerge in flare time. Where was the other howler pilot?

Far downslope and losing ground. Too far to climb back in any reasonable time. That was Rachel, the rammer, wasn't it? With a little skill she could turn the howler and use the larger rear vents to bring her back; but she wasn't showing that skill. She seemed to be trying to back up. Not good at all.

"Grace? Can we take the crawler down to her?"

"We may have to try. Try the intercom first, dear. See if you can talk her back up."

Bronze Legs tried. "Her intercom's off."

"Off? Really? The little idiot—"

"And she's not about to notice the little light. Wait, here she comes." Rachel's howler lifted on emergency power, hovered, then started uphill.

Grace said, "She may have trouble landing."

Then Bronze Legs saw what was happening around them.

To Rachel it seemed that everyone was in panic. Far above her, both crawlers and the power plant had come to a screeching halt. Tough, competent Windstorm had abandoned her own vehicle and was fleeing in terror from nothing visible. The fuxes, the native Medeans, were nowhere in sight. Could they *all* know something Rachel didn't?

She was having her own problems. The damned obsolete sluggish howler refused to back up; it coasted slowly, frictionlessly downhill, further and further from safety. To hell with that. She flipped the override.

The howler went up. Rachel leaned far back, and the howler tilted with her, staying low, following the upward curve of terrain. If the power quit early she wanted some chance to land. But the howler purred nicely uphill, faster now, while Rachel concentrated on her balance. She was marginally aware that the gay orange pennants had all turned to dead black crepe, and that certain round white boulders were cracking, crumbling.

But when things emerged from the boulders, she screamed.

All in an instant the mountains were acrawl with a thousand monsters. Their skins were shiny white. Their eyes were mere slits in heads that were mostly teeth. As Rachel rose toward the precarious safety of the crawlers, the creatures chose their target and converged. They ran with bodies low, tails high, legs an invisible blur. In seconds that meager flat place where the crawlers rested was covered with rock demons.

No safety there.

She flew over the crawlers, glimpsed peering faces behind the windscreens, and kept going. The boulders had been rare near the crest, and the rock demons weren't there yet. Neither was Rachel, of course. She'd get as far as possible before the howler quit. And then what?

She flipped on the headlights and the searchlight too. The rock demons throve in flare time, but even they might fear too much flare sunlight. It was worth a try.

The mountain's rock face grew steeper and steeper. No place to land, unless she could reach the crest. The fans howled.

Here was the ridge, coming level. Rachel cursed venomously. The crest was carpeted in pink, sticky cotton candy. Its proprietors had withdrawn into huge snail shells.

The howl of the fans dropped from contralto toward bass.

Pale six-legged monsters, searching for meat on bare rock, turned big heads to squint as Rachel sank low. They blurred into motion.

The crawler coasted just above the pink froth, riding the ground effect now, not really flying. Strange corpses and strange skeletons were marooned in that sea. The wind from the fans was full of pink froth.

Then she had crossed and was coasting downhill, and it was already too late to land. The howler rode centimeters above the rock, too fast and gaining speed. Here the slope was shallower, and she was still in the pass chosen long ago by Medeans monitoring a tractor probe. But the howler rode too low. If she opened a slot to brake, the skirt would scrape rock, the howler would flip over. Find a level spot—

A quick glance back told her she didn't want to stop anyway. A dozen of the rock demons had crossed the cotton candy. Probably used their siblings for stepping stones after *they* got stuck! Rachel held hard to her sanity and concentrated on staying right side up. The things were holding their own in the race. Maybe they were even catching up.

Bronze Legs squeezed between the crates and the roof to reach the crawler's observation bubble. It was big enough for his head and shoulders. He found one of the rock demons with it forelegs wrapped around the bubble, blocking part of his view while it gnawed at the glass.

Rock demons swarmed on the ground. The fuxes couldn't be seen, but a few rock demons lay unnaturally quiet where the fuxholes were, and Bronze Legs saw a spear thrust through the melee. He called down, "Try the searchlights."

"Won't work," Grace answered. She tried it anyway. Other searchlights joined hers, and the thrashing rock demons blazed painfully bright even through goggles. They turned, squinted at the situation, then came all in a quick rush. The bronze spearhead on Harvester's tail stabbed deep into a straggler. The rock demon's blood jetted an incredible distance. It died almost instantly.

If there were live fuxes under the somewhat tattered silver parasols, they were safe now. All the rock demons were swarming round the vehicle's searchlights. They *liked* the light.

Grace chortled. "Tell me you expected *that*!"

"I wouldn't dare. I feel a lot safer now." The monsters weren't tearing at the lights; they fought each other for a place in the glare. "What do they think they're doing?"

"We've seen this kind of reaction before," Grace answered. "Medean life either loves flares or hates them. All the flare-loving forms act like they're programmed to stay out of shadows during flares. Like, in the shadow of a mountain they'd be in just the conditions they aren't designed for. Most of 'em have high blood pressure, too, and terrific reserves of energy. They have to accomplish a lot in the little time a flare lasts. Be born, eat, grow, mate, give birth—"

"Grace, get on the intercom and find out if everyone's still alive. And see if anyone knows which sun flared."

"Why? What possible difference could it make?"

"Phrixus flares last up to three quarters of an hour. Helle

flares don't last as long. We're going to have to wait it out. And see if Rachel called anyone."

"Right."

Bronze Legs half-listened to the intercom conversation. Along the heatward slopes of the mountains the black flags flew in triumph, growing longer almost as Bronze Legs watched, making sugar while the sun flared. The rock demons milling in the searchlight beams were now hungry enough to be attacking each other in earnest. A vastly larger number of rock demons had deserted the mountainsides entirely, had swarmed straight down to the shoreline. The waves were awash with sea monsters of all sizes; the rock demons were wading out to get them.

Grace called up to him. "Rachel didn't call anyone. Lightning says she made it over the crest."

"Good."

"What do you think she'll do?"

"Nobody knows her very well. Hmm . . . She won't land in the cotton candy. She probably could, because those snails are probably hiding in their shells. Right?"

"But she won't. It'd be too messy. She'll stop on the coldward slope, or beyond, anywhere it's safe to wait it out. If there is anywhere. Do you think she'll find anywhere safe?"

"She won't know what's safe. She won't find anyplace that isn't swarming with *something*, not this far to heatward. The further you look to heatward, the more ferocious the competition gets."

"Then she'll keep going. If she doesn't wreck herself, she'll go straight back to Touchdown City. Let's see, *Morven*'s on the other side of the planet now. Say it'll be up in an hour, and we'll let them know what's happening. That way we'll know she's safe almost as soon as she does. Grace, you don't think she'd try to rejoin us?"

"She can't get lost, and she can't stop, and Touchdown's visible from fifty miles away. She'll just head home. Okay . . ." There was a funny edge of doubt in Grace's voice. She stabbed at an intercom button. "Lightning? Me. You watched Rachel go over the crest, right? Did she have her headlights on?"

Bronze Legs was wondering just how teed off the rammers

would be if Rachel was dead. It took him a moment to see the implications of what Grace was saying.

"The searchlight too? All right, Lightning. The long range sender is on your roof. I want it ready to send a message to *Morven* by the time *Morven* rises, which will be to south of coldward in about an hour. . . . No, don't go out yet. The way the beasts are running around they should die of heatstroke pretty quick. When they fall off the roof, you go."

The rock demons followed Rachel twelve kilometers down-slope before anything distracted them.

The howler was riding higher now, but Rachel wasn't out of trouble. The emergency override locked the vents closed. If she turned it off the power would drop, and so would the howler. She was steering with her weight alone. Her speed would last as long as she was going down. She had almost run out of mountain. The slope leveled off as it approached the river.

The vicious pegasus-type birds had disappeared. The rolling mountainsides covered with feathery wheat were now covered with stubble, stubble with a hint of motion in it, dark flecks that showed and were gone. Millions of mice, maybe?

Whatever: they were meat. The demons scattered in twelve directions across the stubble, their big heads snapping, snapping. Rachel leaned forward across her windscreen to get more speed. Behind her, three rock demons converged on a golden Roman shield . . . on a mock-turtle that had been hidden by feather-wheat and was now quite visible and helpless. The demons turned it over and ripped it apart and ate and moved on.

The howler slid across the shore and onto flowing water.

Each patch of scarlet scum had sprouted a great green blossom. Rachel steered between the stalks by body english. She was losing speed, but the shore was well behind her now.

And all twelve rock demons zipped downhill across the stubble and into the water. Rachel held her breath. Could they *swim*? They were under water, drinking or dispersing heat or both. Now they arched upward to reach the air.

The howler coasted to a stop in midstream.

Rachel nerved herself to switch off the override. The howler dropped, and hovered in a dimple of water, churning a fine mist that rapidly left Rachel dripping wet. She waited. Come what may, at least the batteries were recharging. Give her time and she'd have a howler that could steer and fly.

The heatward shore was black with a million mouse-sized beasties. They'd cleaned the field of feather-wheat; but what did they think they were doing now? Watching Rachel? The rock demons noticed. They waded clumsily out of the water and, once on land, blurred into motion. The shore churned with six-legged white marauders and tiny black prey.

It seemed the fates had given Rachel a break. The water seemed quite empty but for the scarlet scum and its huge blossoms. No telling what might be hugging the bottom while the flare passed. Rachel could wait too. The coldward shore looked safe enough . . . though it had changed. Before the flare, it had been one continuous carpet of chrome yellow bushes. The bushes were still there, but topped now with a continuous sheet of silver blossoms. The clouds of insects swarmed still, though they might be different insects.

Upstream, something was walking toward her on stilts. It came at its own good time, stopping frequently. Rachel kept her eye on it while she tried the intercom.

She got static on all bands. Mountains blocked her from the expedition; other mountains blocked her from Touchdown City. The one sender that could reach *Morven* in orbit was on a crawler. Dammit. She never noticed the glowing pinpoint that meant Bronze Legs had called. It was too dim.

Onshore, two of the rock demons were mating head-to-tail.

The thing upstream seemed to be a great silver Daddy-long-legs. Its legs were slender and almost long enough to bridge the river; its torso proportionately tiny. It paused every so often to reach deep into the water with the thumbless hands on its front legs. The hands were stubby, armored in chitin, startlingly quick. They dipped, they rose at once with something that struggled, they conveyed the prey to its mouth. Its head was wide and flat, like a clam with bulging eyes. It stepped delicately downstream, with all the time in the world . . . and it was bigger than Rachel had realised, and *faster*.

So much for her rest break. She opened the rear vent. The

howler slid across the river and onto shore, and stopped, nudging the bushes.

The Daddy-long-legs was following her. Ten of the dozen rock demons were wading across. As the bottom dipped the six-legged beasts rose to balance on four legs, then two. As bipeds they were impressively stable. Maybe their tails trailed in the mud bottom to serve as anchors. And the mice were coming too. Thousands of them, swimming in a black carpet among the patches of scum.

Rachel used the override for fifteen seconds. It was enough to put her above the silver-topped bushes. The lily-pad-shaped silver blossoms bowed beneath the air blast, but the ground effect held her. She wasn't making any great speed. Bugs swarmed around her. Sticky filaments shot from between the wide silver lily pads, and sometimes found bugs, and sometimes struck the fans or the ground effect skirt.

She looked for the place that had been cleared for a fux encampment. Deadeye would be there, a feisty male biped guarding his nest, if Deadeye still lived. She couldn't find the gap in the bushes. It struck her that that was good luck for Deadeye, considering what was following her.

But she was lonely, and scared.

The Daddy-long-legs stepped delicately among the bushes. Bushes rustled to show where ten rock demons streaked after her, veering to snatch a meal from whatever was under the blossoms, then resuming course. Of the plant-eating not-mice there was no sign, except that here and there a bush had collapsed behind her.

But they were all falling behind as the fuel cells poured power into the howler's batteries.

Rachel oriented herself by Argo and the Jet Stream and headed south and coldward. She was very tired. The land was darkening, reddening . . . and it came to her that the flare was dying.

The flare was dying. The goggles let Bronze Legs look directly at the suns, now, to see the red arc enclosing the bright point of Helle. A bubble of hellfire was rising, cooling, expanding into the vacuum above the lesser hell of a red dwarf star.

They were six-legged rock demons all around them, and a

few on the roofs. All were dead, from heatstroke or dehydration. A far larger number were gathering all along the Ring Sea shore. Now they swarmed uphill in a wave of silver. They paired off as they came, and stopped by twos in the rocks to mate.

The diminished wave swept around the expedition and petered out. Now the mountains were covered with writhing forms: an impressive sight. "They make the beast with twelve legs," Bronze Legs said. "Look at the size of those bellies! Hey, Grace, aren't the beasts themselves bigger than they were?"

"They have to be. They've got to form those eggs. Dammit, don't distract me."

The intercom lit. Grace wasn't about to notice anything so mundane. The paired rock demons were growing quiet, but they were still linked head to tail. Bronze Legs opened the intercom.

Lightning's voice said, "I've got Duty Officer Toffler aboard *Morven*."

"Okay. Toffler, this is Miller. We've got an emergency."

"Sorry to hear it." The male voice sounded sleepy. "What can we do about it?"

"You'll have to call Touchdown City. Can you patch me through, or shall I record a message?"

"Let's check . . ." The voice went away. Bronze Legs watched a nearby pair of rock demons crawling away from each other. The thick torsos seemed different. A belly swelling that had extended the length of the torso was now a prominent swelling between the middle and hind legs. It was happening fast. The beasts seemed gaunt, all bone and skin, except for the great spherical swelling. With fore and middle legs they scratched at the earth, digging, digging.

"Miller, you'd better record. By the time we got their attention they'd be over the horizon. We'll have them in another hour."

"Good—"

"But I don't see how they can help either. Listen, Miller, is there something we can do with an interstellar message laser? At this range we can melt a mountain or boil a lake, and be accurate to—"

"Dammit, Toffler, *we're* not in trouble! Touchdown City's in trouble, and they don't know it yet!"

"Oh? Okay, set to record."

"To Mayor Curly Jackson, Touchdown City. We've weathered the flare. We don't know if the fuxes survived yet. The rammer, Rachel Subramaniam, is on the way to you on a howler. She has no reason to think she's dangerous, but she is. By the time you spot her you'd be too late to stop her. If you don't move damn quick, the human colony on Medea could be dead within the year. You'll need every vehicle you can get your hands on . . ."

The expedition had crossed a great bay of the Ring Sea in twelve hours. Rachel could cross it in three; but she'd be rid of what followed her moments after she left shore. She had heard Lightning mention the parasitic fungus that floated on this arm of the Ring Sea, that was deadly to fuxes and any Medean life . . . unless the flare had burned it away.

The flare was long over. She rode through the usual red-lit landscape, in a circle of the white light from headlights, taillights, searchlight. She hungered and thirsted for the light of farming lamps, the color of Sol, of ship's sunlights; the sign that she had come at last to Touchdown City.

But she hungered more for the fungus that would kill the rock demons and the Daddy-long-legs. She hated them for their persistence, their monstrous shapes, their lust for her flesh. She hated them for being themselves! Let them rot, slow or quick. Then three hours to cross the bay, half an hour more to find and navigate that rubble-strewn pass, and downhill toward the bluewhite light.

That was the shoreline ahead.

Ominously blood-colored beasts milled there. One by one they turned toward the howler.

Rachel cursed horribly and without imagination. She had seen these things before. The expedition's searchlights had pinned a tremendous thousand-legged worm, and these things had been born from its flesh. They were dog-sized, tailless quadrupeds. Flare time must have caught a lot of the great myriapods, brought vast populations of parasites to life, for this many to be still active this long after the flare.

More than active. They leapt like fleas . . . toward Rachel.

She turned to heatward. Weak as she felt now, *one* could knock her out of the saddle.

Her entourage turned with her. Two more rock demons had dropped out. Eight followed, and the great spider, and a loyal population of proto-mice, exposed now that the bushes had ended. And hordes of insects. Rachel's reason told her that she was taking this all too personally. But what did they *see* in her? She wasn't that much meat, and the spider wasn't that hungry. It reached down now and then to pluck a proto-mouse, and once it plucked up a rock demon, with equal nonchalance. The demon raved and snapped and died within the spider's clamshell mouth, but it clawed out an eye, too.

And the demons had the proto-mice for food, but they had to streak down to the water every so often to cool off, and fight their way back through the blood-red quadrupeds, eating what they killed. The mice had fed well on the yellow bushes, and who knew about the tiny might-be-insects? *What did they all want with Rachel?*

After a couple of hours the shore curved south, and now it was white tinged with other colors: a continuous crust of salt. Rachel's climate suit worked well, but her face and hands were hot. The wind was hot with Argo-heat and the heat of a recent flare. The Daddy-long-legs had solved its heat problem. It waded offshore, out of reach of the red parasites, pacing her.

It was five hours before the shore turned sharply to coldward. Rachel turned with it, staying well back from shore, where blood-colored quadrupeds still prowled. She worried now about whether she could find the pass. There would be black, tightly curled ground cover, and trees foliated in gray hair with a spoon-shaped silhouette; and sharp-edged young mountains to the south. But she felt stupid with fatigue, and she had never adjusted to the light and never would: dull red from Argo, pink from two red dwarf suns nearing sunset.

More hours passed. She saw fewer of the red parasites. Once she caught the Daddy-long-legs with another rock demon in its clamshell jaws. The hexapods's own teeth tore at the side of the spider's face . . . the side that was already blind. Flare-loving forms used themselves up fast. Those trees . . .

Rachel swung her searchlight around. The ground cover, the "black man's hair," was gone. A black fog of insects swarmed over bare dirt. But the trees were hairy, with a spoon-shaped silhouette. How far had those trees spread on Medea? She could be in the wrong place. . . .

She turned left, uphill.

There were low mountains ahead, young mountains, all sharp edges. A kilometer short, Rachel turned to parallel them. The pass had been so narrow. She could go right past it. She slowed down, then, impatient, speeded up again. Narrow it had been, but straight. Perhaps she would see farming lamps shining through it. She noticed clouds forming, and began cursing to drive away thoughts of rain.

When the light came it was more than a glimmer.

She saw a sun, a white sun, a *real* sun, shining against the mountains. As if flare time had come again! But Phrixus and Helle were pink dots sinking in the west. She swerved toward the glare. The rising ground slowed her, and she remembered the spider plodding patiently behind her; she didn't turn to look.

The glare grew terribly bright. She slowed further, puzzled and frightened. She pulled the goggles up over her eyes. That was better; but still she saw nothing but that almighty glare at the end of a bare rock pass.

She rode into the pass, into the glare, into a grounded sun. Her eyes adjusted. . . .

The rock walls were lined with vehicles: flyers, tractor probes, trucks, crawlers converted to firefighting and ambulance work, anything that could move on its own was there, and each was piled with farming lamps and batteries, and all the farming lamps were on. An aisle had been left between them. Rachel coasted down the aisle. She thought she could make out man-shaped shadows in the red darkness beyond.

They were human. By the pale mane around his head she recognized Mayor Curly Jackson.

Finally, finally, she slowed the howler, let it sink to the ground, and stepped off. Human shapes came toward her. One was Mayor Curly. He took her arm, and his grip drove pain even through the fog of fatigue. "You vicious little idiot," he said.

She blinked.

He snarled and dropped her arm and turned to face the pass.

Half the population of Touchdown City stood looking down the aisle of light, ignoring Rachel . . . pointedly. She didn't try to shoulder between them. She climbed into the howler's saddle to see.

They were there: half a dozen rock demons grouped beneath the long legs of the spider; a black carpet of proto-mice; all embedded in a cloud of bright motes, insects. The monsters strolled up the aisle of light, and the watching men backed away. It wasn't necessary. Where the light stopped, Rachel's entourage stopped too.

Mayor Curly turned. "Did it *once* occur to you that something might be following your lights? Your *flare-colored* lights? You went through half a dozen domains, and every one had its own predators and its own plant eaters, and you brought them all *here*, you gutless moron! How many kinds of insects are there in that swarm? How many of them would eat our crops down to the ground before it poisoned them? Those little black things on the ground, they're plant-eaters too, aren't they? All flare-loving forms, and you brought them all here to *breed*! The next time a flare goes off would have been the last time any Medean human being had anything to eat! *You'd* be safe, of course. All you'd have to do is fly on to another star . . ."

The only way a human being can turn off her ears is to turn off her mind. Rachel didn't know whether she fainted or not. Probably she was led away rather than carried. Her next memory began some time later, beneath the light of home, with the sounds and the smells of home around her, strapped down in free fall aboard the web ramship *Morven*.

On the curve of the wall the mobile power plant and one of the crawlers had finally left the realms of crusted salt. They ran over baked dirt now. The howler was moored in the center of the ground-effect raft, surrounded by piles of crates. It would be used again only by someone willing to wear a spacesuit. The four remaining fuxes were in the crawlers. Argo was out of camera range, nearly overhead. The view shifted and dipped with the motion of the trailing crawler.

"No, the beasts didn't actually do any harm. We did more damage to ourselves," Mayor Curly said. He wasn't looking at Captain Borg. He was watching the holo wall. A cup of coffee cooled in his hand. "We moved every single farming lamp out of the croplands and set them all going in the pass, right? And the flare-loving life forms just stayed there till they died. They aren't really built to take more than a couple of hours of flare time, what they'd get if both suns flared at once, and they aren't built to walk away from flarelight either. Maybe some of the insects bred. Maybe the big forms were carrying seeds and insect eggs in their hair. We know the six-legged types tried to breed as soon as we turned off the lamps, but they weren't in shape for it by then. It doesn't matter now. I suppose I should . . ."

He turned and looked at her. "In fact, I do thank you most sincerely for melting that pass down to lava. There can't be anything living in it now."

"So you came out of it with no damage."

"Not really. The locusts hurt us. We moved the farming lamps in a hurry, but we took our own good time getting them back in place. That was a mistake. Some flare-hating bugs were just waiting to taste our corn."

"Too bad."

"And a nest of B-70s killed two children in the oak grove."

Captain Borg's mind must have been elsewhere. "You really reamed Rachel out."

"I did," Curly said, without satisfaction and without apology.

"She was almost catatonic. We had to take her back up to *Morven* before she'd talk to anyone. Curly, is there any way to convince her she didn't make a prize idiot of herself?"

"At a guess I'd say no. Why would anyone want to?"

Captain Borg was using her voice of command now. "I dislike sounding childish, especially to you, Curly, but baby talk may be my best option. The problem is that Rachel didn't have any fun on Medea."

"You're breaking my heart."

"She won't even talk about coming down. She didn't like Medea. She didn't like the light, or the animals, or the way the fuxes bred. Too bloody. She went through thirty-odd hours of hell with your power plant expedition, and came back tired to death and being chased by things out of a nightmare, and when she finally got to safety you called her a dangerous in-

competent idiot and made her believe it. She didn't even get
laid on Medea—"

"What?"

"Never mind, it's trivial. Or maybe it's absolutely crucial,
but *skip* it. Curly, I have sampled the official memory tape of
Medea, the one we would have tried to peddle when we got
back into the trade circuit—"

Curly's eyes got big. "O-o-oh shit!"

"It comes to you, does it? That tape was an ugly experience.
It's unpleasant, and uncomfortable, and humiliating, and ex-
hausting, and scary, and there's no sex. That's Rachel's view
of Medea, and there *isn't* any other, and *nobody's* going to
enjoy it."

Curly had paled. "What do we do? Put Rachel's equipment
on somebody else?"

"I wouldn't wear it. No rammer is really manic about her
privacy, but there are limits. What about a Medean?"

"Who?"

"Don't you have any compulsive exhibitionists?"

Curly shook his head. "I'll ask around, but . . . no, maybe
I won't. Doesn't it tell you something, that she couldn't get
screwed? What man could go with a woman, knowing she'll
be peddling the memory of it to millions of strangers? Yuk."

The crawlers had stopped. Human shapes stepped outside,
wearing skintight pressure suits and big transparent bubbles
over their heads. They moved around to the ground-effect raft
and began opening crates.

"It's no good. Curly, it's not easy to find people to make
memory tapes. For a skill tape you need a genuine expert with
twenty or thirty years experience behind him, plus a sharp-
edged imagination and a one track mind and no sense of privacy. And Rachel's a tourist. She's got all of that, and she can
learn new skills at the drop of a hat. She's very reactive, very
emotive."

"And she very nearly wiped us out."

"She'll be making tapes till she dies. And every time something reminds her of Medea, her entire audience is going to
know just what she thinks of the planet."

"What'll happen to us?"

"Oh . . . we could be worried over nothing. I've seen fads

before. This whole memory tape thing could be ancient history by the time we get back to civilization."

Civilization? As opposed to what? Curly knew the answer to that one. He went back to watching the wall.

"And even if it's not . . . I'll be back. I'll bring another walking memory like Rachel, but more flexible. Okay?"

"How long?"

"One circuit, then back to Medea."

Sixty to seventy earthyears. "Good," said Curly, because there was certainly no way to talk her into any shorter journey. He watched men in silver suits setting up the frames for the solar mirrors. There was not even wind in the Hot End, and apparently no life at all. They had worried about that. But Curly saw nothing that could threaten Touchdown City's power supply for hundreds of years to come.

If Medea was to become a backwash of civilization, a land of peasants, then it was good that the farmlands were safe. Curly turned to Janice Borg to say so. But the rammer's eyes were seeing nothing on Medea, and her mind was already approaching Horvendile.

THE LOCUSTS

by Larry Niven and Steve Barnes

There are no men on Tau Ceti IV.

Near the equator on the ridged ribbon of continent which reaches north and south to cover both poles, the evidence of Man still shows. There is the landing craft, a great thick saucer with a rounded edge, gaping doors and vast empty space inside. Ragged clumps of grass and scrub vegetation surround its base, now. There is the small town where they lived, grew old, and died: tall stone houses, a main street of rock fused with atomic fire, a good deal of machinery whose metal is still bright. There is the land itself, overgrown but still showing the traces of a square arrangement that once marked it as farmland.

And there is the forest, reaching north and south along the sprawling ribbon of continent, spreading even to the innumerable islands which form two-thirds of Ridgeback's land mass. Where forest cannot grow, because of insufficient water or because the carefully bred bacteria have not yet built a sufficient depth of topsoil, there is grass, an exceptionally hardy hybrid of Buffalo and Cord with an abnormal number of branching roots, developing a dense and fertile sod.

There are flocks of moas, resurrected from a lost New Zealand valley. The great flightless birds roam freely, sharing their grazing land with expanding herds of wild cattle and buffalo.

There are things in the forest. They prefer it there, but will occasionally shamble out into the grasslands and sometimes

*even into the town. They themselves do not understand why
they go: there is no food, and they do not need building materials or other things which may be there for the scavenging.
They always leave the town before nightfall arrives.*

When men came the land was as barren as a tabletop.

Doc and Elise were among the last to leave the ship. He
took his wife's hand and walked down the ramp, eager to feel
alien loam between his toes. He kept his shoes on. They'd
have to make the loam first.

The other colonists were exceptionally silent, as if each
were afraid to speak. Not surprising, Doc thought. The first
words spoken on Ridgeback would become history.

The robot probes had found five habitable worlds besides
Ridgeback in Earth's neighborhood. Two held life in more or
less primitive stages, but Ridgeback was perfect. There was
one-celled life in Ridgeback's seas, enough to give the planet
an oxygenating atmosphere; and no life at all on land. They
would start with a clean slate.

So the biologists had chosen what they believed was a
representative and balanced ecology. A world's life was stored
in the cargo hold now, in frozen fertilized eggs and stored seeds
and bacterial cultures, ready to go to work.

Doc looked out over his new home, the faint seabreeze
stinging his eyes. He had known Ridgeback would be barren,
but he had not expected the *feel* of a barren world to move
him.

The sky was bright blue, clouds shrouding Tau Ceti, a sun
wider and softer than the sun of Earth. The ocean was a deeper
blue, flat and calm. There was no dirt. There was dust and
sand and rock, but nothing a farming man would call dirt.
There were no birds, no insects. The only sound was that of
sand and small dust-devils dancing in the wind, a low moan
almost below the threshold of human hearing.

Doc remembered his college geology class' fieldtrip to the
Moon. Ridgeback wasn't dead as Luna was dead. It was more
like his uncle's face, after the embalmers got through with him.
It looked alive, but it wasn't.

Jase, the eldest of them and the colony leader, raised his
hand and waited. When all eyes were on him he crinkled his

eyes happily, saving his biggest smile for his sister Cynnie, who was training a holotape camera on him. "We're here, people," his voice boomed in the dead world's silence. "It's good, and it's ours. Let's make the most of it."

There was a ragged cheer and the colonists surged toward the cargo door of the landing craft. The lander was a flattish dome now, its heat shield burned almost through, its Dumbo-style atomic motor buried in dust. It had served its purpose and would never move again. The great door dropped and became a ramp. Crates and machinery began to emerge on little flatbed robot trucks.

Elise put her arm around her husband's waist and hugged him. She murmured, "It's so empty."

"So far." Doc unrolled a package of birth control pills, and felt her flinch.

"Two years before we can have children."

Did she mean it as a question? "Right," he said. They had talked it through too often, in couples and in groups, in training and aboard ship. "At least until Jill gets the ecology going."

"Uh huh." An impatient noise.

Doc wondered if she believed it. At twenty-four, tall and wiry and with seven years of intensive training behind him, he felt competent to handle most emergencies. But children, and babies in particular, were a problem he could postpone.

He had interned for a year at Detroit Memorial, but most of his schooling related directly to General Colonization. His medical experience was no better than Elise's, his knowledge not far superior to that of a 20th century GP. Like his shipmates, Doc was primarily a trained crewman and colonist. His courses in world settling—"funny chemistry," water purification, basic mine engineering, exotic factor recognition, etc.—were largely guesswork. There were no interstellar colonies, not yet.

And bearing children would be an act of faith, a taking possession of the land. Some had fought the delay bitterly. The starship would have been smelling of babies shortly after take-off if they'd had their way.

He offered Elise a pill. "Bacteria and earthworms come first. Men last," he said. "We're too high on the chain. We can't overload the ecology—"

"Uh huh."

"—before we've even got one. And look—"

She took a six-month birth control pill and swallowed it.

So Doc didn't say: suppose it doesn't work out? Suppose we have to go home? He passed out the pills and watched the women take them, crossing names off a list in his head.

The little robot trucks were all over the place now. Their flat beds were endless belts, and they followed a limited repertoire of voiced orders. They had the lander half unloaded already. When Doc had finished his pill pushing he went to work beside Elise, unloading crates. His thirty patients, including himself, were sickeningly healthy. As an unemployed doctor he'd have to do honest work until someone got ill.

He was wrong, of course. Doc had plenty of employment. His patients were doing manual labor in 1.07 gravities. They'd gained an average of ten pounds the moment the landing craft touched down. It threw their coordination and balance off, causing them to strain muscles and gash themselves.

One of the robot trucks ran over Chris' foot. Chris didn't wince or curse as Doc manipulated the bones, but his teeth ground silently together.

"All done here, Chris." Doc smiled. The meteorologist looked at him bleakly from behind wire-rimmed glasses, eyes blinking without emotion. "Hey, you're a better man than I am. If I had a wound like that, I'd scream my head off—"

Something only vaguely like a smile crossed Chris' lips. "Thanks, Doc," he said, and limped out.

Remarkable control, Doc mused. But then again, that's Chris.

A week after landing, Ridgeback's nineteen-hour day caught up with them. Disrupted body rhythms are no joke; adding poor sleep to the weight adjustment led to chronic fatigue. Doc recognized the signs quickly.

"I'm surprised that it took this long," he said to Elise as she tossed, sleepless.

"Why couldn't we have done our adjusting on ship?" she mumbled, opening a bleary eye.

"There's more to it than just periods of light and darkness.

Every planet has its own peculiarities. You just have to get used to them before your sleep cycles adjust."

"Well what am I supposed to do? Jesus, hand me the sleeping pills, wouldja please? I just want to sleep."

"Nope. Don't want anyone hooked on sleeping pills. We've got the 'russian sleep' sets. You'll have one tomorrow." The "russian sleep" headsets were much preferred over chemical sedatives. They produced unconsciousness with a tiny trickle of current through the brain."

"Good," Elise yawned. "Sunset and dawn, they both seem to come too soon."

The colony went up fast. It was all prefabs, makeshift and temporary, the streets cluttered with the tools, machinery and electric cables which nobody had put away because there was no place for them. Gradually places were made. Hydroponic tanks were assembled and stocked, and presently the colonists were back on fresh food.

Much more gradually, the stone houses began to appear.

They blasted their own rock from nearby cliffs with guncotton from the prefab chemical factory. They hauled the fractured stone on the robot trucks, and made concrete to stick it together. There was technology to spare, and endless power from the atomic motor in the landing craft. They took their time with the houses. Prefabs would weather the frequent warm rains for long enough. The stone houses were intended to last much longer. The colonists built thick walls, and left large spaces so that the houses could be expanded when later generations saw fit.

Doc squinted into the mirror, brushing his teeth with his usual precise vertical movements. He jumped when he felt a splash of hot water hit his back. "Cut that out, Elise," he laughed.

She settled back in her bathtub, wrinkling her nose at him. Three years of meagre showers on the ship had left her dying for a real bathtub, where she could waste gallons of water without guilt.

"Spoilsport," she teased. "If you were any kind of fun, you'd come over here and . . ."

"And what?" he asked, interested.

"And rub my back."

"And that's supposed to be fun?"

"I was thinking that we could rub it with you." She grinned, seeing Doc's eyes light up. "And then maybe we could rub you with me..."

Later, they toweled each other off, still tingling. "Look!" Doc said, pulling her in front of the mirror. He studied her, marveling. Had Elise become prettier, or was he seeing her with new eyes? He knew she laughed louder and more often than when they had met years ago in school, she the child of a wealthy family and he a scholarship student who dreamt of the stars. He knew that her body was more firm and alive than it had been in her teens. The same sun that had burnt her body nut-brown had lightened her reddish hair to strawberry blond. She grinned at him from the mirror and asked, "Do you propose to take all the credit?"

He nodded happily. He'd always been fit, but his muscles had been stringy, the kind that didn't show. Now they bulged, handsome curves filling out chest and shoulders, legs strong from lifting and moving rock. His skin had darkened under the probing of a warm, friendly sun. He was sleeping well, and so was she.

All of the colonists were darker, more muscular, with thicker calluses on hands and feet. Under open sky or high ceilings they walked straighter than the men and women of Earth's cities. They talked more boldly and seemed to fill more space. In the cities of Earth, the ultimate luxury had been building space. It was beyond the means of all but the wealthiest. Here, there was land for the taking, and twelve foot ceilings could be built. The house Doc was building for Elise—almost finished now—would be as fine as any her father could have built for her. One that would be passed on to their children, and then to their grandchildren...

She seemed to echo his thought. "One last step. I want a bulge, right here," and she patted her flat abdomen. "Your department."

"And Jill's. We're up to mammals already, and we're adjusting. I've got half the 'russian sleep' sets back in the infirmary already."

*   *   *

The Orion spacecraft was a big, obtrusive object, mace-shaped, cruising constantly across the sky. What had been a fifth of a mile of deuterium snowball, the fuel supply for the starship's battery of laser-fusion motors, was now a thin, shiny skin, still inflated by the residue of deuterium gas. It was the head of the mace. The life support system, ending in motors and shock absorbers, formed the handle.

Roy had taken the ground-to-orbit craft up and was aboard the Orion now, monitoring the relay as Cynnie beamed her holotape up. It was lonely. Once there had been too little room; now there was too much. The ship still smelled of too many people crowded too close for too long. Roy adjusted the view-screen and grinned back at Cynnie's toothy smile.

"This is Year Day on Ridgeback," she said in her smooth announcer's voice. "It was a barren world when we came. Now, slowly, life is spreading across the land. The farming teams have spent this last year dredging mulch from the sea bed and boiling it to kill the native life. Now it grows the tame bacteria that will make our soil." The screen showed a sequence of action scenes: tractors plowing furrows in the harsh dirt; colonists glistening with sweat as they pulled boulders from the ground; and Jill supervising the spreading of the starter soil. Grass seed and earthworms were sown into the trenches, and men and machines worked together to fold them into the earth.

Cynnie had mounted a camera on one of the small flyers for an aerial view. "The soil is being spread along a ten-mile strip," she said, "and grains are being planted. Later we'll have fruit trees and shade trees, bamboo and animal feed."

It was good, Roy thought, watching. It was smooth. Getting it all had been rough enough. Before they were finished the colonists had become damn sick of Roy and Cynnie poking their cameras into their every activity. That sign above the auditorium toilet: Smile! Roy Is Watching!

He'd tried to tell them. "Don't you know who it is that builds starships? It's taxpayers, that's who! And they've got to get something for their money. Sure we're putting on a show for them. If we don't, when election time comes around they may ask for a refund."

Oh, they probably believed him. But the sign was still up.

Roy watched Cynnie interview Jase and Brew in the fields;

watched Angie and Chris constructing the animal pens. Jill thawed some of the fertilized goat eggs and a tape was shown of the wriggling embryos.

"At first," Cynnie reminisced, "Ridgeback was daunting. There was no sound: no crickets, no birdsongs, but no roar of traffic either. By day, the sky is Earthlike enough, but by night the constellations are brighter. It's impossible to forget how far from home we are—we can't even see Sol, invisible somewhere in the northern hemisphere. It's hard to forget that no help of any kind could come in much less than twenty-five years. It would take five years just to refuel the ship. It takes fourteen years to make the trip, although thanks to relativity it was only three years 'ship time.'

"Yes, we are alone." The image of Cynnie's sober face segued to the town hall, a geodesic dome of metal tubing sprayed with plastic. "But it is heartening that we have found, in each other, the makings of a community. We come together for midday meal, discussions, songfests and group worship services."

Cynnie's face was calm now, comforting. "We have no crime, and no unemployment. We're much too busy for marital squabbles or political infighting." She grinned, and the sparkle of her personality brought pleasure to Roy's analytical mind. "In fact, I have work to do myself. So, until next year, this is Cynnie Mitchell on Ridgeback, signing off."

A year and a half after landing, a number of animals were out of incubation with a loss of less than two percent. The mammals drank synthetic milk now, but soon they would be milling in their pens, eating Ridgeback grass and adding their own rich wastes to the cooking compost heaps.

Friday night was community night at the town hall.

From the inside the ribs of the dome were still visible through the sprayed plastic walls, and some of the decorations were less than stylish, but it was a warm place, a friendly, relaxing place where the common bond between the Ridgebackers was strengthened.

Jill, especially, seemed to love the stage, and took every opportunity to mount it, almost vibrating with her infectious energy.

"Everything's right on schedule," she said happily. "The fruit flies are breeding like mad." (Booo!) "And if I hear that again I'm gonna break out the mosquitoes. Gang, there are things we can live without, but we don't know what they are yet. Chances are we'll be raising the sharks sooner or later. We've been lucky so far. Really lucky." She cleared her throat dramatically. "And speaking of luck, we have Chris with some good news for the farmers, and bad news for the sunbathers. Chris?"

There was scattered applause, most vigorously from Chris' tiny wife Angie. He walked to the lectern and adjusted the microphone before speaking.

"We, uh," he took off his glasses, polishing them on his shirt, then replaced them, smiling nervously. "We've been having good weather, people, but there's a storm front moving over the mountains. I think Greg can postpone the irrigation canals for a week, we're going to get plenty wet."

He coughed, and moved the microphone close to his mouth. "June and I are working to program the atmospheric model into the computer. Until we do, weather changes will keep catching us unaware. We have to break down a fairly complex set of thermo and barometric dynamics into something that can be dealt with systematically—wind speed, humidity, vertical motion, friction, pressure gradients, and a lot of other factors still have to be fed in, but we're making progress. Maybe next year we'll be able to tell you how to dress for the tenth anniversary of Landing Day."

There were derisive snorts and laughter, and Chris was applauded back into his seat.

Jase bounded onto the stage and grabbed the mike. "Any more announcements? No? All right, then, we all voted on tonight's movie, so no groans, please. Lights?"

The auditorium dimmed. He slipped from the stage and the twin beams of the holo projector flickered onto the screen.

It was a war movie, shot in flatfilm but optically reconstructed to simulate depth. Doc found it boring. He slipped out during a barrage of cannon fire. He headed to the lab and found Jill there already, using one of the small microscopes.

"Hi hon," he called out, flipping on his desk light. "Working late?"

"Well, I'm maybe just a wee bit more bugged than I let on. Just a little."

"About what?"

"I keep thinking that one day we'll find out that we left something out of our tame ecology. It's just a feeling, but it won't go away."

"Like going on vacation," Doc said, deliberately flippant. "You know you forgot something. You'd just rather it was your toothbrush and not your passport."

She smeared a cover glass over a drop of fluid on a slide and set it to dry. "Yes, it feels like that."

"Do you really have mosquitoes in storage?"

She twinkled and nodded. "Yep. Hornets too."

"Just how good is it going? You know how impatient everyone is."

"No real problems. There sure as hell might have been, but thanks to my superior planning—" she stuck out her tongue at Doc's grimace. "We'll have food for ourselves and all the children we can raise. I've been getting a little impatient myself, you know? As if there's a part of me that isn't functioning at full efficiency."

Doc laughed. "Then I think you'd better tell Greg."

"I'll do better. I'll announce it tonight and let all the fathers-to-be catch the tidings in one shot."

"Oh boy."

"What?"

"No, it has to be done that way. I know it. I'm just thinking about nine months from now. Oh boy."

So it was announced that evening. As Doc might have expected, someone had already cheated. Somehow Nat, the midwestern earthmother blond, had taken a contraceptive pill and, even with Doc watching, had avoided swallowing it. Doc was fairly sure that her husband Brew knew nothing of it, although she was already more than four months along when she confessed.

Nat had jumped the gun, and there wasn't a woman on Ridgeback who didn't envy her. A year and eleven months after Landing Day, Doc delivered Ridgeback's first baby.

Sleepy, exhausted by her hours of labor, Nat looked at her baby with a pride that was only half maternal. Her face was flushed, yellow hair tangled in mats with perspiration and fatigue. She held her baby, swaddled in blankets, at her side. "I can hear them outside. What do they want?" she asked drowsily, fighting to keep her eyelids open.

Doc breathed deeply. Ridiculous, but the scentless air of Ridgeback seemed a little sweeter. "They're waiting for a glimpse of the little crown princess."

"Well, she's staying here. Tell them she's beautiful," Ridgeback's first mother whispered, and dropped off to sleep.

Doc washed his hands and dried them on a towel. He stood above the slumbering pair, considering. Then he gently pried the baby from her mother's grip and took her in his arms. Half-conscious mother's wish or no, the infant must be shown to the colony before they could rest. Especially Brew. He could see the Swede's great broad hands knotting into nervous fists as he waited outside. And the rest of them in a half-crescent around the door; and the inevitable Cynnie and Roy with their holotape cameras.

"It's a girl," he told them. "Nat's resting comfortably." The baby was red as a tomato and looked as fragile as Venetian glass. She and Doc posed for the camera, then Doc left her with Brew to make a short speech.

Elise and Greg, Jill's husband, had both had paramedic training. Doc set up a rotating eight-hour schedule for the three of them, starting with Elise. The group outside was breaking up as he left, but he managed to catch Jase.

"I'd like to be taken off work duties for a while," he told the colony leader, when the two were alone.

Jase gripped his arm. "Something's wrong with the baby?" There was a volume of concern in the question.

"I doubt it, but she is the first, and I want to watch her and Nat. Most of the women are pregnant now. I want to keep an eye on them, too."

"You're not worried about anything specific?"

"No."

When Elise left her shift at the maternity ward, she found him staring at the stone ceiling. She asked, "Insomnia again? Shall I get a 'russian sleep' set?"

"No."

She studied his face. "The baby?"

She'd seen it too, then. "You just left the baby. She's fine, isn't she?"

"They're both fine. Sleeping. Harry?" She was the only one who called him that. "What is it?"

"No, nothing's bothering me. You know everything *I* know. It's just that . . ."

"Well?"

"It's just that I want to do everything right. This is so important. So I keep checking back on myself, because there's no one I can call in to check my work. Can you understand what I'm getting at?"

She pursed her lips. Then said, "I know that the only baby in the world could get a lot more attention than she needs. There shouldn't be too many people around her, and they should all be smiling. That's important to a baby."

Doc watched as she took off her clothes and got into bed. The slight swell of her pregnancy was just beginning to show. Within six months there would be nine more children on Ridgeback, and one would be theirs.

Predictably, Brew's and Nat's daughter became Eve.

It seemed nobody but Doc had noticed anything odd about Eve. Even laymen know better than to expect a newborn child to be pretty. A baby doesn't begin to look like a baby until it is weeks old. The cherubs of the Renaissance paintings of Foucquet or Conegliano were taken from two-year-olds. Naturally Eve looked odd, and most of the colony, who had never seen newborn children, took it in their stride. . . .

But Doc worried.

The ship's library was a world's library. It was more comprehensive, and held more microfilm and holographically encoded information than any single library on earth. Doc spent weeks running through medical tapes, and got no satisfaction thereby.

Eve wasn't sick. She was a "good baby"; she gave no more trouble than usual, and no less. Nat had no difficulty nursing her, which was good, as there were no adult cows available on Ridgeback.

Doc pulled a microfisch chip out of the viewer and yawned irritably. The last few weeks had cost him his adjustment to

Ridgeback time, and gained him . . . well, a kind of general education in pediatrics. There was nothing specific to look for, no *handle* on the problem.

Bluntly put, Eve was an ugly baby.

There was nothing more to say, and nothing to do but wait.

Roy and Cynnie showed their tapes for the year. Cynnie had a good eye for detail. Until he watched the camera view trucking from the landing craft past the line of houses on Main Street, to Brew, to a closeup of Brew's house, Doc had never noticed how Brew's house reflected Brew himself. It was designed like the others: tall and squarish, with a sloped roof and small window. But the stones in Brew's house were twice the size of those in Doc's house. Brew was proud of his strength.

Roy was in orbit on Year Day, but Cynnie stayed to cover the festivities, such as they were. Earth's hypothetical eager audience still hadn't seen Year Day One. Jase spoke for the camera, comparing the celebration with the first Thanksgiving Day in New England. He was right: it was a feast, a display of the variety of foods Ridgeback was now producing, and not much more than that.

His wife June sang a nondenominational hymn, and they all followed along, each in his own key. Nat fed Eve a bit of corncake and fruit juice, and the colonists applauded Eve's gurgling smile.

The folks back on Earth might not have thought it very exciting, but to the Ridgebackers it meant everything. This was food they had grown themselves. All of them had bruises or blisters or calluses from weeding or harvesting. They were more than a community now, they were a world, and the fresh fruit and vegetables, and the hot breads, tasted better than anything they could have imagined.

Six months after the birth of Eve, Doc was sure. There was a problem.

The children of Ridgeback totaled seven. Two of the women had miscarried, fewer than he might have feared, and without complications. Jill was still carrying hers, and Doc was beginning to wonder; but it wasn't serious yet. Jill was big and strong with wide hips and a deep bust. Even now Greg was hard put to keep her from commandeering one of the little flyers and jouncing off to the coastline to check the soil, or inland to supervise the fresh water fish preserve. Give her another week . . .

The night Elise had delivered their child, it had been special. She had had a dry birth, with the water sack rupturing too early, and Doc had had to use a lubrication device. Elise was conscious during the entire delivery, eschewing painkillers for the total experience of her first birth. She delivered safely, for which Doc had given silent thanks. His nerves were scraped to supersensitivity, and he found himself just sitting and holding her hand, whispering affection and encouragement to her, while Greg did much of the work. With Elise's approval he named their son Gerald, shortened to Jerry. Jerry was three weeks old now, healthy and squalling, with a ferocious grip in his tiny hands.

But even a father's pride could not entirely hide the squarish jawline, the eyes, the . . .

All the children had it, all the six recent ones. And Eve hadn't lost it. Doc continued his research in the microlibrary, switching from pediatrics to genetics. He had a microscope and an electron microscope, worth their hundreds of thousands of dollars in transportation costs; he had scrapings of his own flesh and Eve's and Jerry's. What he lacked was a Nobel Prize geneticist to stand behind his shoulder and point out what were significant deviations as opposed to his own poor slide preparation techniques.

He caught Brew looking at him at mealtimes, as though trying to raise the nerve to speak. Soon the big man would break through his inhibitions, Doc could see it coming. Or perhaps Nat would broach the question. Her eldest brother had been retarded, and Doc knew she was sensitive about it. How long could it be before that pain rose to the surface?

And what would he say to them then?

It was not a mutation. One could hardly expect the same mutation to hit all of seven couples in the same way.

It was no disease. The children were phenomenally healthy.

So Doc worked late into the night, sometimes wearing a black scowl as he retraced dead ends. He needed advice, and advice was 11.9 light years away. Was he seeing banshees? Nobody else had noticed anything. Naturally not; the children all looked normal, for they all looked alike. Only Brew seemed disturbed. Hell, it was probably Doc that was worrying Brew, just as it was Doc that worried Elise. He ought to spend more time with Elise and Jerry.

Jill lost her baby. It was stillborn, pitiful in its frailty. Jill turned to Greg as the dirt showered down on the cloth that covered her child, biting her lip savagely, trying to stop the tears. She and her husband held each other for a long moment, then, with the rest of the colonists, they walked back to the dwellings.

The colonists had voted early, and unanimously, to give up coffins on Ridgeback. Humans who died here would give their bodies to the conquest of the planet. Doc wondered if a coffin would have made this ceremony easier, more comforting in its tradition. Probably not, he thought. Dead is dead.

Doc went home with Elise. He'd been spending more time there lately, and less time with the microscopes. Jerry was crawling now, and he crawled everywhere; you had to watch him like a hawk. He could pick his parents unerringly out of a crowd of adults, and he would scamper across the floor, cooing, his eyes alight . . . his deepset brown eyes.

It was a week later that Jase came to him. After eight hours of labor June had finally released her burden. For a newborn infant the body was big and strong, though in any normal context he was a fragile, precious thing. As father, Jase was entitled to see him first. He looked down at his son and said, "He's just like the others." His eyes and his voice were hollow, and at that moment Doc could no longer see the jovial colony leader who called squaredances at the weekly hoedown.

"Of course he is."

"Look, don't con me, Doc. I was eight when Cynnie was born. She didn't look like any of them. And she never looked like Eve."

"Don't you think that's for me to say?"

"Yes. And damned quick!"

Doc rubbed his jaw, considering. If he was honest with himself he had to admit he ached to talk to somebody. "Let's make it tomorrow. In the ship's library."

Jase's strong hand gripped his arm. "Now."

"Tomorrow, Jase. I've got a lot to say, and there are things in the library you ought to see."

"Here," he said, dialling swiftly. A page appeared on the screen, three-quarters illustration, and one-quarter print to explain it. "Notice the head? And the hands. Eve's fingers are longer than that. Her forehead slopes more. But look at these." He conjured up a series of growth states paired with silhouettes of bone structure.

"So?"

"She's maturing much faster than normal."

"Oh."

"At first I didn't think anything about the head. Any infant's head is distorted during passage from the uterus. It goes back to normal if the birth wasn't difficult. And you can't tell much from the features; all babies look pretty much alike. But the hands and arms bothered me."

"And now?"

"See for yourself. Her face is too big and her skull is too small and too flat. And I don't like the jaw, or the thin lips." Doc rubbed his eyes wearily. "And there's the hair. That much hair isn't unheard of at that age, but taken with everything else . . . you can see why I was worried."

"And all the kids look just like her. Even Jase Junior."

"Even Jerry. And Jill's stillbirth."

In the ship's library there was a silence as of mourning.

Jase said, "We'll have to tell Earth. The colony is a failure."

Doc shook his head. "We'd better see how it develops first."

"We can't have normal children, Doc."

"I'm not ready to give up, Jase. And if it's true, we can't go back to Earth, either."

"What? Why?"

"This thing isn't a mutation. Not in us, it can't be. What it could be is a virus replacing some of the genes. A virus is a lot like a free-floating chromosome anyway. If we've got a disease that keeps us from having normal children—"

"That's stupid. A virus here, waiting for us, where there's nothing for it to live on but plankton? You—"

"No, no, no. It had to come with us. Something like the

common cold could have mutated aboard ship. There was enough radiation outside the shielding. Someone sneezes in the airlock before he puts his helmet on. A year later someone else inhales the mutant."

Jase thought it through. "We can't take it back to Earth."

"Right. So what's the hurry? It'd be twenty-four years before they could answer a cry for help. Let's take our time and find out what we've really got."

"Doc, in God's name, what can we tell the others?"

"Nothing yet. When the time comes I'll tell them."

Those few months were a busy time for Ridgeback's doctor. Then they were over. The children were growing, and most of the women were pregnant, including Angie and Jill, who had both had miscarriages. Never again would all the women of Ridgeback be having children in one ear-shattering population explosion.

Now there was little work for Doc. He spoke to Jase, who put him on the labor routines. Most of the work was agricultural, with the heavy jobs handled by machines. Robot trucks, trailing plows, scored rectangular patterns across the land.

The fenced bay was rich in Earthborn plankton, and now there were larger forms to eat the plankton. Occasionally Greg opened the filter to let discolored water spread out into the world, contaminating the ocean.

At night the colonists watched news from Earth, 11.9 years in transit, and up to a year older before Roy boarded the starship to beam it down. They strung the program out over the year in hour segments to make it last longer. There were no wars in progress, to speak of; the Procyon colony project had been abandoned; Macrostructures Inc. was still trying to build an interstellar ramjet. It all seemed very distant.

Jase came whistling into Doc's lab, but backed out swiftly when he saw that he had interrupted a counselling session with Cynnie and Roy. Doc was the closest thing the colony had to a marriage therapist. Jase waited outside until the pair had left, then trotted in.

"Rough day?"

"Yeah. Jase, Roy and Cynnie don't fight, do they?"

"They never did. They're like twins. Married people do get to be like each other, but those two overdo it sometimes."

"I knew it. There's something wrong, but it's not between them." Doc rubbed his eyes on his sleeve. "They were sounding me out, trying to get me talking about the children without admitting they're scared. Anyway... what's up?"

Jase brought his hands from behind his back. He had two bamboo poles rigged for fishing. "What say we exercise our manly prerogatives?"

"Ye gods! In our private spawning ground?"

"Why not? It's big enough. There are enough fish. And we can't let the surplus go; they'd starve. It's a big ocean."

By now the cultivated strip of topsoil led tens of miles north and south along the continent. Jill claimed that life would spread faster that way, outward from the edges of the strip. The colony was raising its own chicken eggs and fruit and vegetables. On Landing Day they'd been the first in generations to taste moa meat, whose rich flavor had come *that* close to making the New Zealand bird extinct. Why shouldn't they catch their own fish?

They made a full weekend of it. They hauled a prefab with them on the flyer and set it up on the barren shore. For three days they fished with the springy bamboo poles. The fish were eager and trusting. They ate some of their catch, and stored the rest for later.

On the last day Jase said, "I kept waiting to see you lose some of that uptight look. You finally have, a little, I think."

"Yeah. I'm glad this happened, Jase."

"Okay. What about the children?"

He didn't need to elaborate. Doc said, "They'll never be normal."

"Then what are they?"

"I dunno. How do you tell people who came twelve light years to build a world that their heirs will be..." he groped for words. "Whatever. Changed. Animals."

"Christ. What a mess."

"Give me time to tell Elise... if she hasn't guessed by now. Maybe she has."

"How long?"

"A week, maybe. Give us time to be off with Jerry. Might make it easier if we're with him."

"Or harder."

"Yeah, there's that." He cast his line out again. "Anyway, she'll keep the secret, and she'd never forgive me if I didn't tell her first. And you'd better tell June the night before I make the big announcement." The words seemed to catch in his throat and he hung his head, miserable.

Tentatively Jase said, "It's absolutely nobody's fault."

"Oh, sure. I was just thinking about the last really big announcement I helped to make. Years ago. Seems funny now, doesn't it? 'It's safe, people. You can start dreaming now. Go ahead and have those babies, folks. It's all right . . .'" His voice trailed off and he looked to Jase in guilty confusion. "What could I do, Jase? It's like thalidomide. In the beginning, it all looked so wonderful."

Jase was silent, listening to the sound of water lapping against the boat. "I just hate to tell Earth, that's all," he finally said in a low voice. "It'll be like giving up. Even if we solve this thing, they'd never risk sending another ship."

"But we've got to warn them."

"Doc, what's *happening* to us?"

"I don't know."

"How hard have you—no, never mind." Jase pulled his line in, baited it and sent it whipping out again. Long silences are in order when men talk and fish.

"Jase, I'd give anything I have to know the answer. Some of the genes look different in the electron microscope. Maybe. Hell, it's all really too fuzzy to tell, and I don't really know what it means anyway. None of my training anticipated anything like *this*. *You* try to think of something."

"Alien invasion."

Pause. "Oh, really?"

Jase's line jumped. He wrestled in a deep sea bass and freed the hook. He said, "It's the safest, most painless kind of invasion. They find a world they want, but there's an intelligent species in control. So they design a virus that will keep us from bearing intelligent children. After we're gone they move in at their leisure. If they like they can use a countervirus, so the children can bear human beings again for slaves."

The bamboo pole seemed dead in Doc's hands. He said, "That's uglier than anything I've thought of."

"Well?"

"Could be. Insufficient data. If it's true, it's all the more reason to warn Earth. But Ridgeback is doomed."

Jerry had his mother's hair, sunbleached auburn. He had too much of it. On his narrow forehead it merged with his brows... his shelf of brow, and the brown eyes watching from way back. He hardly needed the shorts he was wearing; the hair would have been almost enough. He was nearly three.

He seemed to sense something wrong between his parents. He would spend some minutes scampering through the grove of sapling fruit trees, agile as a child twice his age; then suddenly return to take their hands and try to tug them both into action.

Doc thought of the frozen fertilized eggs of dogs in storage. Jerry with a dog... the thought was repulsive. Why? Shouldn't a child have a dog?

"Well, of course I guessed *something*," Elise said bitterly. "You were always in the library. When you were home, the way that you looked at Jerry... and me, come to think of it. I see now why you haven't taken me to bed much lately." She'd been avoiding his eyes, but now she looked full at him. "I *do* see. But, Harry, couldn't you have asked me for help? I have some medical knowledge, and, and I'm your wife, and Jerry's mother, damn it Harry!"

"Would you believe I didn't want you worrying?"

"Oh, really? How did it work?"

Her sarcasm cut deep. Bleeding, he said, "Nothing worked."

Jerry came out of the trees at a tottering run. Doc stood up, caught him, swung him around, chased him through the trees... came back puffing, smiling, holding his hand. He almost lost the smile, but Elise was smiling back, with some effort. She hugged Jerry, then pulled fried chicken from the picnic basket and offered it around.

She said, "That alien invasion idea is stupid."

"Granted. It'd be easy to think someone has 'done' it to us."

"Haven't you found anything? Isn't there anything I can help with?"

"I've found a lot. All the kids have a lower body temperature, two point seven degrees. They're healthy as horses, but hell, who would they catch measles from? Their brain capacity is too small, and not much of it is frontal lobe. They're hard to toilet train and they should have started babbling, at least, long ago. What counts is the brain, of course."

Elise took one of Jerry's small hands. Jerry crawled into her lap and she rocked him. "His hands are okay. Human. His eyes . . . are brown, like yours. His cheekbones are like yours, too. High and a little rounded."

Doc tried to smile. "His eyes look a little strange. They're not really slanted enough to suspect mongolism, but I'll bet there's a gene change. But where do I go from there? I can see differences, and they're even consistent, but there's no precedent for the analysis equipment to extrapolate from." Doc looked disgusted. Elise touched his cheek, understanding.

"Can you teach me to use an electron microscope?"

Doc sat at the computer console, watching over Jill's shoulder as she brought out the Orion vehicle's image of Ridgeback. The interstellar spacecraft doubled as a weather eye, and the picture, once drab with browns and grays, now showed strips of green beneath the fragmented cloud cover. If Ridgeback was dead, it certainly didn't show on the screen.

"Well, we've done a fair old job." Jill grinned and took off her headset. Her puffy natural had collected dust and seeds and vegetable fluff until she gave up and shaved it off. The tightly curled mat just covered her scalp now, framing her chocolate cameo features. "The cultivated strip has spread like weeds. All along the continent now I get CO_2-oxygen exchange. It jumped the ridges last year, and now I get readings on the western side."

"Are you happy?"

"No," she said slowly. "I've done my job. Is it too much to want a child too? I wouldn't care about the . . . problem. I just want . . ."

"It's nobody's fault," Doc said helplessly.

"I know, I know. But two miscarriages. Couldn't they have

known back on Earth? Wasn't there any way to be sure? Why did I have to come all this way..." She caught herself and smiled thinly. "I guess I should count my blessings. I'm better off than poor Angie."

"Poor Angie," Doc echoed sadly. How could they have known about Chris? The night Doc announced his conclusions about the children, there had been tears and harsh words, but no violence. But then there was Chris.

Chris, who had wanted a child more than any of them could have known. Who had suffered silently through Angie's first miscarriage, who hoped and prayed for the safe delivery of their second effort.

It had been an easy birth.

And the morning after Doc's speech, the three of them, Chris, Angie and the baby, were found in the quiet of their stone house, the life still ebbing from Chris' eyes and the gaps in his wrists.

"I'm sorry," he said over and over, shaking his head as if he were cold, his watery brown eyes dulling. "I just couldn't take it. I just... I just..." and he died. The three of them were buried in the cemetery outside of town, without coffins.

The town was different after the deaths, a stifling quiet hanging in the streets. Few colonists ate at the communal meals, choosing to take their suppers at home.

In an effort to bring everyone together, Jase encouraged them to come to town hall for Movie Night.

The film was "The Sound of Music." The screen erupted with sound and color, dazzling green Alps and snow-crested mountains, happy song and the smiling faces of normal, healthy children.

Half the colonists walked out.

Most of the women took contraceptives now, except those who chose not to tamper with their estrogen balance. For these, Doc performed painless menstrual extractions bimonthly.

Nat and Elise insisted on having more children. Maybe the problem only affected the firstborn, they argued. Doc fought the idea at first. He found himself combatting Brew's sullen withdrawal, Nat's frantic insistence, and a core of hot anger in his own wife.

Earth could find a cure. It was possible. Then their grand-children would be normal again, the heirs to a world.

He gave in.

But all the children were the same. In the end, Nat alone had not given up. She had borne five children, and was carrying her sixth.

The message of failure was halfway to Earth, but any reply was still nineteen years away. Doc had adapted the habit of talking things over with Jase, hoping that he would catch some glimpse of a solution.

"I still think it's a disease," he told Jase, who had heard that before, but didn't mention it. The bay was quiet and their lines were still. They talked only during fishing trips. They didn't want the rest of the colony brooding any more than they already were. "A mutant virus. But I've been wondering, could the changes have screwed us up? A shorter day, a longer year, a little heavier gravity. Different air mixture. No common cold, no mosquito bites; even that could be the key."

On a night like this, in air this clear, you could even see starglades casting streaks across the water. A fish jumped far across the bay, and phosphorescence lit that patch of water for a moment. The Orion vehicle, mace-shaped, rose out of the west, past the blaze of the Pleiades. Roy would be rendez-vousing with it now, preparing for tomorrow's Year Day cel-ebration.

Jase seemed to need these trips even more than Doc. After the murders the life seemed to have gone out of him, only flashes of his personality coming through at tranquil times like these. He asked, "Are you going to have Jill breed mosquitoes?"

". . . Yes."

"I think you're reaching. Weren't you looking at the genes in the cytoplasm?"

"Yeah. Elise's idea, and it was a good one. I'd forgotten there were genes outside the cell nucleus. They control the big things, you know: not the shape of your fingers, but how many you get, and where. But they're hard to find, Jase. And maybe we found some differences between our genes and the chil-dren's, but even the computer doesn't know what the difference *means*."

"Mosquitoes." Jase shook his head. "We know there's a fish down that way. Shall we go after him?"

"We've got enough. Have to be home by morning. Year Day."

"What exactly are we celebrating *this* time?"

"Hell, you're the mayor. You think of something." Doc sulked, watching the water ripple around his float. "Jase, we can't give up—"

Jase's face was slack with horror, eyes cast up to the sky. Doc followed his gaze, to where a flaring light blossomed behind the Orion spacecraft.

"Oh my God," Jase rasped, "Roy's up there."

Throwing his bamboo pole in the water, Jase started the engine and raced for shore.

Doc studied the readouts carefully. "Mother of God," he whispered. "How many engines did he fire?"

"Six." Jill's eyes were glued to the screen, her voice flat. "If he was aboard, he . . . well, there isn't much chance he survived the acceleration. Most of the equipment up there must be junk now."

"But what if he *did* survive? Is there a chance?"

"I don't know. Roy was getting set to beam the messages down, but said that he had an alarm to handle first. He went away for a while, and . . ." she seemed to search for words. She whispered, "Boôm."

"If he was outside the ship, in one of the little rocket sleds, he could get to the shuttle vehicle."

Jase walked heavily into the lab.

"What about Cynnie? What did she say?" Doc asked quickly.

Jase's face was blank of emotion. "She talked to him before the . . . accident."

"And?"

"It's all she would say. I'm afraid she took it pretty bad. This was sort of the final straw." His eyes were hollow as he reminisced. "She was always a brave kid, you know? Anything I could do, she'd be right behind me, measuring up to big brother. There's just a limit, that's all. There's just a limit."

Doc's voice was firm, only a slight edge of unease breaking

through his control. "I think we had better face it. Roy is dead. The Orion's ruined, and the shuttle-craft is gone anyway."

"He could be alive..." Jill ventured.

Doc tried to take the sting out of his voice, and was not entirely successful. "Where? On the ship, crushed to a paste? Not on the shuttle. It's tumbling further from the Orion every second. There's no one on it. In one of the rocket sleds?" His face softened, and they could see that he was afraid to have hope. "Yes. Maybe that. Maybe on one of the sleds."

They nodded to each other, and they and the other colonists spent long hours on the telescope hoping, and praying.

But there was nothing alive up there now. Ridgeback was entirely alone.

Cynnie never recovered. She would talk only to her brother, refusing even to see her child. She was morose and ate little, spending most of her time watching the sky with something like terrified awe in her eyes.

And one day, seven months after the accident, she walked into the woods and never returned.

Doc hadn't seen Jerry for three weeks.

The children lived in a community complex which had some of the aspects of a boarding school. The colonists took turns at nursing duty. Jill spent most of her time there since she and Greg were on the outs. Lately, Elise had taken up the habit too. Not that he blamed her; he couldn't have been very good company the last few months.

Parents took their children out to the T-shaped complex whenever they felt like it, so that some of the children had more freedom than others. But by and large they all were expected to live there eventually.

Brew was coming out of the woods with a group of six children when Doc stumbled out into the sunlight and saw Jerry.

He wore a rough pair of coveralls that fit him well enough, but he would have looked ludicrous if there had been anything to laugh about. Soft brown fur covered every inch of him. As Doc appeared he turned his head with a bird-quick movement, saw his father, and scampered over. Jerry bounced into him, wrapped long arms tight about his rib cage and said, eagerly, "Daddy."

There was a slight pause.

"Hello, Jerry." Doc slowly bent to the ground, looking into his son's eyes.

"Daddy Doc, Daddy Doc," he chattered, smiling up at his father. His vocabulary was about fifteen words. Jerry was six years old and much too big for his age. His fingers were very long and strong, but his thumbs were small and short and inconsequential. Doc had seen him handle silverware without much trouble. His nose pugged, jaw massive with a receding chin. There were white markings in the fur around his eyes, accentuating the heavy supraorbital ridges, making the poor child look like—

The poor child. Doc snorted with self-contempt. *Listen to me. Why not my child?*

Because I'm ashamed. Because we lock our children away to ease the pain. Because they look like—

Doc gently disengaged Jerry's fingers from his shirt, turned and half-ran back to the ship. Shivering, he curled up on one of the cots and cursed himself to sleep.

Hours later he roused himself and, woozy with fatigue, he went looking for Jase. He found him on a work detail in the north fields, picking fruit.

"I'm not sure," he told Jase. "They're not old enough for me to be sure. But I want your opinion."

"Show me," said Jase, and followed him to the library.

The picture on the tape was an artist's rendering of Pithecanthropus erectus. He stood on a grassy knoll looking warily out at the viewer, his long-fingered hand clutching a sharp-edged throwing rock.

"I'll smack your head," said Jase.

"I'm wrong, then?"

"You're calling them apes!"

"I'm not. Read the copy. Pithicanthropus was a small-brained Pleistocene primate, thought to be a transitional stage between ape and man. You got that? Pith is also called Java Man."

Jase glared at the reader. "The markings are different. And there is the fur—"

"Forget 'em. They're nothing but guesswork. All the artist had to go on were crumbling bones and some broken rocks."

"Broken rocks?"

"Pith used to break rocks in half to get an edged weapon. It was about the extent of his tool-making ability. All we know about what he looked like comes from fossilized bones—very much like the skeleton of a stoop shouldered man with foot trouble, topped with the skull of an ape with hydrocephalus."

"Very nice. Will Eve's children be fish?"

"I don't know, dammit. I don't know anything at all. Look, Pith isn't the only candidate for missing link. Homo Habilis looked a lot more like us and lived about two million years ago. Kenyapithicus Africanus resembled us less, but lived eighteen million years earlier. So I can't say what we've got here. God only knows what the next generation will be like. That depends on whether the children are moving backwards or maybe sideways. I don't know, Jase, I just don't *know*!" The last words were shrill, and Doc punctuated them by slamming his fist against a wire window screen. Then, because he could think of nothing more to say, he did it again. And again. And—

Jase caught his arm. Three knuckles were torn and bleeding. "Get some sleep," he said, eyes sad. "I'll have them send Earth a description of Eve the way she is now. She's oldest, and best developed. We'll send them all we have on her. It's all we can do."

Momentum and the thoroughness of their training had kept them going for eight years. Now the work of making a world slowed and stopped.

It didn't matter. The crops and the meat animals had no natural enemies on Ridgeback. Life spread along the continent like a green plague. Already it had touched some of the islands.

Doc was gathering fruit in the groves. It was a shady place, cool, quiet, and it made for a tranquil day's work. There was no set quota. You took home approximately a third of what you gathered. Sometimes he worked there, and sometimes he helped with the cattle, examining for health and pregnancy, or herding the animals with the nonlethal sonic stunners.

He wished that Elise were here with him, so they could laugh together, but that was growing infrequent now. She was growing more involved with the nursery, and he spent little of his time there.

Jill's voice hailed him from the bottom of the ladder. "Hey up there, Doc. How about a break?"

He grinned and climbed down, hauling a sack of oranges.

"Tired of spending the day reading, I guess," she said lightly. She offered him an apple. He polished it on his shirt and took a bite. "Just needed to talk to somebody."

"Kinda depressed?"

"Oh, I don't know. I guess it's just getting hard to cope with some of the problems."

"I guess there have been a few."

Jill gave a derisive chuckle. "I sure don't know Greg anymore. Ever since he set up the brewery and the distillery, he doesn't really want to see me at all."

"Don't take it so hard," Doc comforted. "The strain is showing on all of us. Half the town does little more than read or play tapes or drink. Personally, I'd like to know who smuggled the hemp seeds on board."

Jill laughed, which he was glad for, then her face grew serious again. "You know, there'd probably be more trouble if we didn't need someone to look after the kids." She paused, looking up at Doc. "I spend a lot of my time there," she said unnecessarily.

"Why?" It was the first time he'd asked. They had left the groves and were heading back into town along the gravel road that Greg and Brew and the others had built in better days.

"We . . . I came here for a reason. To continue the human race, to cross a new frontier, one that my children could have a part in. Now, now that we know that the colony is doomed, there's just no motive to anything. No reason. I'm surprised that there isn't more drinking, more carousing and foursomes and divorces and everything else. Nothing seems to matter a whole lot. Nothing at all."

Doc took her by the shoulders and held her. Go on and cry, he silently said to her. God, I'm tired.

* * *

The children grew fast. At nine Eve reached puberty and seemed to shoot skyward. She grew more hair. She learned more words, but not many more. She spent much of her time in the trees in the children's complex. The older girls grew almost as fast as she did, and the boys.

Every Saturday Brew and Nat took some of the children walking. Sometimes they climbed the foothills at the base of the continental range; sometimes they wandered through the woods, spending most of their efforts keeping the kids from disappearing into the trees.

One Saturday they returned early, their faces frozen in anger. Eve and Jerry were missing. At first they refused to discuss it, but when Jase began organizing a search party, they talked.

They'd been ready to turn for home when Eve suddenly scampered into the trees. Jerry gave a whoop and followed her. Nat had left the others with Brew while she followed after the refugees.

It proved easy to find them, and easier still to determine what they were doing with each other when she came upon them.

Eve looked up at Nat, innocent eyes glazed with pleasure. Nat trembled for a moment, horrified, then drove them both away with a stick, screaming filth at them.

Over Nat's vehement objections and Brew's stoney refusal to join, Jase got his search party together and set off. They met the children coming home. By that time Nat had talked to the other mothers and fathers at the children's complex.

Jase called a meeting. There was no way to avoid it now, feelings were running too deep.

"We may as well decide now," he told them that night. "There's no question of the children marrying. We could train them to mouth the words of any of our religions, but we couldn't expect them to understand what they were saying. So the question is, shall we let the children reproduce?"

He faced an embarrassed silence.

"There's no question of their being too young. In biological terms they aren't, or you could all go home. In our terms, they'll never be old enough. Anyone have anything to say?"

"Let's have Doc's opinion," a hoarse voice called. There was a trickle of supportive applause.

Doc rose, feeling very heavy. "Fellow colonists..." The smile he was trying on for size didn't fit his face. He let it drop. There was a desperate compassion in his voice. "This world will never be habitable to mankind until we find out what went wrong here. I say let our children breed. Someday someone on Earth may find out how to cure what we've caught. Maybe he'll know how to let our descendants breed men again. Maybe this problem will only last a generation or two, then we'll get human babies again. If not, well, what have we lost? Who else is there to inherit Ridgeback?"

"No!" The sound was a tortured meld of hatred and venom. That was Nat, sunhaired loving mother of six, with her face a strained mask of frustration. "I didn't risk my life and leave my family and, and train for years and bleed and sweat and toil so my labor could fall to...to...a bunch of goddamned *monkeys*!"

Brew pulled her back to her seat, but by now the crowd was muttering and arguing to itself. The noise grew louder. There was shouting. The yelling, too, grew in intensity.

Jase shouted over the throng. "Let's talk this out peacefully!"

Brew was standing, screaming at the people who disagreed with him and Natalie. Now it was becoming a shoving match, and Brew was getting more furious.

Doc pushed his way into the crowd, hoping to reach Brew and calm him. The room was beginning to break down into tangled knots of angry, emotionally charged people.

He grabbed the big man's arm and tried to speak, but the Swede turned bright baleful eyes on him and swung a heavy fist.

Doc felt pain explode in his jaw and tasted blood. He fell to the ground and was helped up again, Brew standing over him challengingly. "Stay out of our lives, *Doctor*," he sneered, openly now. "You've never helped anything before. Don't try to start now."

He tried to speak but felt the pain, and knew his jaw was fractured. A soft hand took his arm and he turned to see Elise, big green eyes luminous with pity and fear. Without struggling, he allowed her to take him to the ship infirmary.

As they left the auditorium he could hear the shouting and struggling, Jase on the microphone trying to calm them, and the coldly murderous voices that screamed for "no monkey Grandchildren."

He tried to turn his head towards the distant sound of argument as Elise set the bone and injected quick-healing serums. She took his face and kissed him softly, with more affection than she had shown in months, and said, "They're afraid, Harry." Then kissed him again, and led him home.

Doc raged inwardly at his jaw that week. Its pain prevented him from joining in the debate which now flared in every corner of the colony.

Light images swam across his closed eyes as the sound of fists pounding against wood roused him from dreamless sleep. Doc threw on a robe and padded barefoot across the cool stone floor of his house, peering at the front door with distaste before opening it. Jase was there, and some of the others, sombre and implacable in the morning's cool light.

"We've decided, Doc," Jase said at last. Doc sensed what was coming. "The children are not to breed. I'm sorry, I know how you feel—" Doc grunted. How could Jase know how he felt when he wasn't sure himself? "We're going to have to ask you to perform the sterilizations . . ." Doc's hearing faded down to a low fuzz, and he barely heard the words. This is the way the world ends. . . .

Jase looked at his friend, feeling the distaste between them grow. "All right. We'll give you a week to change your mind. If not, Elise or Greg will have to do it." Without saying anything more they left.

Doc moped around that morning, even though Elise swore to him that she'd never do it. She fussed over him as they fixed breakfast in the kitchen. The gas stove burned methane reclaimed from waste products, the flame giving more heat control than the microwaves some of the others had. Normally Doc enjoyed scrambling eggs and wok-ing fresh slivered vegetables into crisp perfection, but nothing she said or did seemed to lift him out of his mood.

He ate lightly, then got dressed and left the house. Although she was concerned, Elise did not follow him.

He went out to the distillery, where Greg spent much of his time under the sun, drunk and playing at being happy. "Would you?" The pain still muffled Doc's words. "Would you sterilize them?"

Greg looked at him blearily, still hung over from the previous evening's alcoholic orgy. "You don't understand, man." There was a stirring sound from the sheltered bedroom behind the distillery, and a woman's waking groan. Doc knew it wasn't Jill. "You just don't understand."

Doc sat down, wishing he had the nerve to ask for a drink. "Maybe I don't. Do you?"

"No. No, I don't. So I'll follow the herd. I'm a builder. I build roads, and I build houses. I'll leave the moralizing to you big brains."

Doc tried to say something and found that no words would come. He needed something. He needed . . .

"Here, Doc. You know you want it." Greg handed him a cannister with a straw in it. "Best damn vodka in the world." He paused, and the slur dropped from his voice. "And this is the world, Doc. For us. For the rest of our lives. You've just got to learn to roll with it." He smiled again and mixed himself an evil-looking drink.

Greg's guest had evidently roused herself and dressed. Doc could her hear now, singing a snatch of song as she left. He didn't want to recognize the voice.

"Got any orange juice?" Doc mumbled, after sipping the vodka.

Greg tossed him an orange. "A real man works for his pleasures."

Doc laughed and took another sip of the burning fluid. "Good lord. What *is* that mess you're drinking?"

"It's a Black Samurai. Sake and soy sauce."

Doc choked. "How can you drink that?"

"Variety, my friend. The stimulation of the bizarre."

Doc was silent for a long time. Senses swimming he watched the sun climb, feeling the warmth as morning melted into afternoon. He downed a slug of his third screwdriver and said irritably, "You can't do it, Greg. If you sterilize the children, it's over."

"So what? It's over anyway. If they wanna let a drunk slit the pee pees of their . . . shall we say atavistic progeny? Yeah, that sounds nice. Well, if they want me to do it, I guess I'll have to do it." He looked at Doc very carefully. "I do have my sense of civic duty. How about you, Doc?"

"I tried." He mumbled, feeling the liquor burning his throat, feeling the light-headedness exert its pull. "I tried. And I've failed."

"You've failed so far. What were your goals?"

"To keep—" he took a drink. Damn, that felt good. "To keep the colony healthy. That's what. It's a disaster. We're at each other's throats. We kill our babies—"

Doc lowered his head, unable to continue.

They were both silent, then Greg said, "If I've gotta do it, I will, Doc. If it's not me, it'll be someone else who reads a couple of medical texts and wants to play doctor. I'm sorry."

Doc sat, thinking. His hands were shaking. "I can't do that." He couldn't even feel the pain anymore.

"Then do what you gotta do, man," and Greg's voice was dead sober.

"Will you . . . can you help me?" Doc bit his lip. "This is *my* civic duty, you know?"

"Yea, I know." He shook his head. "I'm sorry. I wish I could help."

A few minutes passed, then Doc said drunkenly, "There's got to be a way. There just has to be."

"Wish I could help, Doc."

"I wish you could too," Doc said sincerely, then rose and staggered back to his house.

It rained the night he made his decision, one of the quick, hot rains that swept from the coast to the mountains in a thunderclap of fury. It would make a perfect cover.

He gathered his medical texts, a Bible and a few other books, regretting that most of the information available to him was electronically encoded. Doc took one of the silent stunners from the armory. The nonlethal weapons had only been used as livestock controllers. There had never been another need, until now. From the infirmary he took a portable medical kit, stocking it with extra bandages and medicine, then took it all to the big cargo flyer.

It was collapsible, with a fabric fusilage held rigid by highly compressed air in fabric structural tubing. He put it in one of the soundless electric trucks and inflated it behind the children's complex.

There was plenty of room inside the fence for building and for a huge playground with fruit trees and all the immemorial toys of the very young. After the children had learned to operate a latch, Brew had made a lock for the gate and given everyone a key. Doc clicked it open and moved in.

He stayed in the shadows, creeping close to the main desk where Elise worked.

You can't follow where I must go, he thought regretfully. *You and I are the only fully trained medical personnel. You must stay with the others. I'm sorry, darling.*

And he stunned her to sleep silently, moving up to catch her head as it slumped to the table. For the last time, he gently kissed her mouth and her closed eyes.

The children were in the left wing—one room for each sex, with floors all mattress and no covers, because they could not be taught to use a bed. He sprayed the sound waves up and down the sleeping forms. The parabolic reflector leaked a little, so that his arm was numb to the elbow when he was finished. He shook his hand, trying to get some feeling back into it, then gave up and settled into the hard work of carrying the children to the flyer.

He hustled them through the warm rain, bending under their weight but still working swiftly. Doc arranged them on the fabric floor in positions that looked comfortable—the positions of sleeping men rather than sleeping animals. For some time he stood looking down at Jerry his son and at Lori his daughter, thinking things he could not afterwards remember.

He flew North. The flyer was slow and not soundless; it must have awakened people, but he'd have some time before anyone realized what had happened.

Where the forest had almost petered out he hovered down and landed gently enough that only a slumbering moan rose from the children. Good. He took half of them, including Jerry and Lori, and spread them out under the trees. After he had made sure that they had cover from the air he took the other packages, the books and the medical kit, and hid them under a bush a few yards away from the children.

He stole one last look at them, his heirs, small and defenseless, asleep. He could see Elise in them, in the color of their hair, as Elise could see him in their eyes and cheeks.

Kneading his shoulder, he hurried back to the ship. There was more for him to do.

Skipping the ship off again, he cruised thirty miles west, near the stark ridge of mountains, their sombre grey still broken only sparsely by patches of green. There he left the other seven children. Let the two groups develop separately, he thought. They wouldn't starve, and they wouldn't die of exposure, not with the pelts they had grown. Many would remain alive, and free. He hoped Jerry and Lori would be among them.

Doc lifted the flyer off and swept it out to the ocean. Only a quarter mile offshore were the first of the islands, lush now with primitive foliage. They spun beneath him, floating brownish-green upon a still blue sea.

Now he could feel his heartbeat, taste his fear. But there was resolve, too, more certain and calm than any he had known in his life.

He cut speed and locked the controls, setting the craft on a gradual decline. Shivering already, he pulled on his life jacket and walked to the emergency hatch, screwing it open quickly.

The wind whipped his face, the cutting edge of salt narrowing his eyes. Peering against the wall of air pressure he was able to see the island coming up on him now, looming close. The water was only a hundred feet below him, now eighty, sixty...

The rumbling of the shallow breakers joined with the tearing wind, and, fighting his fear, he waited until the last possible moment before hurling himself from the doorway.

He remembered falling.

He remembered hitting the water at awful speed, the spray ripping into him, the physical impact like the blow of a great hand. When his head broke surface Doc wheezed for air, swallowed salty liquid and thrashed for balance.

In the distance, he saw the flash of light, and a moment

later heard the shattering roar as the flyer spent itself on the rocky shore.

Jase was tired. He was often tired lately, although he still managed to get his work done.

The fields had only recently become unkempt, as Marlow and Billie and Jill and the others grew more and more inclined to pick their vegetables from their backyard gardens.

So just he and a few more still rode out to the fields on the tractors, still kept close watch on the herds, still did the hand-pruning so necessary to keep the fruit trees healthy.

The children were of some help. Ten years ago a few of them had been captured around the foothill area. They had been sterilized, of course, and taught to weed, and carry firewood, and a few other simple tasks.

Jase leaned on his staff and watched the shaggy figures moving along the street, sweeping and cleaning.

He had grown old on this world, their Ridgeback. He regretted much that had happened here, especially that night thirty-some years before when Doc had taken the children.

Taken them—where? Some argued for the islands, some for the West side of the mountain range. Some believed that the children had died in the crash of the flyer. Jase had believed that, until the adult Piths were captured. Now, it was hard to say what happened.

It was growing chill now, the streetlights winking on to brighten the long shadows a setting Tau Ceti cast upon the ground. He drew his coat tighter across his shoulders and walked back to his house. It was a lonelier place to be since June had died, but it was still home.

Fumbling with the latch, he pushed the door open and reached around for the light switch. As it flicked on, he froze.

My God.

"Hello, Jase." The figure was tall and spare, clothes ragged, but greying hair and beard cut squarely. Three of the children were with him.

After all this time . . .

"Doc . . ." Jase said, still unbelieving. "It is you, isn't it?"

The bearded man smiled uncertainly, showing teeth that

were white but chipped. "It's been a long time, Jase. A very long time."

The three Piths were quiet and alert, sniffing the air of this strange place.

"Are these—?"

"Yes. Jerry and Lori. And Eve. And a small addition." One of the three—God, could it be Eve? sniffed up to Jase. The soft golden fur on her face was tinged with grey, but she carried a young child at her breast.

Jerry stood tall for a preman, eyeing Jase warily. He carried a sharpened stick in one knobby hand.

Jase sat down, speechless. He looked up into the burning eyes of the man he had known thirty years before. "You're still officially under a death sentence, you know."

Doc nodded his head. "For kidnapping?"

"Murder. No one was sure what had happened to you, whether you or any of the children had survived."

Doc, too, sat down. For the first time the light in his eyes dimmed. "Yes. We survived. I swam to shore after crashing the flyer, and found the place where I had left the children." He thought for a moment, then asked quietly. "How is Elise? And all the others?"

Jase was unable to raise his eyes from the floor. "She died three years ago, Doc. She was never the same after you left. She thought you were dead. That the children were dead. Couldn't you have at least told her about your plan? Or gotten her a message?"

Doc's fingers played absently with his beard as he shook his head. "I couldn't involve her. I couldn't. Could you . . . show me where she's buried, Jase?"

"Of course."

"What about the others?"

"Well, none of the people were the same after the children left. Some just seemed to lose purpose. Brew's dead. Greg drank himself under. Four of the others have died." Jase paused, thinking. "Do any of the others know you're here?"

"No. I slipped in just at dusk. I wasn't sure what kind of a reception I'd get."

"I'm still not sure." Jase hesitated. "Why did you do it?"

The room was quiet, save for a scratching sound as Jerry fingered an ear. Fleas? Absurd. Jill had never uncrated them.

"I had to know, Jase," he said. There was no uncertainty in his voice. In fact, there was an imperious quality he had never had in the old days. "The question was: Would they breed true? Was the Pith effect only temporary?"

"Was it?"

"No. It persisted. I had to know if they were regressing or evolving, and they remained the same in subsequent generations, save for natural selection, and there isn't much of that."

Jase watched Lori, her stubby fingers untangling mats in her fur. Her huge brown eyes were alive and vital. She was a lovely creature, he decided. "Doc, what are the children?"

"What do you think?"

"You know what I think. An alien species wants our worlds. In a hundred years they'll land and take them. What they'll do with the children is anybody's guess. I—" He couldn't bring himself to look at Eve. "I wish you'd sterilized them, Doc."

"Maybe you do, Jase. But, you see, I don't believe in your aliens."

Jase's breath froze in his throat.

"They might want our world," said Doc, "but why would they want our life forms? Everything but Man is spreading like a plague of locusts. If someone wants Ridgeback, why haven't they done something about it? By the time they land, terrestrial life will have an unstoppable foothold. Look at all the thousands of years we've been trying to stamp out just one life form, the influenza viruses.

"No, I've got another idea. Do you know what a locust is?"

"I know what they are. I've never seen one."

"As individuals they're something like a short grasshopper. As individuals, they hide or sleep in the daytime and come out at night. In open country you can hear them chirping after dusk, but otherwise nobody notices them. But they're out there, eating and breeding and breeding and eating, getting more numerous over a period of years, until one day there are too many for the environment to produce enough food.

"Then comes the change. On Earth it hasn't happened in a long time because they aren't allowed to get that numerous.

But it used to be that when there were enough of them, they'd grow bigger and darker and more aggressive. They'd come out in the daytime. They'd eat everything in sight, and when all the food was gone, and when there were enough of them, they'd suddenly take off all at once.

"That's when you'd get your plague of locusts. They'd drop from the air in a cloud thick enough and broad enough to darken the sky, and when they landed in a farmer's field he could kiss his crops goodbye. They'd raze it to the soil, then take off again, leaving nothing."

Jase took off his glasses and wiped them. "I don't see what it is you're getting at."

"Why do they do it? Why were locusts built that way?"

"Evolution, I guess. After the big flight they'd be spread over a lot of territory. I'd say they'd have a much bigger potential food supply."

"Right. Now consider this. Take a biped that's man shaped, enough so to use a tool, but without intelligence. Plant him on a world and watch him grow. Say he's adaptable; say he eventually spread over most of the fertile land masses of the planet. Now what?

"Now an actual physical change takes place. The brain expands. The body hair drops away. Evolution had adapted him to his climate, but that was when he had hair. Now he's got to use his intelligence to keep from freezing to death. He'll discover fire. He'll move out into areas he couldn't live in before. Eventually he'll cover the whole planet, and he'll build spacecraft and head for the stars."

Jase shook his head. "*But why would they change back*, Doc?"

"Something in the genes, maybe. Something that didn't mutate."

"Not *how*, Doc. We know it's possible. *Why*?"

"We're going back to being grasshoppers. Maybe we've reached our evolutionary peak. Natural selection stops when we start protecting the weak ones, instead of allowing those with defective genes to die a natural death."

He paused, smiling. "I mean, look at us, Jase. You walk with a cane now. I haven't been able to read for five years, my eyes have weakened so. And we were the best Earth had to offer; the best minds, the finest bodies. Chris only squeaked by with his glasses because he was such a damn good meteorologist."

Jase's face held a flash of long-forgotten pain. "And I guess they still didn't choose carefully enough."

"No," Doc agreed soberly. "They didn't. On Earth we protected the sick, allowed them to breed, instead of letting them die . . . with pacemakers, with insulin, artificial kidneys and plastic hip joints and trusses. The mentally ill and retarded fought in the courts for the right to reproduce. Okay, it's humane. Nature isn't humane. The infirm will do their job by dying, and no morality or humane court rulings or medical advances will change the natural course of things for a long, long time."

"How long?"

"I don't know how stable they are. It could be millions of years, or . . . ?" Doc shrugged. "We've changed the course of our own development. Perhaps a simpler creature is needed to colonize a world. Something that has no choice but to change or die. Jase, remember the Cold War?"

"I read about it."

"And the Belt Embargo? Remember diseromide, and smog, and the spray-can thing, and the day the fusion seawater distillery at San Francisco went up and took the Bay area with it, and four states had to have their water flown in for a month?"

"So?"

"A dozen times we could have wiped out all life on Earth. As soon as we've used our intelligence to build spacecraft and seed another world, intelligence becomes a liability. Some old anthropologist even had a theory that a species needs abstract intelligence before it can prey on its own kind. The development of fire gave Man time to sit back and dream up ways to take things he hadn't earned. You know how gentle the children are, and you can remember how the carefully chosen citizens of Ridgeback acted the night we voted on the children's right to reproduce."

"So you gave that to them, Doc. They are reproducing. And when we're gone they'll spread all over the world. But are they *human*?"

Doc pondered, wondering what to say. For many years he

had talked only to the children. The children never interrupted, never disagreed . . . "I had to know that too. Yes. They're human."

Jase looked closely at the man he had called friend so many years ago. Doc was so sure. He didn't discuss; he lectured. Jase felt an alienness in him that was deeper than the mere passage of time.

"Are you going to stay here now?"

"I don't know. The children don't need me any more, though they've treated me like a god. I can't pass anything on to them. I think our culture has to die before theirs can grow."

Jase fidgetted, uncomfortable. "Doc. Something I've got to tell you. I haven't told anyone. It's thirty years now, and nobody knows but me."

Doc frowned. "Go on."

"Remember the day Roy died? Something in the Orion blew all the motors at once? Well, he talked to Cynnie first. And she talked to me, before *she* disappeared. Doc, he got a laser message from Earth, and he knew he couldn't ever send it down. It would have destroyed us. So he blew the motors."

Doc waited, listening intently.

"It seems that every child being born on Earth nowadays bears an uncanny resemblance to Pithicanthropus erectus. They were begging us to make the Ridgeback colony work. Because Earth is doomed."

"I'm glad nobody knew that."

Jase nodded. "If intelligence is bad for us, it's bad for Earth. They've fired their starships. Now they're ready for another cycle."

"Most of them'll die. They're too crowded."

"Some will survive. If not there, then, thanks to you, here." He smiled. A touch of the old Jase in his eyes. "They'll *have* to become men, you know."

"Why do you put it like that?"

"Because Jill uncrated the wolves, to help thin out the herds."

"They'll cull the children, too," Doc nodded. "I couldn't help them become men, but I think that will do it. They will have to band together, and find tools, and fire." His voice took on a dreamy quality. "Eventually, the wolves will come out of the darkness to join them at their campfires, and Man will have dogs again." He smiled. "I hope they don't overbreed them like we did on earth. I doubt if chihuahuas have ever forgotten what we did to them."

"Doc," Jase said, urgently, "will you trust me? Will you wait for a minute while I leave? I...I want to try something. If you decide to go there may never be another chance."

Doc looked at him, mystified. "Alright, I'll wait."

Jase limped out of the door. Doc sat, watching his charges, proud of their alertness and flexibility, their potential for growth in the new land.

There was a creaking as the door swung open.

The woman's hair had been blond, once. Now it was white, heavy wrinkles around her eyes and mouth, years of hardship and disappointment souring what had once been beauty.

She blinked, at first seeing only Doc.

"Hello, Nat," he said to her.

She frowned. "What...?" Then she saw Eve.

Their eyes locked, and Nat would have drawn back save for Jase's insistent hand at her back.

Eve drew close, peering into her mother's face as if trying to remember her.

The old woman stuttered, then said, "Eve?" The Pith cocked her head and came closer, touching her mother's hand. Nat pulled it back, eyes wide.

Eve cooed, smiling, holding her baby out to Nat.

At first she flinched, then looked at the child, so much like Eve had been, so much...and slowly, without words or visible emotion, she took the child from Eve and cradled it, held it, and began to tremble. Her hand stretched out helplessly, and Eve came closer, took her mother's hand and the three of them, mother, child and grandchild, children of different worlds, held each other. Nat cried for the pain that had driven them apart, the love that had brought them together.

Doc stood at the edge of the woods, looking back at the colonists who waved to them, asking for a swift return.

Perhaps so. Perhaps they could, now. Enough time had passed that understanding was a thing to be sought rather than avoided. And he missed the company of his own kind.

No, he corrected himself, the children *were* his kind. As he had told Jase, without explaining, he knew that they were human. He had tested it the only way he could, by the only means available.

Eve walked beside him, her hand seeking his. "Doc," she cooed, her birdlike singsong voice loving. He gently took their child from her arms, kissing it.

At over sixty years of age, it felt odd to be a new father, but if his lover had her way, as she usually did, his strange family might grow larger still.

Together, the five of them headed into the forest, and home.

YET
ANOTHER
MODEST
PROPOSAL:
The Roentgen Standard

It happened around the time of World War I. The Director of Research for Standard Oil was told, "There's all this goo left over when we refine oil. It's terrible stuff. It ruins the landscape, and covering it with dirt only gets the dirt gooey. Find something to do with it."

So he created the plastics industry.

He turned useless, offensive goo into wealth. He was not the first in history to do so. Consider oil itself: useless, offensive goo, until it was needed to lubricate machinery, and later to fuel it. Consider some of the horrid substances that go into cosmetics: mud, organic goop of all kinds, and stuff that comes out of a sick whale's head. Consider sturgeon caviar: American fishermen are still throwing it away! And the Japanese consider cheese to be what it always started out to be: sour milk.

Now: present plans for disposal of expended nuclear fuel involve such strategies as

1) Diluting and burying it.

2) Pouring it into old, abandoned oil wells. The Soviets tell us that it ought to be safe; after all, the *oil* stayed there for millions of years. We may question their sincerity: the depleted oil wells they use for this purpose are all in Poland.

3) The Pournelle method. The No Nukes types tell us that stretches of American desert have already been rendered useless for thousands of years because thermonuclear bombs were tested there. Let us take them at their word. Cart the nuclear wastes

200

out into a patch of cratered desert. Put several miles of fence around it, and signs on the fence:

IF YOU CROSS THIS FENCE YOU WILL DIE

Granted, there will be people willing to cross the fence. Think of it as evolution in action. Average human intelligence goes up by a fraction of a percent.

4) Drop the radioactive wastes, in canisters, into the seabed folds where the continental plates are sliding under each other. The radioactives would disappear back into the magma from which they came.

Each of these solutions gets rid of the stuff; but at some expense, and no profit. What the world needs now is another genius. We need a way to turn radioactive wastes into wealth.

And I believe I know the way.

Directly. Make coins out of it.

Radioactive money has certain obvious advantages.

A healthy economy depends on money circulating *fast*. Make it radioactive and it will certainly circulate.

Verifying the authenticity of money would become easy. Geiger counters, like pocket calculators before them, would become both tiny and cheap due to mass production. You would hear their rapid clicking at every ticket window. A particle accelerator is too expensive for a counterfeiter; counterfeiting would become a lost art.

The economy would be boosted in a number of ways. Lead would become extremely valuable. Even the collection plates in a church would have to be made of lead (or gold). Bank vaults would have to be lead lined, and the coins separated by dampers. Styles of clothing would be affected. Every purse, and one pocket in every pair of pants, would need to be shielded in lead. Even so, the concept of "money burning a hole in your pocket" would take on new meaning.

Gold would still be the mark of wealth. Gold blocks radiation as easily as lead. It would be used to shield the wealthy from their money.

The profession of tax collector would carry its own, well deserved penalty. So would certain other professions. An Arab oil sheik might still grow obscenely rich, but at least we could count on his spending it as fast as it comes in, lest it go up in a fireball. A crooked politician would have to take bribes by credit card, making it easier to convict him. A bank robber would be conspicuous, staggering up to the teller's window in his heavy lead-shielding clothing. The successful pickpocket would also stand out in a crowd. A thick lead-lined glove would be a dead giveaway; but without it, he could be identified by his sickly, faintly glowing hands. Society might even have to revive an ancient practice, amputating the felon's hand as a therapeutic measure, before it kills him.

Foreign aid could be delivered by ICBM.

Is this just another crazy utopian scheme? Or could the American people be brought to accept the radioactive standard as money? Perhaps we could. It's got to be better than watching green paper approach its intrinsic value. The cost of making and printing a dollar bill, which used to be one and a half cents, is rising inexorably toward one dollar. (If only we could count on its stopping there! But it costs the same to print a twenty . . .)

At least the radioactive money would have intrinsic value. What we have been calling "nuclear waste," our descendants may well refer to as "fuel." It is dangerous precisely because it undergoes fission . . . because it delivers power. Unfortunately, the stuff *doesn't* last "thousands of years." In six hundred years, the expended fuel is no more radioactive than the ore it was mined from.

Dropping radioactives into the sea is wasteful. We can ensure that they will still be around when the Earth's oil and coal and plutonium have been used up, by turning them into money, now.

MORE TALES
FROM THE
DRACO TAVERN...

FOLK
TALE

A lot of what comes out of Xenobiology these days is classified, and it *doesn't* come out. The Graduate Studies Complex is in the Mojave Desert. It makes security easier.

Sireen Burke's smile and honest blue retina prints and the microcircuitry in her badge got her past the gate. I was ordered out of the car. A soldier offered me coffee and a bench in the shade of the guard post. Another searched my luggage.

He found a canteen, a sizable hunting knife in a locking sheath, and a microwave beamer. He became coldly polite. He didn't thaw much when I said that he could hold them for awhile.

I waited.

Presently Sireen came back for me. "I got you an interview with Dr. McPhee," she told me on the way up the drive. "Now it's your baby. He'll listen as long as you can keep his interest."

Graduate Studies looked like soap bubbles: foamcrete sprayed over inflation frames. There was little of military flavor inside. More like a museum. The reception room was gigantic, with a variety of chairs and couches and swings and resting pits for aliens and humans: designs borrowed from the Draco Tavern without my permission.

The corridors were roomy too. Three chirpsithra passed us, eleven feet tall and walking comfortably upright. One may have known me, because she nodded. A dark glass sphere rolled through, nearly filling the corridor, and we had to step into what looked like a classroom to let it pass.

McPhee's office was closet-sized. He certainly didn't interview aliens here, at least not large aliens. Yet he was a mountainous man, six feet four and barrel-shaped and covered with black hair: shaggy brows, full beard, a black mat showing through the V of his blouse. He extended a huge hand across the small desk and said, "Rick Schumann? You're a long way from Siberia."

"I came for advice," I said, and then I recognized him. "B-beam McPhee?"

"Walter, but yes."

The Beta Beam satellite had never been used in war; but when I was seven years old, the Pentagon had arranged a demonstration. They'd turned it loose on a Perseid meteor shower. Lines of light had filled the sky one summer night, a glorious display, the first time I'd ever been allowed up past midnight. The Beta Beam had shot down over a thousand rocks.

Newscasters had named Walter McPhee for the Beta Beam when he played offensive guard for Washburn University.

B-beam was twenty-two years older, and bigger than life, since I'd last seen him on a television set. There were scars around his right eye, and scarring distorted the lay of his beard. "I was at Washburn on an athletic scholarship," he told me. "I switched to Xeno when the first chirpsithra ships landed. Got my doctorate six years ago. And I've never been in the Draco Tavern because it would have felt too much like goofing off, but I've started to wonder if that isn't a mistake. You get everything in there, don't you?"

I said it proudly. "Everything that lands on Earth visits the Draco Tavern."

"Folk too?"

"Yes. Not often. Four times in fifteen years. The first time, I thought they'd want to talk. After all, they came a long way—"

He shook his head vigorously. "They'd rather associate with other carnivores. I've talked with them, but it's damn clear they're not here to have fun. Talking to local study groups is a guest-host obligation. What do you know about them?"

"Just what I see. They come in groups, four to six. They'll

talk to glig, and of course they get along with chirpsithra. Everything does. This latest group was thin as opposed to skeletal, though I've seen both—"

"They're skeletal just before they eat. They don't associate with aliens then, because it turns them mean. They only eat every six days or so, and of course they're hungry when they hunt."

"You've seen hunts?"

"I'll show you films. Go on."

Better than I'd hoped. "I need to see those films. I've been invited on a hunt."

"Sireen told me."

I said, "This is my slack season. Two of the big interstellar ships took off Wednesday, and we don't expect another for a couple of weeks. Last night there were no aliens at all until—"

"This all happened last night?"

"Yeah. Maybe twenty hours ago. I told Sireen and Gail to go home, but they stayed anyway. The girls are grad students in Xeno, of course. Working in a bar that caters to alien species isn't a job for your average waitress. They stayed and talked with some other Xenos."

"We didn't hear what happened, but we saw it," Sireen said. "Five Folk came in."

"Anything special about them?"

She said, "They came in on all fours, with their heads tilted up to see. One alpha-male, three females and a beta-male, I think. The beta had a wound along its left side, growing back. They were wearing the usual: translators built into earmuffs, and socks, with slits for the fingers on the forefeet. Their ears were closed tight against the background noise. They didn't try to talk till they'd reached a table and turned on the sound baffle."

I can't tell the Folk apart. They look a little like Siberian elkhounds, if you don't mind the head. The head is big. The eyes are below the jawline, and face forward. There's a nostril on top that closes tight or opens like a trumpet. They weigh about a hundred pounds. Their fingers are above the callus, and they curl up out of the way. Their fur is black, sleek, with white markings in curly lines. We can't say their word for themselves; their voices are too high and too soft. We call them the Folk because their translators do.

I said, "They stood up and pulled themselves onto ottomans. I went to take their orders. They were talking in nearly supersonic squeaks, with their translators turned off. You had to strain to hear anything. One turned on his translator and ordered five glasses of milk, and a drink for myself if I would join them."

"Any idea why?"

"I was the closest thing to a meat eater?"

"Maybe. And maybe the local alpha-male thought they should get to know something about humans as opposed to grad students. Or—" McPhee grinned. "Had you eaten recently?"

"Yeah. Someone finally built a sushi place near the spaceport. I can't do my own cooking, I'd go *nuts* if I had to run an alien restaurant too—"

"Raw flesh. They smelled it on your breath."

Oh. "I poured their milk and a double Scotch and soda. I don't usually drink on the premises, but I figured Sireen or Gail could handle anything that came up.

"It was the usual," I said. "What's it like to be human. What's it like to be Folk. Trade items, what are they missing that could improve their life-styles. Eating habits. The big one did most of the talking. I remember saying that we have an ancestor who's supposed to have fed itself by running alongside an antelope while beating it on the head with a club till it fell over. And he told me that his ancestors traveled in clusters— he didn't say *packs*—and followed herds of plant-eaters to pull down the slow and the sick. Early biological engineering, he said."

McPhee looked worried. "Do the Folk expect you to outrun an antelope?"

"Oboy!" That was a terrible thought. "No, we talked about that too, how brains and civilization cost you other abilities. Smell, for humans. I got a feeling . . . he wanted to think we're carnivores unless we run out of live meat. I tried not to disillusion him, but I had to tell him about cooking, that we like the taste, that it kills parasites and softens vegetables and meat—"

"Why?"

"He asked. Jesus, B-beam, you don't lie to aliens, do you?"

He grinned. "I never have. I'm never sure what they want to hear."

"Well, I never lie to customers. —And he talked about the hunts, how little they test the Folk's animal abilities, how the whole species is getting soft...I guess he saw how curious I was. He invited me on a hunt. Five days from now."

"You've got a problem anyone in this building would kill for."

"Ri-ight. But what the hell do they *expect* of me?"

"Where does it take place? The Folk have an embassy not fifty miles from here."

"Yeah, and it's a hunting ground too, and I'll be out there next Wednesday, getting my own meal. I may have been a little drunk. I did have the wit to ask if I could bring a companion."

"And?" B-beam looked like he was about to spring across the desk into my lap.

"He said yes."

"That's my Nobel Prize calling," said B-beam. "Rick Schumann, will you accept me as your, ah, second?"

"Sure." I didn't have to think hard. Not only did he have the knowledge; he looked like he could strangle a grizzly bear; which might be what they expected of us.

The Folk had arrived aboard a chirpsithra liner, five years after the first chirp landing.

They'd leased a stretch of the Mojave. They'd rearranged the local weather and terrain, over strenuous objections from the Sierra Club, and seeded it with a hundred varieties of plants and a score of animals. Meanwhile they toured the world's national parks in a 727 with a redesigned interior. The media had been fascinated by the sleek black killing machines. They'd have given them even more coverage if the Folk had been more loquacious.

Three years of that, and then the public was barred from the Folk hunting ground. IntraWorld Cable sued, citing the public's right-to-know. They lost. Certain guest species would leave Earth, and others would kill, to protect their privacy.

IntraWorld Cable would have killed to air this film.

The sunset colors were fading from the sky . . . still a Mojave desert sky, though the land was an alien meadow with patches of forest around it. Grass stood three feet tall in places, dark green verging on black. Alien trees grew bent, as if before a ferocious wind; but they bent in different directions.

Four creatures grazed near a stream. None of the Folk were in view.

"The Folk don't give a damn about privacy," B-beam said. "It's pack thinking, maybe. They don't mind our taking pictures. I don't think they'd mind our broadcasting everything we've got, world wide. It was all the noisy news helicopters that bothered them. Once we realised that, we negotiated. Now there's one Xenobiology Department lifter and some cameras around the fences."

The creatures might have been a gazelle with ambitions to be a giraffe, but the mouth and eyes and horns gave them away.

Alien. The horns were big and gaudy, intricately curved and interwined, quite lovely and quite useless, for the tips pointed inward. The neck was long and slender. The mouth was like a shovel. The eyes, like Folk eyes, were below the jaw hinges; though they faced outward, as with most grazing beasts. The creatures couldn't look up. Didn't the Folk planet have birds of prey? Or heights from which something hungry might leap?

B-beam reclined almost sleepily in a folding chair too small for him. He said, "We call it a melk, a mock elk. Don't picture it evolving the usual way. Notice the horns? Melks were shaped by generations of planned breeding. Like a show poodle. And the grass, we call it *fat grass*."

"Why? Hey—"

"Seen them?"

I'd glimpsed a shadow flowing among the trees. The melks had sensed something too. Their heads were up, tilted *way* up to let them see. A concealed nostril splayed like a small horn.

Three Folk stood upright from the grass, and screamed like steam-whistles.

The melks scattered in all directions. Shadows flowed in the black grass. One melk found two Folk suddenly before it, shrieking. The melk bellowed in despair, wheeled and made for the trees. Too slow. A deer could have moved much faster.

The camera zoomed to follow it.

Into the trees—and into contact with a black shadow. I glimpsed a forefoot/hand slashing at the creature's vulnerable throat. Then the shadow was clinging to its back, and the melk tried to run from the forest with red blood spilling down its chest. The rest of the Folk converged on it.

They tore it apart.

They dragged it into the trees before they ate.

Part of me was horrified . . . but not so damn horrified as all that. Maybe I've been with aliens too long. Part of me watched, and noticed the strange configuration of the ribcage, the thickness and the familiar design of legs and knees, and the *convenient* way the skull split to expose brain when two Folk pulled the horns apart. The Folk left nothing but bone. They split the thick leg bones with their jaws, and gnawed the interiors. When they were finished they rolled the bones into a neat pile and departed at a waddle.

B-beam said, "That's why we don't give these films to the news. Notice anything?"

"Too much. The one they picked, it wasn't just the smallest. The horns weren't right. Like one grew faster than the other."

"Right."

"None of the Folk were carrying anything or wearing anything. No knives, no clothes, not even those sock-gloves. What do they do in winter?"

"They still hunt naked. What else?"

"The rest drove it toward that one hidden in the woods."

"There's one designated killer. Once the prey's fate is sealed, the rest converge. There are other meat sources. Here—"

There was a turkey-sized bird with wonderful irridescent patterns on its small wings and enormous spreading tail. It flew, but not well. The Folk ran beneath it until it ran out of steam and had to come down into their waiting hands. The rest drew back for the leader to make the kill. B-beam said, "They killed four that day. Want to watch? It all went just about the same way."

"Show me."

I thought I might see . . . right. The third attempt, the bird was making for the trees with the Folk just underneath. It might make it. Could the Folk handle trees? But the Folk broke off, far short of the trees. The bird fled to safety while they converged on another that had landed too soon, and frightened it into panicky circles . . .

Enough of that. I said, "B-beam, the Folk sent some stuff to the Draco Tavern by courier. Your gate Security has it now. I think I'd better get it back. A microwave beamer and a hunting knife and canteen, and it all looks like it came from Abercrombie and Fitch."

He stared at me, considering. "*Did* they. What do you think?"

"I think they're making allowances because I'm human."

He shook his head. "They make things easy for themselves. They cull the herds, but they kill the most difficult ones too. Anything that injures a Folk, dies. So okay, they've made things easy for us too. I doubt they're out to humiliate us. They didn't leave extra gear for your companion?"

"No."

An instructor led us in stretching exercises, isometrics, duck-waddles, sprints, and an hour of just running, for two hours each day. There was a spa and a masseur, and I needed them. I was blind with exhaustion after every session . . . yet I sensed that they were being careful of me. The game was over if I injured myself.

B-beam put us on a starvation diet. "I want us thinking hungry, thinking like Folk. Besides, we can both stand to lose a few pounds."

I studied Folk physiology more closely than I would have stared at a customer. The pointed mouths show two downpointing daggers in front, then a gap, then teeth that look like two conical canines fused together. They look vicious. The eyes face forward in deep sockets below the hinges of the jaw: white with brown irises, oddly human. Their fingers are short and thick, tipped with thick claws, three to a forefoot, with the forward edge of the pad to serve as a thumb. Human hands are better, I think. But if the eyes had been placed like a wolf's, they couldn't have *seen* their hands while standing up, and they wouldn't be tool users.

My gear was delivered. I strung the canteen and the beamer and the sheath knife on a loop of line. I filled the canteen with water, changed my mind and replaced it with Gatorade, and left it all in a refrigerator.

I watched three more hunts. Once they hunted melk again. Once it was pigs. That wasn't very interesting. B-beam said, "Those were a gift. We mated pigs to wild boars, raised them in bottles and turned them loose. The Folk were polite, but I don't think they like them much. They're too easy."

The last film must have been taken at night, light-amplified, for the moon was blazing like the sun. The prey had two enormous legs with too many joints, a smallish torso slung horizontally between the shoulders, and tiny fingers around a strange mouth. Again, it looked well fed. It was in the forest, eating into a hanging melon-sized fruit without bothering to pick it. I said, "That doesn't look . . . right."

B-beam said, "No, it didn't evolve alongside the Folk. Different planet. Gligstith(click)tcharf, maybe. We call them *stilts*."

It was faster than hell and could jump too, but the Folk were spread out and they were always in front of it. They kept it running in a circle until it stepped wrong and lost its balance.

One Folk zipped toward it. The stilt tumbled with its legs folded and stood up immediately, but it still took too long. The designated killer wrapped itself around one leg; its jaws closed on the ankle. The stilt kicked at its assailant, a dozen kicks in a dozen seconds. Then the bone snapped and the rest of the Folk moved in.

"Do you suppose they'll wear translators when they hunt with us?"

"I'd guess they won't. I know some Folk words and I've been boning up. And I've got a horde of students looking for anything on Folk eating habits. I've got a suspicion . . . Rick, why are we doing this?"

"We ought to get to know them."

"Why? What have we seen that makes them worth knowing?"

I was hungry and I ached everywhere. I had to think before I answered. "Oh . . . enough. Eating habits aside, the Folk aren't totally asocial. They're *here*, and they aren't xenophobes . . .

B-beam, suppose they *don't* have anything to teach us? They're still part of a galactic civilization, and we want to be out there with them. I just want humanity to look good."

"Look good... yeah. I did wonder why you didn't even *hesitate*. Have you ever been hunting?"

"No. You?"

"Yeah, my uncles used to take me deer hunting. Have you ever killed anything? Hired out as a butcher, for instance?"

"...No."

And I waited to say, *Sure, I can kill an animal, no sweat. Hell, I promised!* But he didn't ask; he only looked.

I never did mention my other fear. For all I know, it never occurred to anyone else that B-beam and I might be the prey.

Intelligent beings, if gullible. Armed, but with inadequate weapons. Betrayed, and thus enraged, likely to fight back. The Folk eat Earthborn meat. Surely we would make more interesting prey than the boar-pigs!

But it was plain crazy. The chirpsithra enforced laws against murder. If humans were to disappear within the Mojave hunting park, the Folk might be barred from the chirp liners! They wouldn't dare.

The Folk came for us at dawn. We rode in the Xenobiology lifter. We left the air ducts wide open. The smell of five Folk behind us was rich and strange: not quite an animal smell, but something else, and not entirely pleasant. If the Folk noticed our scent, they didn't seem to mind.

B-beam seemed amazingly relaxed. At one point he told me, casually, "We're in danger of missing a point. We're here to have fun. The Folk don't know we've been sweating and moaning, and they won't. You're being honored, Rick. Have fun."

At midmorning we landed and walked toward a fence.

It was human-built, posted with signs in half a dozen languages. NO ENTRY. DANGER! B-beam took us through the gate. Then the Folk waited. B-beam exchanged yelps with them, then told me. "You're expected to lead."

"Me? Why?"

"Surprise. You're the designated killer."

"Me?" It seemed silly . . . but it was their hunt. I led off. "What are we hunting?"

"You make that decision too."

Well inside the fence, we crossed what seemed a meandering dune, varying from five to eight meters high, curving out of sight to left and right. Outside the dune was desert. Inside, meadow.

A stream poured out of the dune. Further away and much lower, its returning loop flowed back into the dune. The dune hid pumps. It might hide defenses.

The green-black grass wasn't thin like grass; it was a succulent, like three-foot-tall fingers of spineless cactus, nice to the touch. *Fat grass*. Sawgrass would have been a real problem. We wore nothing but swim suits (we'd argued about even that) and the items strung on a line across my shoulders.

Any of the Folk, or B-beam himself, would have made a better killer than one middle-aged bartender.

Of course I had the beamer, and it would kill; but it wouldn't kill fast. Anything large would be hurt and angry long before it fell over.

All five Folk dropped silently to their bellies. I hadn't seen anything, so I stayed upright, but I was walking carefully. Naked humans might not spook the prey anyway. They'd be alert for Folk.

B-beam's eyes tried to see everywhere at once. He whispered, "I got my report on Folk eating habits."

"Well?"

"They drink water and milk. They've never been seen eating. They don't *buy* food—"

"Pets?"

"—Or pets, or livestock. I thought of that—"

"Missing Persons reports?"

"Oh, for Christ's sake, Rick! No, this the *only* way they eat. It's not a hunt so much as a formal dinner party. The rules of etiquette are likely to be rigid."

Rigid, hell. I'd watched them tearing live animals apart.

Water gurgled ahead. The artificial stream ran everywhere. "I never wondered about the canteen," I said. "Why a canteen?"

B-beam yelped softly. A Folk squeaked back. Yelp, and

squeak, and B-beam tried to suppress a laugh. "You must have talked about drinking wine with meals."

"I did. Is there supposed to be *wine* in this thing?"

B-beam grinned. Then lost the grin. "The canteen isn't for the hunt, it's for afterward. What about the knife and beamer?"

"Oh, come on, the Foik *gave* me . . . uh." Butterflies began breeding in my stomach. Humans cook their food. Sushi and Sashimi and Beef Tartar are exceptions. I'd said so, that night. "The beamer's for cooking. If I use it to kill the prey . . . we'll be disgraced?"

"I'm not sure I want to come right out and ask. Let's see . . ."

The high-pitched squeaking went on for some time. B-beam was trying to skirt the edges of the subject. The butterflies in my belly were turning carnivorous. Presently he whispered, "Yup. Knife too. Your teeth and nails are visibly inadequate for carving."

"Oh, Lord."

"The later you back out, the worse it'll be. Do it *now* if—"

Two melks were grazing beyond a rise of ground. I touched B-beam's shoulder and we sank to our bellies.

The melks were really too big. They'd weigh about what I did: a hundred and eighty pounds. I'd be better off chasing a bird. Better yet, a boar-pig.

Then again, these *were* meat animals, born to lose. And we'd need four or five birds for this crowd. I'd be totally winded long before we finished. B-beam's exercise program had given me a good grasp of my limits . . . not to mention a raging hunger.

The purpose of this game was to make humans—me— look good. Wasn't it? Anyway, there wasn't a bird or a pig in sight.

We crept through the fat grass until we had a clear view. That top-heavy array of horns would make a handle. If I could get hold of the horns, I could break the melk's long, slender neck.

The thought made me queasy.

"The smaller one," I whispered. B-beam nodded. He yelped softly, and got answers. The Folk flowed away through the fat grass. I crept toward the melks on hands and toes.

Three Folk stood up and shrieked.

The melks shrieked too, and tried to escape. Two more Folk stood up in front of the smaller one. I stayed down, scrambling through the grass stalks, trying to get ahead of it.

It came straight at me. *And now I must murder you.*

I lunged to the attack. It spun about. A hoof caught my thigh and I grunted in pain. The melk leapt away, then froze as B-beam dashed in front of it waving his arms. I threw myself at its neck. It wheeled and the cage of horns slammed into me and knocked me on my ass. It ran over me and away.

I was curled around my belly, trying to remember how to breathe. B-beam helped me to my feet. It was the last place I wanted to be. "Are you all right?"

I wheezed, "Hoof. Stomach."

"Can you move?"

"Nooo! Minute. Try again."

My breath came back. I walked around in a circle. The Folk were watching me. I straightened up. I jogged. Not good, but I could move. I took off the loop of line that held canteen and beamer and knife, and handed them to B-beam. "Hold these."

"I'm afraid they may be the mark of the leader."

"Bullshit. Folk don't carry anything. Hold 'em so I can fight." I wanted to be rid of the beamer. It was too tempting.

We'd alerted the prey in this area. I took us along the edge of the forest, where the fat grass thinned out and it was easier to move. We saw nothing for almost an hour.

I saw no birds, no stilts, no boar-pigs. What I finally did see was four more melks drinking from the stream. It was a situation very like the first I'd seen on film.

I'd already proved that a melk was more than my equal. My last-second qualms had slowed me not at all. I'd been beaten because my teeth and claws were inadequate; because I was not a wolf, not a lion, not a Folk.

I crouched below the level of the fat grass, studying them. The Folk studied me. B-beam was at my side, whispering, "We're in no hurry. We've got hours yet. Do you think you can handle a boar-pig?"

"If I could find one I might catch it. But how do I kill it? With my teeth?"

The Folk watched. What did they expect of me?

Suddenly I knew.

"Tell them I'll be in the woods." I pointed. "Just in there. Pick a melk and run it toward me." I turned and moved into the woods, low to the ground. When I looked back everyone was gone.

These trees had to be from the Folk world. They bent to an invisible hurricane. They bent in various directions, because the Mojave wasn't giving them the right signals. The trunks had a teardrop-shaped cross section for low wind resistance. Maybe the Folk world was tidally locked, with a wind that came always from one direction . . .

I dared not go too far for what I needed. The leafy tops of the trees were just in reach, and I plunged my hands in and felt around. The trunk was straight and solid; the branches were no thicker than my big toe, and all leaves. I tried to rip a branch loose anyway. It was too strong, and I didn't have the leverage.

Through the bent trunks I watched melks scattering in panic. But one dashed back and forth, and found black death popping up wherever it looked.

There was fallen stuff on the ground, but no fallen branches. To my right, a glimpse of white—

The melk was running toward the wood.

I ran deeper among the trees. White: bones in a neat pile. Melk bones. I swept a hand through to scatter them. Damn! The leg bones had all been split. What now?

The skull was split too, hanging together by the interwined horns. I stamped on the horns. They shattered. I picked up a massive half-skull with half a meter of broken horn for a handle.

The melk veered just short of the woods. I sprinted in pursuit. Beyond, B-beam half-stood, his eyes horrified. He shouted, "Rick! No!"

I didn't have time for him. The melk raced away, and nothing popping up in its face was going to stop it now. I was gaining . . . it was fast . . . too damn fast . . . I swung the skull at a flashing hoof, and connected. Again. Throwing it off, slowing it just enough. The half-skull and part-horn made a good bludgeon. I smacked a knee, and it wheeled in rage and caught me across the face and chest with its horns.

I dropped on my back. I got in one grazing blow across the neck as it was turning away, and then it was running and I rolled to my feet and chased it again. There was a feathery feel to my run. My lungs and legs thought I was dying. But the melk shook its head as it ran, and I caught up far enough to swing at its hooves.

This time it didn't turn to attack. Running with something whacking at its feet, it just gradually lost ground. I delivered a two-handed blow to the base of its neck. Swung again and lost my balance and tumbled, caught the roll on my shoulder, had to go back for the skull. Then I ran, floating, recovering lost ground, and suddenly realised that the grass was stirring all around me. I was surrounded by the black shadows of the Folk.

I caught up.

A swing at the head only got the horns. I hammered at the neck, just behind the head. It tumbled, and tried to get to its feet, and I beat it until it fell over. I used the skull like an ax ... murdering it ... and suddenly black bodies flowed out of the fat grass and tore at the melk. B-beam got a good grip on the horns and snapped the neck.

I sat down.

He handed me the line: knife, beamer, canteen. He was almost as winded as I was. He whispered, "Damn fool, you weren't—"

"Wrong." I didn't have breath for more. I drank from my canteen, paused to gasp, drank again. Then I turned the beamer on a meaty thigh. The Folk must have been waiting for me to make my choice. They now attacked the forequarters.

I crouched, panting, holding the beamer on the meat until it sizzled, until it smoked, until the smell of it told my belly it was ready.

The heaving of my chest had eased. I handed the knife to B-beam. "Carve us some of that. Eat as much as you can. Courtesy to our hosts."

He did. He gave me a chunk that I needed both hands to hold. It was too hot; I had to juggle it. B-beam said, "You used a weapon."

"I used a club," I said. I bit into the meat. Ecstacy! The famine was over. I hadn't cooked it enough, and so what? I swallowed enough to clear my mouth and said, "Humans don't use teeth and claws. The Folk know that. They wanted to see us in action. *My* evolution includes a club."

THE
GREEN
MARAUDER

I was tending bar alone that night. The chirpsithra interstellar liner had left Earth four days earlier, taking most of my customers. The Draco Tavern was nearly empty.

The man at the bar was drinking gin and tonic. Two glig—grey and compact beings, wearing furs in three tones of green—were at a table with a chirpsithra guide. They drank vodka and consomme, no ice, no flavorings. Four farsilshree had their bulky, heavy environment tanks crowded around a bigger table. They smoked smoldering yellow paste through tubes. Every so often I got them another jar of paste.

The man was talkative. I got the idea he was trying to interview the bartender and owner of Earth's foremost multi-species tavern.

"Hey, not me," he protested. "I'm not a reporter. I'm Greg Noyes, with the *Scientific American* television show."

"Didn't I see you trying to interview the glig, earlier tonight?"

"Guilty. We're doing a show on the formation of life on Earth. I thought maybe I could check a few things. The glig-stith(click)optok—" He said that slowly, but got it right. "—have their own little empire out there, don't they? Earthlike worlds, a couple of hundred. They must know quite a lot about how a world forms an oxygenating atmosphere." He was careful with those polysyllabic words. Not quite sober, then.

"That doesn't mean they want to waste an evening lecturing the natives."

He nodded. "They didn't know anyway. Architects on vacation. They got me talking about my home life. I don't know how they managed that." He pushed his drink away. "I'd better switch to espresso. Why would a thing that *shape* be interested in my sex life? And they kept asking me about territorial imperatives—" He stopped, then turned to see what I was staring at.

Three chirpsithra were just coming in. One was in a floating couch with life support equipment attached.

"I thought they all looked alike," he said.

I said, "I've had chirpsithra in here for close to thirty years, but I can't tell them apart. They're all perfect physical specimens, after all, by their own standards. I never saw one like *that*."

I gave him his espresso, then put three sparkers on a tray and went to the chirpsithra table.

Two were exactly like any other chirpsithra: eleven feet tall, dressed in pouched belts and their own salmon-colored exoskeletons, and very much at their ease. The chirps claim to have settled the entire galaxy long ago—meaning the useful planets, the tidally locked oxygen worlds that happen to circle close around cool red-dwarf suns—and they act like the reigning queens of wherever they happen to be. But the two seemed to defer to the third. She was a foot shorter than they were. Her exoskeleton was as clearly artificial as dentures: alloplastic bone worn on the outside. Tubes ran under the edges from the equipment in her floating couch. Her skin between the plates was more gray than red. Her head turned slowly as I came up. She studied me, bright-eyed with interest.

I asked, "Sparkers?" as if chirpsithra ever ordered anything else.

One of the others said, "Yes. Serve the ethanol mix of your choice to yourself and the other native. Will you join us?"

I waved Noyes over, and he came at the jump. He pulled up one of the high chairs I keep around to put a human face on a level with a chirpsithra's. I went for another espresso and a Scotch and soda and (catching a soft imperative *hoot* from the farsilshree) a jar of yellow paste. When I returned they were deep in conversation.

"Rick Schumann," Noyes cried, "meet Ftaxanthir and Hrofilliss and Chorrikst. Chorrikst tells me she's nearly two *billion* years old!"

I heard the doubt beneath his delight. The chirpsithra could be the greatest liars in the universe, and how would we ever know? Earth didn't even have interstellar probes when the chirps came.

Chorrikst spoke slowly, in a throaty whisper, but her translator box was standard: voice a little flat, pronunciation perfect. "I have circled the galaxy numberless times, and taped the tales of my travels for funds to feed my wanderlust. Much of my life has been spent at the edge of lightspeed, under relativistic time-compression. So you see, I am not nearly so old as all that."

I pulled up another high chair. "You must have seen wonders beyond counting," I said. Thinking: *My God, a short chirpsithra! Maybe it's true. She's a different color, too, and her fingers are shorter. Maybe the species has actually changed since she was born!*

She nodded slowly. "Life never bores. Always there is change. In the time I have been gone, Saturn's ring has been pulled into separate rings, making it even more magnificent. What can have done that? Tides from the moons? And Earth has changed beyond recognition."

Noyes spilled a little of his coffee. "You were here? When?"

"Earth's air was methane and ammonia and oxides of nitrogen and carbon. The natives had sent messages across interstellar space . . . directing them toward yellow suns, of course, but one of our ships passed through a beam, and so we established contact. We had to wear life support," she rattled on, while Noyes and I sat with our jaws hanging, "and the gear was less comfortable then. Our spaceport was a floating platform, because quakes were frequent and violent. But it was worth it. Their cities—"

Noyes said, "Just a minute. Cities? We've never dug up any trace of, of nonhuman cities!"

Chorrikst looked at him. "After seven hundred and eighty million years, I should think not. Besides, they lived in the offshore shallows in an ocean that was already mildly salty. If the quakes spared them, their tools and their cities still deteriorated rapidly. Their lives were short too, but their memories were inherited. Death and change were accepted facts for them, more than for most intelligent species. Their works of philosophy gained great currency among my people, and spread to other species too."

Noyes wrestled with his instinct for tact and good manners, and won. "How? How could anything have evolved that far? The Earth didn't even have an oxygen atmosphere! Life was just getting started, there weren't even trilobites!"

"They had evolved for as long as you have," Chorrikst said with composure. "Life began on Earth one and a half billion years ago. There were organic chemicals in abundance, from passage of lightning through the reducing atmosphere. Intelligence evolved, and presently built an impressive civilization. They lived slowly, of course. Their biochemistry was less energetic. Communication was difficult. They were not stupid, only slow. I visited Earth three times, and each time they had made more progress."

Almost against his will, Noyes asked, "What did they look like?"

"Small and soft and fragile, much more so than yourselves. I cannot say they were pretty, but I grew to like them. I would toast them according to your customs," she said. "They wrought beauty in their cities and beauty in their philosophies, and their works are in our libraries still. They will not be forgotten."

She touched her sparker, and so did her younger companions. Current flowed between her two claws, through her nervous system. She said, "Sssss . . ."

I raised my glass, and nudged Noyes with my elbow. We drank to our predecessors. Noyes lowered his cup and asked, "What happened to them?"

"They sensed worldwide disaster coming," Chorrikst said, "and they prepared; but they thought it would be quakes. They built cities to float on the ocean surface, and lived in the undersides. They never noticed the green scum growing in certain tidal pools. By the time they knew the danger, the green scum was everywhere. It used photosynthesis to turn carbon dioxide into oxygen, and the raw oxygen killed whatever it touched, leaving fertilizer to feed the green scum.

"The world was dying when we learned of the problem. What could we do against a photosynthesis-using scum growing beneath a yellow-white star? There was nothing in chirpsithra libraries that would help. We tried, of course, but we were unable to stop it. The sky had turned an admittedly lovely transparent blue, and the tide pools were green, and the offshore cities were crumbling before we gave up the fight. There was an attempt to transplant some of the natives to a suitable world; but biorhythm upset ruined their mating habits. I have not been back since, until now."

The depressing silence was broken by Chorrikst herself. "Well, the Earth is greatly changed, and of course your own evolution began with the green plague. I have heard tales of humanity from my companions. Would you tell me something of your lives?"

And we spoke of humankind, but I couldn't seem to find much enthusiasm for it. The anaerobic life that survived the advent of photosynthesis includes gangrene and botulism and not much else. I wondered what Chorrikst would find when next she came, and whether she would have reason to toast our memory.

WAR
MOVIE

Ten, twenty years ago my first thought would have been, *Great-looking woman! Tough-looking, too. If I make a pass, it had better be polite.* She was in her late twenties, tall, blond, healthy-looking, with a squarish jaw. She didn't look like the type to be fazed by anything; but she had stopped, stunned, just inside the door. Her first time here, I thought. Anyway, I'd have remembered her.

But after eighteen years tending bar in the Draco Tavern, my first thought is generally, *Human. Great! I won't have to dig out any of the exotic stuff.* While she was still reacting to the sight of half a dozen oddly-shaped sapients indulging each its own peculiar vice, I moved down the bar to the far right, where I keep the alcoholic beverages. I thought she'd take one of the bar stools.

Nope. She looked about her, considering her choices—which didn't include empty tables; there was a fair crowd in tonight—then moved to join the lone qarasht. And I was already starting to worry as I left the bar to take her order.

In the Draco it's considered normal to strike up conversations with other customers. But the qarasht wasn't acting like it wanted company. The bulk of thick fur, pale blue striped with black in narrow curves, had waddled in three hours ago. It was on its third quart-sized mug of Demerara Sours, and its sense cluster had been retracted for all of that time, leaving it deaf and blind, lost in its own thoughts.

It must have felt the vibration when the woman sat down. Its sense cluster and stalk rose out of the fur like a python rising from a bed of moss. A snake with no mouth: just two big wide-set black bubbles for eyes and an ear like a pink blossom set between them, and a tuft of fine hairs along the stalk to serve for smell and taste, and a brilliant ruby crest on top. Its translator box said, quite clearly, "Drink, not talk. My last day."

She didn't take the hint. "You're going home? Where?"

"Home to the organ banks. I am *shishishorupf*—" A word the box didn't translate.

"What's it mean?"

"Your kind has bankruptcy laws that let you start over. My kind lets me start over as a dozen others. Organ banks." The alien picked up its mug; the fur parted below its sense cluster stalk, to receive half a pint of Demerara Sour.

She looked around a little queasily, and found me at her shoulder. With some relief she said, "Never mind, I'll come to the bar," and started to stand up.

The qarasht put a hand on her wrist. The eight skeletal fingers looked like two chicken feet wired together; but a qarasht's hand is stronger than it looks. "Sit," said the alien. "Barmonitor, get her one of these. Human, why do you not fight wars?"

"What?"

"You used to fight wars."

"Well," she said, "sure."

"We could have been fourth-level wealthy," the qarasht said, and slammed its mug to the table. "You would still be a single isolated species had we not come. In what fashion have you repaid our generosity?"

The woman was speechless; I wasn't. "Excuse me, but it wasn't the qarashteel who made first contact with Earth. It was the chirpsithra."

"We paid them."

"What? Why?"

"Our ship *Far-Stretching Sense Cluster* passed through Sol system while making a documentary. It confuses some species that we can make very long entertainments, and sell them to billions of customers who will spend years watching them, and reap profits that allow us to travel hundreds of light-years and spend decades working on such a project. But we are very long-lived, you know. Partly because we are able to keep the organ banks full," the qarasht said with some savagery, and it drank again. Its sense-cluster was weaving a little.

"We found dramatic activity on your world," it said. "All over your world, it seemed. Machines hurled against each other. Explosives. Machines built to fly, other machines to hurl them from the sky. Humans in the machines, dying. Machines blowing great holes in populated cities. It fuddles the mind, to think what such a spectacle would have cost to make ourselves! We went into orbit, and we recorded it all as best we could. Three years of it. When we were sure it was over, we returned home and sold it."

The woman swallowed. She said to me, "I think I need that drink. Join us?"

I made two of the giant Demerara Sours and took them back. As I pulled up a chair the qarasht was saying, "If we had stopped then we would still be moderately wealthy. Our recording instruments were not the best, of course. Worse, we could not get close enough to the surface for real detail. Our atmosphere probes shivered and shook and so did the pictures. Ours was a low-budget operation. But the ending was superb! Two cities half-destroyed by thermonuclear explosions! Our recordings sold well enough, but we would have been mad not to try for more.

"We invested all of our profits in equipment. We borrowed all we could. Do you understand that the nearest full-service spaceport to Sol system is sixteen-squared light years distant? We had to finance a chirpsithra diplomatic expedition in order to get Local Group approval and transport for what we needed . . . and because we needed intermediaries. Chirps are very good at negotiating, and we are not. We did not tell them what we really wanted, of course."

The woman's words sounded like curses. "Why negotiate? You were doing fine as Peeping Toms. Even when people saw your ships, nobody believed them. I expect they're saucer-shaped?"

Foo fighters, I thought, while the alien said, "We needed more than the small atmospheric probes. We needed to mount hologram cameras. For that we had to travel all over the Earth, especially the cities. Such instruments are nearly invisible. We spray them across a flat surface, high up on your glass-slab-style towers, for instance. And we needed access to your libraries, to get some insight into *why* you do these things."

The lady drank. I remembered that there had been qarashteel everywhere the chirpsithra envoys went, twenty-four years ago when the big interstellar ships arrived; and I took a long pull from my Sour.

"It all looked so easy," the qarasht mourned. "We had left instruments on your moon. The recordings couldn't be sold, of course, because your world's rotation permits only fragmentary glimpses. But your machines were becoming better, *more* destructive! We thanked our luck that you had not destroyed yourselves before we could return. We studied the recordings, to guess where the next war would occur, but there was no discernable pattern. The largest land mass, we thought—"

True enough, the chirps and their qarashteel entourage had been very visible all over Asia and Europe. Those cameras on the Moon must have picked up activity in Poland and Korea and Vietnam and Afghanistan and Iran and Israel and Cuba and, and . . . bastards. "So you set up your cameras in a tearing hurry," I guessed, "and then you waited."

"We waited and waited. We have waited for thirty years . . . for twenty-four of your own years, and we have nothing to show for it but a riot here, a parade there, an attack on a children's vehicle . . . robbery of a bank . . . a thousand people smashing automobiles or an embassy building . . . rumors of war, of peace, some shouting in your councils . . . how can we sell any of this? On Earth my people need life support to the tune of six thousand dollars a day. I and my associates are *shishishorupf* now, and I must return home to tell them."

The lady looked ready to start her own war. I said, to calm her down, "We make war movies too. We've been doing it for over a hundred years. They sell fine."

Her answer was an intense whisper. "I never liked war movies. And that was us!"

"Sure, who else—"

The qarasht slammed its mug down. *"Why have you not fought a war?"*

She broke the brief pause. "We would have been ashamed."

"Ashamed?"

"In front of you. Aliens. We've seen twenty alien species on Earth since that first chirp expedition, and none of them seem to fight wars. The, uh, qarasht don't fight wars, do they?"

The alien's sense cluster snapped down into its fur, then slowly emerged again. "Certainly we do not!"

"Well, think how it would look!"

"But for you it is natural!"

"Not really," I said. "People have real trouble learning to kill. It's not built into us. Anyway, we don't have quite so much to fight over these days. The whole world's getting rich on the widgetry the chirps and the thtopar have been selling us. Long-lived, too, on glig medicines. We've all got more to lose." I flinched, because the alien's sense cluster was stretched across the table, staring at us in horror.

"A lot of our restless types are out mining the asteroids," the woman said.

"And, hey," I said, "remember when Egypt and Saudi Arabia were talking war in the UN? And all the aliens moved out of both countries, even the glig doctors with their geriatrics consulting office. The sheiks didn't like that one damn bit. And when the Soviets—"

"Our doing, all our own doing," the alien mourned. Its sense cluster pulled itself down and disappeared into the fur, leaving just the ruby crest showing. The alien lifted its mug and drank, blind.

The woman took my wrist and pulled me over to the bar. "What do we do *now*?" she hissed in my ear.

I shrugged. "Sounds like the emergency's over."

"But we can't just let it go, can we? You don't really think we've given up war, do you? But if we knew these damn aliens were waiting to make *movies* of us, maybe we would! Shouldn't we call the newspapers, or at least the Secret Service?"

"I don't think so."

"Somebody has to know!"

"Think it through," I said. "One particular qarasht company may be defunct, but those cameras are still there, all over the world, and so are the mobile units. Some alien receiving company is going to own them. What if they offer . . . say Iran, or the Soviet Union, one-tenth of one percent of the gross profits on a war movie?"

She paled. I pushed my mug into her hands and she gulped hard at it. Shakily she asked, "Why didn't the qarasht think of that?"

"Maybe they don't think enough like men. Maybe if we just leave it alone, they never will. But we sure don't want any human entrepreneurs making suggestions. Let it drop, lady. Let it drop."

THE
REAL
THING

If the IRS could see me now! Flying a light-sail craft, single-handed, two million miles out from a bluish-white dwarf star. Fiddling frantically with the shrouds, guided less by the instruments than by the thrust against my web hammock and the ripples in the tremendous, near-weightless mirror sail. Glancing into the sun without blinking, then at the stars without being night-blind, dipping near the sun without being fried; all due to the quick-adjusting goggles and temp-controlled skin-tight pressure suit the chirpsithra had given me.

This entire trip was deductible, of course. The Draco Tavern had made me a good deal of money over the years, but I never could have paid for an interstellar voyage otherwise. As the owner of the Draco Tavern, Earth's only multi-species bar, I was quite legitimately touring the stars to find new products for my alien customers.

Would Internal Revenue object to my actually enjoying myself?

I couldn't make myself care. The trip out on the chirpsithra liner: that alone was something I'd remember the rest of my life. This too, if I lived. Best not to distract myself with memories.

Hroyd System was clustered tightly around its small, hot sun. Space was thick with asteroids and planets and other sailing ships. Every so often some massive piece of space junk bombed the sun, or a storm would bubble up from beneath the photosphere, and my boat would surge under the pressure of the flare. I had to fiddle constantly with the shrouds.

The pointer was aimed at black space. Where *was* that damned spaceport? Huge and massive it had seemed, too big to lose, when I spun out my frail silver sail and launched . . . how long ago? The clock told me: twenty hours, though it didn't feel that long.

The spaceport was coin-shaped, spun for varying gravities. Maybe I was trying to see it edge-on? I tilted the sail to lose some velocity. The fat sun expanded. My mind felt the heat. If my suit failed, it would fail all at once, and I wouldn't have long to curse my recklessness. Or—Even chirpsithra-supplied equipment wouldn't help me if I fell into the sun.

I looked outward in time to see a silver coin pass over me. Good enough. Tilt the sail forward, pick up some speed . . . pull my orbit outward, slow down, *don't move the sail too fast or it'll fold up*! Wait a bit, then tilt the sail to spill the light; drop a bit, wait again . . . watch a black coin slide across the sun. Tilt to slow, tilt again to catch up. It was another two hours before I could pull into the spaceport's shadow, fold the sail and let a tractor beam pull me in.

My legs were shaky as I descended the escalator to Level 6.

There was Earth gravity on 6, minus a few percent; and also a multi-species restaurant bar. I was too tired to wonder about the domed boxes I saw on some of the tables. I wobbled over to a table, turned on the privacy bubble and tapped *tee tee hatch nex ool*, carefully. That code was my life. A wrong character could broil me, freeze me, flatten me, or have me drinking liquid methane or breathing prussic acid.

An Earthlike environment formed around me. I peeled off my equipment and sank into a web, sighing with relief. I still ached everywhere. What I really needed was sleep. But it had been glorious!

A warbling whistle caused me to look up. My translator said, "Sir or madam, what can I bring you?"

The bartender was a small, spindly Hroydan, and his environment suit glowed at dull red heat. I said, "Something alcoholic."

"Alcohol? What is your physiological type?"

"Tee tee hatch nex ool."

"Ah. May I recommend something? A liqueur, Opal Fire."

Considering the probable distance to the nearest gin-and-tonic . . . "Fine. What proof is it?" I heard his translator skip a word, and amplified: "What percent ethyl alcohol?"

"Thirty-four, with no other metabolic poisons."

About seventy proof? "Over water ice, please."

He brought a clear glass bottle. The fluid within did indeed glitter like an opal. Its beauty was the first thing I noticed. Then, the taste, slightly tart, with an overtone that can't be described in any human language. A crackling aftertaste, and a fire spreading through my nervous system. I said, "That's *wonderful*! What about side effects?"

"There are additives to compensate: thiamin and the like. You will feel no ugly aftereffects," the Hroydan assured me.

"They'd love it on Earth. Mmm . . . what's it cost?"

"Quite cheap. Twenty-nine chirp notes per flagon. Transport costs would be up to the chirpsithra. But I'm sure Chignthil Interstellar would sell specs for manufacture."

"This could pay for my whole trip." I jotted the names: chirp characters for *Opal Fire* and *Chignthil Interstellar*. The stuff was still dancing through my nervous system. I drank again, so it could dance on my taste buds too.

To hell with sleep; I was ready for another new experience. "These boxes—I see them on all the tables. What are they?"

"Full-sensory entertainment devices. Cost is six chirp notes for use." He tapped keys and a list appeared: titles, I assumed, in alien script. "If you can't read this, there is voice translation."

I dithered. Tempting; dangerous. But a couple of these might be worth taking back. Some of my customers can't use anything I stock; they pay only cover charges. "How versatile is it? Your customers seem to have a lot of different sense organs. Hey, would this thing actually give me alien senses?"

The bartender signalled negative. "The device acts on your central nervous system; I assume you have one? There at the top? Ah, good. It feeds you a story skeleton, but your own imagination puts you in context and fills in the background details. You live a programmed story, but largely in terms familiar to you. Mental damage is almost unheard of."

"Will I know it's only an entertainment?"

"You might know from the advertisements. Shall I show you?" The Hroydan raised the metal dome on a many-jointed arm and poised it over my head. I felt the heat emanating from him. "Perhaps you would like to walk through an active volcano?" He tapped two buttons with a black metal claw, and everything changed.

The Vollek merchant pulled the helmet away from my head. He had small, delicate-looking arms, and a stance like a tyrannosaur: torso horizontal, swung from the hips. A feathery down covered him, signalling his origin as a flightless bird. "How did you like it?"

"Give me a minute." I looked about me. Afternoon sunlight spilled across the tables, illuminating alien shapes. The Draco Tavern was filling up. It was time I got back to tending bar. It had been nearly empty (I remembered) when I agreed to try this stunt.

I said, "That business at the end—?"

"We end all of the programs that way when we sell to Level Four civilizations. It prevents disorientation."

"Good idea." Whatever the reason, I didn't feel at all confused. Still, it was a hell of an experience. "I couldn't tell it from the real thing."

"The advertisement would have alerted an experienced user."

"You're actually manufacturing these things on Earth?"

"Guatemala has agreed to license us. The climate is so nice there. And so I can lower the price per unit to three thousand dollars each."

"Sell me two," I said. It'd be a few years before they paid for themselves. Maybe someday I really would have enough money to ride the chirpsithra liners . . . if I didn't get hooked myself on these full-sensory machines. "Now, about Opal Fire. I can't believe it's really that good—"

"I travel for Chignthil Interstellar too. I have sample bottles."

"Let's try it."

LIMITS

I never would have heard them if the sound system hadn't gone on the fritz. And if it hadn't been one of those frantically busy nights, maybe I could have done something about it . . .

But one of the big chirpsithra passenger ships was due to leave Mount Forel Spaceport in two days. The chirpsithra trading empire occupies most of the galaxy, and Sol system is nowhere near its heart. A horde of passengers had come early in fear of being marooned. The Draco Tavern was jammed.

I was fishing under the counter when the noises started. I jumped. Two voices alternated: a monotonal twittering, and a bone-vibrating sound like a tremendous door endlessly opening on rusty hinges.

The Draco Tavern used to make the Tower of Babel sound like a monolog, in the years before I got this sound system worked out. Picture it: thirty or forty creatures of a dozen species including human, all talking at once at every pitch and volume, and all of their translating widgets bellowing too! Some species, like the srivinthish, don't talk with sound, but they also don't notice the continual *skreek*ing from their spiracles. Others sing. They *call* it singing, and they say it's a religious rite, so how can I stop them?

Selective damping is the key, and a staff of technicians to keep the system in order. I can afford it. I charge high anyway, for the variety of stuff I have to keep for anything that might wander in. But sometimes the damping system fails.

I found what I needed—a double-walled cannister I'd never needed before, holding stuff I'd been calling *green kryptonite*—and delivered glowing green pebbles to four aliens in globular environment tanks. They were at four different tables, sharing conversation with four other species. I'd never seen a rosyfin before. Rippling in the murky fluid within the transparent globe, the dorsal fin was triangular, rose-colored, fragile as gossamer, and ran from nose to tail of a body that looked like a flattened slug.

Out among the tables there was near-silence, except within the bubbles of sound that surrounded each table. It wasn't a total breakdown, then. But when I went back behind the bar the noise was still there.

I tried to ignore it. I certainly wasn't going to try to fix the sound system, not with fifty-odd customers and ten distinct species demanding my attention. I set out consomme and vodka for four glig, and thimble-sized flasks of chilled fluid with an ammonia base, for a dozen chrome yellow bugs each the size of a fifth of Haig Pinch. And the dialog continued: high twittering against grating metallic bass. What got on my nerves was the way the sounds seemed always on the verge of making sense!

Finally I just switched on the translator. It might be less irritating if I heard it in English.

I heard: "—noticed how often they speak of limits?"

"Limits? I don't understand you."

"Lightspeed limit. Theoretical strengths of metals, of crystals, of alloys. Smallest and largest masses at which an unseen body may be a neutron star. Maximum time and cost to complete a research project. Surface-to-volume relationship for maximum size of a creature of given design—"

"But every sapient race learns these things!"

"We find limits, of course. But with humans, the limits are what they seek first."

So they were talking about the natives, about us. Aliens often do. Their insights might be fascinating, but it gets boring fast. I let it buzz in my ear while I fished out another dozen flasks of ammonia mixture and set them on Gail's tray along with two Stingers. She went off to deliver them to the little yellow bugs, now parked in a horseshoe pattern on the rim of their table, talking animatedly to two human sociologists.

"It is a way of thinking," one of the voices said. "They set enormously complex limits on each other. Whole professions, called *judge* and *lawyer*, devote their lives to determining which human has violated which limit where. Another profession alters the limits arbitrarily."

"It does not sound entertaining."

"But all are forced to play the game. You must have noticed: the limits they find in the universe and the limits they set on each other bear the same name: law."

I had established that the twitterer was the one doing most of the talking. Fine. Now who were they? Two voices belonging to two radically different species . . .

"The interstellar community knows all of these limits in different forms."

"Do we know them all? Goedel's Principle sets a limit to the perfectability of mathematical systems. What species would have sought such a thing? Mine would not."

"Nor mine, I suppose. Still—"

"Humans push their limits. It is their first approach to any problem. When they learn where the limits lie, they fill in missing information until the limit breaks. When they break a limit, they look for the limit behind that."

"I wonder . . ."

I thought I had them spotted. Only one of the tables for two was occupied, by a chirpsithra and a startled-looking woman. My suspects were a cluster of three: one of the rosyfins, and two compact, squarish customers wearing garish designs on their exoskeletal shells. The shelled creatures had been smoking tobacco cigars under exhaust hoods. One seemed to be asleep. The other waved stubby arms as it talked.

I heard: "I have a thought. My savage ancestors used to die when they reached a certain age. When we could no longer breed, evolution was finished with us. There is a biological self-destruct built into us."

"It is the same with humans. But my own people never die unless killed. We fission. Our memories go far, far back."

"Though we differ in this, the result is the same. At some point in the dim past we learned that we could postpone our deaths. We never developed a civilization until individuals could live long enough to attain wisdom. The fundamental limit was lifted from our shells before we set out to expand into the world, and then the universe. Is this not true with most of the space-traveling peoples? The Pfarth species choose death only when they grow bored. Chirpsithra were long-lived before they reached the stars, and the gligstith(click)optok went even further, with their fascination with heredity-tailoring—"

"Does it surprise you, that intelligent beings strive to extend their lives?"

"Surprise? No. But humans still face a limit on their lifespans. The death limit has immense influence on their poetry. They may think differently from the rest of us in other ways. They may find truths we would not even seek."

An untranslated metal-on-metal scraping. Laughter? "You speculate irresponsibly. Has their unique approach taught them anything we know not?"

"How can I know? I have only been on this world three local years. Their libraries are large, their retrieval systems poor. But there is Goedel's Principle; and Heisenberg's Uncertainty Principle is a limit to what one can discover at the quantum level."

Pause. "We must see if another species has duplicated that one. Meanwhile, perhaps I should speak to another visitor."

"Incomprehension. Query?"

"Do you remember that I spoke of a certain gligstith-(click)optok merchant?"

"I remember."

"You know their skill with water-world biology. This one comes to Earth with a technique for maintaining and restoring the early-maturity state in humans. The treatment is complex, but with enough customers the cost would drop, or so the merchant says. I must persuade it not to make the offer."

"Affirmative! Removing the death-limit would drastically affect human psychology!"

One of the shelled beings was getting up. The voices chopped off as I rounded the bar and headed for my chosen table, with no clear idea what I would say. I stepped into the bubble of sound around two shelled beings and a rosyfin, and said, "Forgive the interruption, sapients—"

"You have joined a wake," said the tank's translator widget.

The shelled being said, "My mate had chosen death. He wanted one last smoke in company." It bent and lifted its dead companion in its arms and headed for the door.

The rosyfin was leaving too, rolling his spherical fishbowl toward the door. I realised that its own voice hadn't penetrated the murky fluid around it. No chittering, no bone-shivering bass. I had the wrong table.

I looked around, and there were still no other candidates. Yet *somebody* here had casually condemned mankind—me!—to age and die.

Now what? I might have been hearing several voices. They all sound alike coming from a new species; and some aliens never interrupt each other.

The little yellow bugs? But they were with humans.

Shells? My voices had mentioned shells . . . but too many aliens have exoskeletons. Okay, a chirpsithra would have spoken by now; they're garrulous. Scratch any table that includes a chirp. Or a rosyfin. Or those srivinthish: I'd have heard the *skreek* of their breathing. Or the huge grey being who seemed to be singing. That left . . . half a dozen tables, and I couldn't interrupt that many.

Could they have left while I was distracted?

I hot-footed it back to the bar, and listened, and heard nothing. And my spinning brain could find only limits.

ABOUT THE AUTHOR

Larry Niven was born on April 30, 1938, in Los Angeles, California. In 1956, he entered the California Institute of Technology, only to flunk out a year and a half later after discovering a bookstore jammed with used science-fiction magazines. He graduated with a B.A. in mathematics (minor in psychology) from Washburn University, Kansas, in 1962, and completed one year of graduate work in mathematics at UCLA before dropping out to write. His first published story, "The Coldest Place," appeared in the December 1964 issue of *Worlds of If*.

Larry Niven's interests include backpacking with the Boy Scouts, science-fiction conventions, supporting the conquest of space, and AAAS meetings and other gatherings of people at the cutting edge of the sciences.

He won the Hugo Award for Best Short Story in 1966 for "Neutron Star," and in 1974 for "The Hole Man." The 1975 Hugo Award for Best Novelette was given to "The Borderland of Sol." His novel *Ringworld* won the 1970 Hugo Award for Best Novel, the 1970 Nebula Award for Best Novel, and the 1972 Ditmar, an Australian award for Best International Science Fiction.